MISTRESS
for Hire

Also by Niobia Bryant

MISTRESS SERIES
Message from a Mistress
Mistress No More
Mistress, Inc.
The Pleasure Trap

FRIENDS & SINS SERIES
Live and Learn
Show and Tell
Never Keeping Secrets

STRONG FAMILY SERIES
Heated
Hot Like Fire
Give Me Fever
The Hot Spot
Red Hot
Strong Heat

Make You Mine
Want, Need, Love

Reckless (with Cydney Rax and Grace Octavia)
Heat Wave (with Donna Hill and Zuri Day)

Published by Kensington Publishing Corp.

MISTRESS
for Hire

NIOBIA BRYANT

KENSINGTON PUBLISHING CORP.

www.kensingtonbooks.com

DAFINA BOOKS are published by

Kensington Publishing Corp.
119 West 40th Street
New York, NY 10018

All Kensington titles, imprints, and distributed lines are available at special quantity discounts for bulk purchases for sales promotion, premiums, fund-raising, and educational or institutional use.

Special book excerpts or customized printings can also be created to fit specific needs. For details, write or phone the office of the Kensington Sales Manager: Kensington Publishing Corp., 119 West 40th Street, New York, NY 10018. Attn. Sales Department. Phone: 1-800-221-2647.

ISBN-13: 978-1-4967-1652-1
ISBN-10: 1-4967-1652-3
First Kensington Trade Paperback Printing: October 2018

eISBN-13: 978-1-4967-1653-8
eISBN-10: 1-4967-1653-1
First Kensington Electronic Edition: October 2018

10 9 8 7 6 5 4 3 2 1

Printed in the United States of America

Thank you, Lord, for blessing me
with the gift of storytelling, for the wisdom to utilize
that gift,
and for the readers who support and (hopefully) enjoy it.
And always, for my angel in heaven, my mama,
Letha "Bird" Bryant

Dear Readers,

The first book in the Mistress series, *Message from a Mistress*, was published back in 2010, and I never imagined that seven years later, I would be writing my fifth book following the shenanigans of the one and only Jessa Bell née Logan. That first book was eventually adapted to film, and by the time this new book, *Mistress for Hire*, hits the stores, the movie will have aired on Centric (now known as BET Her). Now that is hella dope.

I just wanted to take a moment and thank you, the readers, for the tremendous support for this series over the years and for the way it has forever changed my life. Sometimes I am so moved by the support for all my books, across all genres, that I get emotional. There are a lot of good books available to spend your hard-earned money on, and I am forever humbled that you spend some on mine.

Here's to your support and the infinite ink in my pen. Teamwork makes the dream work.

Best,
N.
P.S. Happy reading!

Prologue

Shit. Did I almost die?

With a little grunt filled with fatigue, she wiped her face with her hands. She winced at the tiny pinch of pain and looked down at the intravenous line in the bend of her arm. She licked her full lips to relieve the dryness and then released a long, drawn-out breath as she sat up in the hospital bed.

Gotta slow up. I like to get fucked up but not high enough to kiss Jesus. Shit.

"Miss Smith, how are you feeling this morning?"

She began to remove the tape holding the IV needle.

"Miss Smith?"

She looked up and was surprised at the nurse standing at the foot of the bed. "Miss Smith?" *she asked, her throat raw and pained as she spoke.* Who the hell is that?

The dreadlock-wearing nurse nodded and gently smiled at her. "Do you remember who you are, where you are, what day it is, and why you are here?"

"I'm Miss Smith," she lied, not bothering with the other questions

as she swung her bare legs over the side of the bed. "Did anyone wait with me?"

"Honey, your friends didn't even come with you. They gave your name to the paramedics and said they found you passed out in the bathroom of the club."

Figures. Nothing ever stops the party with that crew.

The nurse shook her head as she pulled on latex gloves and came over to smooth back down the edges of the tape.

"Can I have some ice water, please?" she asked the nurse, fighting the urge to knock the woman's hands off her.

"Sure." She picked up the water container from the overbed table and removed the lid to look inside it. "The ice melted. Be right back."

As soon as the door closed behind her, "Miss Smith" quickly worked to undo the tape and free the IV needle from her arm. At first, she was a little unsteady on her feet, but still she moved as quickly as she could to look through the drawers and cabinets until she found her clothes and purse in a large plastic bag. Stuffing the sack under her arm, she peeked her head out the door of the room. She spotted a door to the stairway at the end of the hall. With one last cursory check that all was clear, she headed for it, thankful for the bright yellow no-slip socks as she hurried over the polished floor.

Quickly she dressed in the wide-leg gold silk pants, white sequined halter top, ostrich feather coat, and heels that were more suited for the party she attended last night than day wear. She frowned and ignored the rancid smell of her own vomit dried to the material. She paused, vaguely remembering hurling in the middle of the dance floor.

As she walked down the stairs, she dug the box cutter she always carried for protection from her clutch and cut the hospital band from her arm. She tossed it in the air, and it floated gently to the stairs behind her.

Her eyes locked on the natural light flooding through the windows and the doors of the hospital, she took quick steps toward it, praying she didn't look like what she was—a patient sneaking out of the hospital. Everything to the left and right of her seemed blurry because of her focus on the door. It was freedom to her and she craved it.

When she finally reached the lobby of the hospital, she gripped the door handle and paused, closing her eyes and taking deep breaths as she fought the unbalance she felt. The unsteadiness. "Shit," she swore, wetting her lips with her tongue and opening the door with as much energy as she could muster.

A man on the other side of the door eyed her through the glass as he opened it and stepped back to allow her to exit.

"Thank you," she said with a half-smile and in a voice barely above a whisper as she stepped outside and took a deep breath of the chilly November air.

Swiping at the sweat building on her nape beneath her curly hair, she moved on unsteady feet toward the bright yellow of one of the taxis parked on the street. From the moment, she slumped onto the backseat and gave the driver her address until she felt the taxi jerk as it stopped, she shifted somewhere between being sleep and being awake. She raised her head from the headrest and looked out the window at her apartment building.

"Fifteen dollars," the driver said in a Haitian accent.

Nodding, she dug a twenty-dollar bill from her purse and pushed it into his waiting hand. Something from her purse fell to the floor of the cab and she bent down to pick it up. Her lip curled in anger as she looked down at the photo. The woman pictured in it was notorious. "Jessa Bell, you slick, no-good bitch you," she muttered in disgust, climbing from the car and closing the door with a jut of her hip.

As she tore the picture up, she wished it was just as easy to destroy Jessa Bell. Even through her fatigue and lack of clear thought, her gut burned with the heat of her anger. With a flick of her wrist, the pieces were freed into the air. She gave them one glance over her shoulder as they were caught by the wind before she entered the building.

Chapter 1

Six months later
2015

"Don't go, baby."

Jessa Bell pushed her newly golden-streaked, chestnut locks back from her face as she looked down at the man she straddled in the middle of her king-sized bed. She raised her arms high above her head, lifting her full breasts higher as she stretched. "I have to," Jessa said regretfully. "The responsibilities of being the boss."

One of his large hands slid up her toned thigh and around her shapely hip to massage her buttocks. He slid the tip of his thick middle finger inside her pussy from behind. She shivered and arched her back, lifting her backside to give him better access. They both moaned as he gently stroked her throbbing clit with his index finger. She spread her knees wider and pressed her hands against his strong chest as she circled her hips.

None of the thrill he gave her had diminished since they'd become secret lovers. His touch was electrifying and *almost* addictive.

She leaned in to dangle her breasts just above his hungry

mouth, allowing him a few precious moments to suck one deep brown nipple between his lips before she rose, leaving him hard and wanting on the bed. Naked, Jessa gave him one last seductive and flirty glance over her shoulder before picking up her red satin gown from the floor to pull on as she crossed the gleaming ebony hardwood floors to the door connecting the master suite to the nursery.

Her four-year-old daughter, Delaney, was a late sleeper. Jessa was surprised to find her bed was empty. Tying the belt of her robe, she quickly crossed the room decorated in cream with splashes of pink and walked out into the wide hall. She checked her mother Darla's bedroom at the opposite end of the hall but that room was empty as well, with nothing but the scent of the smoke from the cigarettes she snuck clinging to the air.

"Damn," she swore in annoyance, entering the room to push all the windows open wide.

Jessa was headed to the exit but paused at the nightstand to open the top drawer and remove her pill organizer. She replaced it after ensuring her mother had taken her daily dose of her antipsychotic medicine. She did a cursory check for alcohol or drugs while she was at it.

"Thank God," she muttered, when her search didn't turn up anything.

Her mother's bipolar condition without meds and with alcohol spelled disaster.

Pausing to check her reflection in the mirror over her dresser drawers, she ran the tips of her crimson red fingernails through her hair and smoothed her microbladed brows before she left the room.

The ends of her robe slightly lifted behind her, exposing her brown legs as she rushed down one side of the double wrought iron stairs of the grand foyer. She headed down the long, wide hall leading to the den and kitchen. The loud sounds of some kiddie cartoon on the television reached her.

Jessa felt relief to see both her mother and her daughter. Darla sat on one of the six high-back stools surrounding the island, and Delaney sat on the center of the granite top. She forced herself to relax.

"Hi, Mama," Delaney said, reaching out to offer Jessa one of the grapes she was eating from a pile on a paper towel between her open legs.

Jessa smiled and felt her heart swell with love for her daughter as she came over and pressed kisses to her plump cheeks and neck. That caused a fit of giggles.

"I got up and got her since you had *company*."

Jessa momentarily paused at the censure in her mother's voice. Deciding to ignore her, Jessa slid the paper towel out of her daughter's reach and picked her up to securely sit her in her monogrammed high chair at the end of the island. She grabbed a knife, cut all the grapes into halves, and slid them into one of her colorful bowls before sitting them before Delaney along with her no spill cup filled with apple juice.

I will do right by you. I won't fuck it.

Jessa bent down to a press a kiss to the soft ebony curls of her daughter's head. Her heart swelled with love that completely outmeasured the hate she harbored for her baby's father, Eric Hall. She was determined to be a lioness and protect her cub. *The sins of the parents will not visit upon my child. His nor mine.*

"How'd you sleep, Ma?" Jessa asked, acutely aware that her parents had made no such promises to her growing up.

Their relationship could easily be likened to the ups and down of a roller-coaster ride. Jessa had been raised by her grandmother since she was six, when her mother, a high-strung woman who loved men more than she loved herself or her daughter, had left her behind. The notoriety Jessa gained from her lover attempting to take her life after she ended their scandalous affair had brought Darla back into her life three years ago. Jessa's appearances on the local news and national talk shows had given Darla the motivation that she hadn't had in over twenty years to find the daughter she abandoned.

Ding-dong.

Jessa looked over her shoulder at Delaney's newest nanny, Winifrid, waving at them through one of the glass panes of the side door entrance. *Thank God.*

Jessa felt better with Delaney being closely supervised by her nanny while she was at work. She and her mother were in the middle of one of the lows of their relationship, and Jessa tried not to feel guilty about those heated moments when she wished she'd left her mother to live in her brownstone in Harlem that resembled the homes on *Hoarders.*

"Good morning, Ms. Bell," Winifrid said after Darla let her in.

Jessa gave the slender white woman a welcoming smile. "I'm running late, so I'm going to head back upstairs to get ready for work and then I'm right out the door, Winifrid. Just email your plans for you and Delaney today," she said over her shoulder as she padded across the tiled floor of the kitchen.

"And bye to you, too," Darla said sarcastically.

Jessa stopped and turned to eye her mother. She could tell from the tightness of her mouth that she was annoyed. With a lick of her lips, Jessa made her way around the island to come over and hug her mother with one arm as she pressed a kiss to her brow. "Good-bye, Ma," she said, pushing warmth into her tone.

Darla smiled, reaching out to playfully swat her daughter's behind.

"I have to go," Jessa said, moving to allow herself one more kiss to her daughter's cheek before heading out of the kitchen.

"I hope you find your panties."

Jessa did not break her stride at her mother's words as she retraced her steps back to her bedroom. The bed was empty, but as she neared her en suite bathroom she could hear the shower running. She glanced at his tall frame blurred by the steam and frosted glass. She made a point of ignoring the enticing sight.

"You gonna join me?"

And his inviting words.

"No," she told him, thankful for the heated floors as she crossed the room to fill the Jacuzzi tub. They had been among the main selling points when she purchased the beautiful four-bedroom, three-and-half-bathroom colonial in Carmel, a moderate-sized city in upstate New York. *Well, that and the need to get away.*

Taking a small breath that symbolized far more than its size, Jessa used both hands to brush her shoulder-length hair from her face as she studied her reflection. It had been five years since she left the upscale gated community of Richmond Hills, New Jersey, behind, but the indelible memories remained. Her eyes clouded over as she lightly stroked her throat with her fingers.

Five years ago, when she sent identical text messages to her three friends, Renee, Aria, and Jaime, taunting them that she was running away with one of their husbands, she'd never guessed where it would lead her life. Her intention with the message? To punish Renee and Aria with the lie for what she considered their faulty friendships and to give the coup de grâce to Jaime's marriage to Eric. Much more followed. Much more than even she anticipated.

Eric never left Jaime as he promised, and when *she* ended the marriage instead, Jessa ending their affair had been the straw shattering his sanity. He began stalking her with a ferocity that both scared and disgusted her. And then the man she once loved had tried to kill her. She flinched at the vision of her former lover's face filled with irrational rage as he attempted to choke the life from her. Their adulterous love had turned into his obsession that swung between hatred and a desperation to have her. Just madness.

Pow.

The echo of the fatal gunshot he delivered to his own head in the moments before she slipped into unconsciousness seemed to still ring out around her.

Jessa released a terrified squeal at the feel of strong hands suddenly on her shoulders.

"You okay?" her lover asked.

She forced herself to relax as she nodded and gave him a smile in the mirror before she moved away from his strength and heat to climb into the large tub. "I'll see you later, okay?" she said to him, shifting her eyes away from the sight of his body naked, damp, and far too enticing.

With a chuckle, he strode to the door, his muscles flexing with each movement. "Maybe sooner," he said.

After allowing herself one quick peek at his strong buttocks, she turned off the flowing water before leaning back to rest her head against the rim, enjoying the feel of the steaming water against her smooth skin. She knew she had a busy day ahead of her and was already running behind on meetings, but she needed a few precious moments alone to regain her balance.

Nearly an hour had passed by the time Jessa came back down to the foyer with its grand ceiling and elaborate chandelier of scrolled ironwork that perfectly suited the neutral décor and rich wood trimmings. Tucking her clutch under her arm, she left the house through one of the towering glass and metal front doors.

Her lover was gone, and her circular stone-paved drive was free of his Harley-Davidson motorcycle. That suited her just fine. Playtime was over.

Jessa climbed behind the wheel of her new convertible Porsche—like her nails and her lipstick, it was cherry red and glossy. It was May and there was just enough bite in the air to keep her from putting down the top during her forty-five-minute commute to Manhattan. Like every other morning, she was anxious to get to work, and she tapped her nails against the steering wheel to release some of her energy as she drove.

The notoriety that came calling after the attempt on her life had pushed her into the reality TV–, Instagram-, and blog-post-driven world of fame. Even as she struggled with her own redemption in the wake of the damage she caused to so many lives, she had stepped into the spotlight. News interviews. Talk shows. A *New York Times* best-selling book, *The Mistress Memoirs*. Book tour. Endorsements. Infamy.

And enough money to eventually start her own business where she could combine her experience as a mistress with her need to redeem herself.

Jessa was thankful for the on-site parking at the thirty-story building in the Garment District of Manhattan. She pulled her car into her reserved spot next to the silver BMW of her partner and friend, Keegan Connor. She grabbed her crocodile Birkin and strode over to the elevator. Offering the man standing there a smile, she stepped on when the door opened and he stepped back to allow her to enter first.

"Do you work in the building?" he asked.

She held her bag with both hands and gave him a look. Tall, handsome enough in a blond hair, blue eye kind of way, and surely wealthy enough from the cut of his clothing, but not for her. "No," she lied. "Going to visit the hubby."

He gave her a nod of understanding before focusing on his phone.

When the lift stopped at the twelfth floor, he gave her one last appreciative look before walking away.

White boy looking like a treat. With a soft bite of her bottom lip, she enjoyed the view of him until the door closed.

Her thoughts refocused on work when she stepped off onto the twentieth floor and walked the short distance to the frosted glass door of her office suite. She opened it and paused. Her stylish waiting area was filled with beautiful women of all shapes, sizes, and nationalities.

For a second most of them diverted their attention away from the phones or magazines they were idly flipping through to glance at her. They all looked away, probably assuming she was there for the same purpose as them.

Wrong.

"Good morning, ladies," Jessa said, her voice soft but authoritative. "I will be with you all in just a moment."

She smiled when they all looked to her again. Sat up a little straighter. Tried to make eye contact. Respected the head bitch in charge.

Jessa strode across the wood plank flooring colored in bright red and felt invigorated.

"Good morning, Ms. Bell," said Felisha, their freckled and petite shortbread-colored receptionist, handing her a stack of mail.

Jessa eyed her. "Are we all set?" she asked.

Felisha nodded.

"Give me five minutes and start showing them in," she instructed before walking down the short hall leading to their two offices and conference room. She stopped at the door of Keegan's office and cleared her throat.

Keegan looked up, pushing her turquoise spectacles atop her bright red hair. She smiled and sat back in her chair. "Well, look who the cat finally drug in," she teased, her Texas accent still in place.

"I couldn't get out of bed," Jessa said, sifting through the mail and stepping inside the small but stylish white office with bold splashes of color to set the incoming bills on her desk.

Keegan snorted in derision. "Who was in it?" she asked, with a playful but sly look.

Jessa just shrugged. "I'm ready to start the interviews if you are," she said, purposefully changing the subject.

"Good, these ladies have been waiting for more than an

hour, darlin'," Keegan said, rising to come around the modern glass desk and hand her a list of names.

"Patience is key in this business," Jessa said as they walked to the conference room together.

Keegan had gone from being Jessa's interior decorator to her friend and now her business partner. She was a godsend in the days after Jessa sent that text and blew up her friendships. They were both in their mid-thirties and had a sense of humor. That was where the similarities ended.

Keegan was a white Southern belle with a brash tongue who was good in business.

Jessa was a black city girl with more than enough city slick to get what she wanted when she wanted it.

Together they ran Mistress, Inc., and business was booming.

"Send in the first applicant," Jessa said via the intercom once they settled in their seats behind the oval-shaped conference table.

"Remember beauty and brains, sugar," Keegan said to her just before the door opened and the first young lady entered the room.

Jessa eyed her and then dismissed her, drawing a line through her name on the sign-up sheet. She was pretty enough and had the right build, but her eyes revealed her lack of confidence. *Not a good start to the day.*

"And you're twenty-five, Lori?" Keegan asked, checking the head shot she handed her.

"I will be in two—"

"Thanks, Lori," Jessa said, dismissing her.

Lori looked surprised.

Keegan looked annoyed.

"Good luck with your acting career," Jessa said with a stiff smile before turning her attention to the next name on the list. She pressed the button on the intercom. "Next, Felisha."

"You are messier than cow dung, darling," Keegan drawled.

One by one, beautiful out-of-work actresses entered the conference room and took a seat before them. And one by one, Jessa was more and more disappointed. She knew exactly what she was looking for, and that hadn't walked into the room yet.

A tall brunette entered with more breasts than hips. Jessa dropped her pen and swiveled in the chair to look out the windows at the sun beating down on the skyscrapers. The city that never sleeps was filled with those who creeped, and the wives or husbands of cheating mates wanted help exposing them. It was beyond hiring private detectives or personally snooping through phones and social media accounts. Some wanted control.

That's where Mistress, Inc., filled the void.

Jessa reached for her iPad from her Birkin and logged into the security system software. The camera in the waiting room showed eight more applicants waiting. She eyed each one and then sighed. The door to the outer office opened and her eyes shifted to watch a woman walk in wearing a strapless black jumpsuit that suited her small breasts and wide hips. Jessa arched a brow. She was beautiful, poised, and magnetic. Every other woman in the room watched her, and their envy was clear.

The woman used slender hands to swoop her bone-straight hair over one shoulder before she smiled at Felisha and handed over her application.

Jessa turned off the tablet and eyed the young woman sitting before them with a mass of honey-colored curls that suited her light brown complexion. She double-checked her name. Lacey Adams.

"And you understand that you are not to have a sexual relationship with any client," Keegan said. "This is not a cathouse. We're serving up justice, not kitty-cat."

Jessa bit back a smile at Keegan's snark.

"Yes, I understand," Lacey said with a nod.

Keegan looked to her. Jessa said nothing.

"Okay, Lacey, we'll be in touch," Keegan said, sitting back in her chair as the woman rose and left the conference room.

"Hire her," Jessa said, rising to walk around the table and leave the conference room herself. She walked straight to the new woman and extended her hand. *She's more beautiful in person.*

She rose and matched Jessa's intense stare with one of her own.

"You are?" Jessa asked.

"Charli Cole," she said, her voice soft and husky.

Men love that.

"You're hired," Jessa said.

Charli gave her a smooth smile that spread across her pretty face like soft butter on a hot roll.

Jessa gave her one last look before turning and walking away.

Chapter 2

Two months later

Jessa grabbed her daughter close to her and pressed kisses to her neck.

Delaney laughed and sighed before she pressed chubby cheeks to Jessa's face. "Love you, Mama," she said, her eyes still bright with joviality.

Jessa smiled. "Love you, Del," she said softly, her guilt paining her.

And I love Georgia, too.

Jessa released her four-year old, and Delaney went running across her brightly colored playroom to her nanny, Winifrid. Watching them, she pulled her knees to her chest and wrapped her arms around them before settling her chin in the groove between her knees. *Is it possible to love someone you have never met?*

For so long, Jessa had forced herself to forget the daughter she bore at thirteen. The baby she was never allowed to see. The baby born from a rape by her own father.

Please, no, Daddy! No!

Jessa flinched, hating the vile and violent memory imprinted on her life. Never would she forget the smell of the liquor on his breath, the dazed look in his eyes, or the feel of his body on hers. In. hers.

"Shit," she swore, forcing herself to breathe.

Well over twenty years had passed, but still the pain clung. As did her thoughts of Georgia.

Is she okay?

Was she normal?

Does she wonder about me?

Sometimes she wished she didn't know her name.

Over the years, the pain and shame of her past had finally begun to lose some of its bite until Eric Hall Sr. used his wealth and influence to unveil her childhood secret to force her hand during the contentious custody battle for Delaney after Eric's suicide. Although she eventually defeated Hall's tactics by videotaping and blackmailing him with his attempts to bed her—his deceased son's ex-mistress and mother to his grandchild—she was unable to be freed of her thoughts of the child she was forced to give up.

Georgia.

Eric Sr. gave up her first name but redacted all other info about her from the file. He saw it as punishment to keep information from her, like the grandchild she kept from him and his wife.

He didn't know he freed her.

As much as she had begun to ponder her daughter's whereabouts and well-being, Jessa had not attempted to locate her. She had the resources to do so but felt that if Georgia discovered she was born of incestuous rape, it would do nothing but cripple her. She could only hope that Georgia's life was far better without the knowledge of the shattered foundation upon which she was born.

And now her second child might one day have to grapple with being born of an adulterous affair, and her father killing himself after thinking he had killed her mother. She was hell-bent and determined to hide that truth from her daughter; she could only hope another round of the karma she wrought wouldn't take that decision out of her hands.

She made no excuses for choices she made. Alienations. Betrayals.

But she was not whole. Her being had been shattered. Once as a child when she stood at a window and waited for the return of her mother, and then again with her innocence lost to her very own father. And once more when her husband died and the happily-ever-after she dreamt of was snatched away.

Hurt people liked to hurt people, and she had hurt plenty.

Self-reflection was hard, especially when seen through the lens of truth.

Jessa released a heavy breath, thinking of the many moments where she chose wrong over right. When she had lashed out in anger, been petty, or wanted to see lives implode at her hand. *I am a horrible person.*

"Was," she mouthed. "I *was* a horrible person."

Right?

She wasn't sure and she needed to be sure. She joined a church, paid her tithes, and felt she was providing an invaluable service to marriage through her business. She forgave her mother and tried her best to build a good relationship with her. She was a good mother to Delaney. She was a better friend to Keegan than she had been to Renee, Aria, and most definitely, Jaime. Her days of being a mistress were over. She *was* a better person.

Right?

"Mama. Mama. Ma-ma."

"Huh?" she said, turning away from where she had been staring out the window. Her eyes landed on Delaney and she was taken aback by how much of Eric she saw in her round little face.

"This is all your fault."

"You need me just like I need you."

"You destroyed me."

"You complete me."

"Both you bitches used me."

"Anything you want. It's yours. Just say the word."

"I hate you."

"I love you."

She trembled as she remembered the look of rage on his face as he tried to choke the life from her body. In the moments before she'd lost consciousness, she thought she was dying, even as he tried to revive her. When she'd heard the gunshot echo throughout the room, she knew he'd killed himself and prayed he would join her in hell.

"Look, Mama."

And now I'm raising our child.

She forced a smile as she rose to her feet and walked over to look down at her beloved child behind the wheel of her bright red Power Wheels Porsche. "Winifrid, it's not too hot today. Why not take her outside and let her enjoy the lawn," she said, nervously stroking her palm with her thumb. "I have to run an errand, but I should be back in an hour."

"Yes, ma'am."

Jessa left the room and entered her suite, grabbing her bag and making sure her phone was in the back pocket of her wide-leg denim pants before she stepped into the hall, ignored the loud soul music blaring from her mother's room, and made her way down the stairs to leave her home.

She paused as she entered her car.

Why the name Georgia? Was her new family from there?

Some days her daughter didn't cross her mind, and others— like today—she felt drowned by the weight of her past.

She closed the driver's side door and started the car, leaning forward to pull her iPhone from her back pocket. She dialed with her thumb as she drove down the short driveway and turned out onto the street.

Jessa rolled her eyes at her neighbors unloading their tan Honda crossover. They waved and smiled at her. "Hey, you boring assholes," she sang lightly as she gave them a forced smile and waved in return.

Suburbia still sucked.

"Hello, Jessa."

She glanced up at her rearview mirror. "I need to see you," she said, her eyes showing her hope that he was available.

"It's last minute."

"It's urgent," she countered.

He chuckled. It was deep and rich. "It always is."

Jessa frowned so deeply her arched brows dipped.

"Come on, Jessa."

She ended the call. "It always is," she mimed sarcastically as her car accelerated.

Soon she turned onto the driveway of the New Hope megachurch and parked next to a black Mercedes Benz with the license plate REV1.

As she made her way inside the expansive white building with floor-to-ceiling windows, her heels clicked against the tiled floors, breaking up the quiet. A side door opened and she stumbled backward in surprise before smiling at the tall and broad handsome man standing there. He had the same kind of dark and delicious handsomeness as Morris Chestnut, Lance Gross, or Kofi Siriboe.

Their body type, too.

She allowed herself a quick up-and-down glance at him in loose-fitting, distressed denims and a burnt orange V-neck T-shirt that accentuated his smooth chocolate complexion.

"Is it okay if we meet in here?" he asked, stepping back against the door to push it open wider.

"No problem, Reverend Dell," Jessa said, fighting the devil tempting her to brush her body against his as she passed him.

When she moved to Carmel she had wanted to maintain her newfound ties to church and her salvation, so she visited several churches before settling in at New Hope. She was proud to note it was Reverend Evan Dell's concise delivery of the Word and not the fit of his suit that drew her. In time he had become her religious mentor and counselor. Thankfully, she ignored any urges to seduce him and was grateful for his advice.

"It's good to see you, Jessa," Rev Dell said, waving his hand to offer her a seat on the first polished wood pew before sitting as well. "It's been a long time."

She crossed her legs and set her phone face down on the seat beside her. "I know I've missed a few Sundays," she said. "But my tithes are paid faithfully, right?"

He tossed his head back and chuckled.

Her eyes dipped down to his smooth throat. She forced her eyes away. *I rebuke you, devil. Get from me.*

"I prefer your presence on the pew to your check in the church's bank account," he assured her. "You can't buy your way into heaven."

Right. "I'll be to church Sunday," she promised.

Jessa saw him as a gauge of her success in becoming a better person than she used to be, and felt properly chastised.

"Are we alone?" she asked, remembering the reason for her impromptu visit.

He nodded, hanging his bent arm over the top of the pew.

His demeanor and advice always comforted her. Outside of keeping the secret of the child she'd had at thirteen, she was frankly honest with him during their monthly sessions.

"I'm having difficulties forgiving myself for my past," she began, nervously twisting the five-carat ring on her middle finger. She took a deep, steadying breath. "When I was thirteen, I gave birth to a daughter that my grandmother forced me to give up for adoption."

His handsome face filled with concern as he reached over to take one of her hands into his. "Take a breath, Jessa," he advised.

She did, closing her eyes as her pain fought its way through the level of numbness she tried to maintain. Her tears rose with a quickness. "I feel guilty because I do not want to find her. I do not want to be in her life," she admitted, her voice slightly shaky.

"You *don't?*" he asked.

She slid her hand out of his when his fingertips against her skin felt all too warm. "No. I think it's best we both move on with our lives as it is."

"Why is that?' Reverend Dell asked, his eyes assessing her but not judging.

She took another breath, a deep one that filled her lungs but did nothing to steady her. "Discovering that she shares the same father as her birth mother is a bit much," she drawled, trying and failing at humor at that moment.

He looked perplexed.

"Rape," she supplied, her voice calmer than she felt.

His face filled with understanding and horror.

Jessa fought hard not to succumb to her pain and rising tears. She swallowed over a lump in her throat.

"Breathe deep," he urged again.

She shook her head, denying his request. "I'm breathing just fine, Rev," she said. "It's my soul I'm worried about. Am I a horrible person?"

Revered Dell crossed his arms over his solid chest. "No, you are not. Besides, I am not here to judge you, Jessa," he insisted. "Life is all about tough decisions."

She rolled her eyes heavenward. "But you're one of the mainlines to heaven, and I'm telling you that I want to know I'm not a horrible person."

"Jessa—"

"Like, I know there's a balance. Karma and all that," she said, rising to her feet to pace in front of the grand pulpit. "I pay tithes. I come to church. I'm a good mother . . . this time.

I'm good to my crazy mother. I help catch cheating husbands—
well, wives, too. A cheat is a cheat."

"Jessa—"

"What else does God want me to do?" Jessa asked, her
face stricken.

"Jessa—"

She pointed up to the sky and looked up. "And *you* know
I deserve major points for not seducing him," she stressed
before pointing her finger at the reverend.

"Jessa!" he roared, jumping to his feet.

She cut her eyes over to him before she forced a smile and
shrugged. "No disrespect, Rev," she said. "And don't worry,
I'm not throwing anything at you but tithes, offerings, and
my problem. I got enough damn sins to bear."

She winced and glanced upward again. "Sorry, God."

Reverend Dell cleared his throat.

"Yeah, you, too," she said, her tone distracted as she
pressed her hands on her hips and tapped the toe of one of
her heels against the hardwood floors.

He came over to lightly grab her shoulders.

The look she gave him was incredulous. "For God cannot
be tempted by evil, nor does he tempt anyone." She quoted
the Bible, leaning back to avoid his platonic touch.

He dropped his hands. "I didn't mean anything—"

She waved her fingers at him. "I know that, but temptation
is temptation, and I need five feet at all times, Rev," she said.
"Just being honest."

He nodded and stepped back, looking uncomfortable.
Her honesty obviously disconcerted him. "I think we should
pray," he offered, before kneeling before the altar.

She joined him, clasping her hands together under her
chin. As she tried her very best to focus on his prayers, Jessa
wished she wasn't more confused leaving her counseling than
she'd been coming in.

★ ★ ★

That Monday, Jessa was in a meeting with a client but kept finding it difficult to focus on anything but the myriad of emotions swirling around her like a tornado. *Come on, Jessa, get your shit together.*

She cleared her throat and turned slightly in her red swivel chair to fully face Mrs. Meredith Peabody. She was in her late twenties, stylish, beautiful, and obviously living well on her husband's ridiculous wealth as a real estate developer. She'd come in two weeks ago after a referral from another satisfied client who decided to use the intel on her husband's affair with their nanny to renegotiate her prenuptial agreement.

"I'm sorry to tell you that your husband did make a very obvious play for our decoy," Jessa said, reaching across the desk to grasp the woman's trembling hand.

She eased away from Jessa's touch.

I'm not here offering friendship.

Jessa understood. To many of the wives, she was a necessary evil: a former mistress helping them to catch their philandering spouses. Still, a mistress. A woman who had shattered the life of a wife, making her a common enemy.

"I can only assume you have proof," Meredith said, reaching inside her couture bag for an embroidered handkerchief.

Jessa gave the attractive ash-blond woman a well-practiced woeful look. "Yes, we do," she said, opening her Louis Vuitton iPad case to lightly swipe the dark screen. "Are you ready?"

Meredith shook her head, tucking her straight hair behind her ear and flashing a huge diamond ring.

Jessa raised her finger from the tablet, allowing her a moment before she shattered the woman's world. *She assumed she was young, probably blowing and swallowing him on call, and that her older husband wasn't looking for more.*

She had been wrong.

"I came to you just two weeks ago and he fucked up already?" she said, her eyes glassy with her hurt.

Meredith hadn't thought her husband was cheating. She came to Mistress, Inc., to test him to see *if* he would, and he failed.

"It took a week and a half for our investigator to learn his schedule," Jessa told her, her tone soft to lessen the blow of the truth of her words. "He fell for the bait after one night."

"Did they have sex?" Meredith asked, her blue-green eyes on Jessa.

"No," she stressed, shaking her head. "Our agents are bait, but we let the fish off the hook before they bite. I promise you that."

Jessa tapped the screen and then lifted her chin toward the sixty-inch television on the wall across from her desk.

Meredith turned in her chair.

Jessa's eyes darted between the screen and her client's profile as she watched her husband's eyes on Charli Cole as soon as she walked into the restaurant where he was enjoying dinner with friends. His eyes remained on her even as she passed their table. And while she was seated alone nearby.

It was clear he couldn't take his eyes off her in the white dress she wore.

Jessa felt the pain and embarrassment of her client. She couldn't imagine sitting there and watching her husband lust for another woman.

The light from the all-too-revealing video footage hit against the edge of Meredith's tear before it raced down her face. Her eyes flittered about, missing nothing, seeming not to blink as her husband left behind his dinner mates. From the moment Charli accepted his offer to sit and dine with her, all through their flirtatious conversation, and up until they danced together as he pressed a kiss to her neck that echoed loudly through Charli's mic pack.

"I want to lay inside you all night—"

"Stop it," Meredith cried out, pressing her handkerchief to her face as she lowered her head.

Jessa turned off the television with one tap. "What are you going to do?" she asked, her curiosity ever piqued about that moment when a spouse discovers an infidelity.

Meredith released a heavy breath.

"We didn't discover any signs of infidelity *yet*," Jessa advised her, settling back in her chair and locking her fingers in her lap. "Take some time. Think it through. Don't be silly in your choices. If you are going to leave, then this is your proof. If you are going to stay, then in your case, that video and his knowledge that you will go to all ends to be respected can go a long way to tame a dog before he shits on you."

Jessa gave her a smile that was calculating.

Meredith looked taken aback.

"You're thinking I'm cold, right? A bitch, right?" Jessa asked with a little shake of her head. "No, *life's* the cold bitch."

Meredith rose to her feet. "I would like the file and the video, please."

Jessa stood as well. "Our receptionist has a copy awaiting you at her desk upon receipt of the remaining balance on your account of ten thousand dollars," she said, extending her hand. "Let us know if we can be of any further service, Meredith."

She shook Jessa's hand and walked to the door, pausing before she opened it. "Maybe there was just something about *her*?" she asked, sounding hopeful as she looked back over her tanned, slender shoulder.

Naiveté of the twenties. Jessa was happy to leave that type of blind trust behind in her youth.

Life will teach her better.

"Our agent will *never* see him again," Jessa assured her.

Meredith nodded and took her leave.

Jessa reclaimed her seat and used her tablet to check the interior security camera and watched as the woman paid her fee in cash to Felisha and left with the manila envelope clutched to her chest.

Knock-knock.

"Come in," she called, looking up as their private detective Robert "Hammer" Young entered. He looked the part of an investigator in all black T-shirt and cargo pants, his mirrored sunglasses in place and his silver-flecked hair and beard cut low.

He'd been Mistress, Inc.'s full-time private investigator since the business's inception. He was good at his job and looked even better. Both she and Keegan had found the man attractive—even with him being over ten years older—and they swore neither would cross the line with him and possibly ruin a great working relationship.

"I have the quarterly reports on my regulars," Hammer said, coming in to place the stack of files on her desk before sitting down.

She pushed them to the edge of her desk. "To hell with those files, come fuck me," she said, removing the skimpy black lace panties she wore as he quickly rose to lock her office door.

Sorry, Keegan.

Jessa had been able to resist her desire for him for all of a week.

She tossed her undergarment at him. He caught it with one hand and pressed it to his face as she came around her desk, hitched her floral-print satin pencil skirt up around her waist, and leaned against the edge of the desk. She was already anxious and ready for him.

Hammer dropped his pants to his ankles and walked over to her, stroking his dick to hardness as he hotly eyed her spread legs. "I thought you said no sex in the office?" he asked, slightly cocky as he reached her and bent his strong legs to thrust his hardness inside her.

She gasped and flung her head back, not answering his question, as he stroked deep inside her with speed and strength. She wrapped her legs around his back, the heel of her foot pressing against his buttocks as he clenched and released the hard flesh with each thrust. Her entire body felt alive as her heart pounded wildly and her clit swelled to life against the base of his hard dick. "Hurry, Keegan and I have a meeting at one," she gasped, as he leaned forward and pressed hot kisses to the length of her soft neck.

He stopped.

She looked at him. "What?" she asked,

"Fuck Keegan," he said, still deeply implanted inside her.

Jessa arched a brow. "No, finish fucking me," she stressed.

Their eyes locked.

She bit her bottom lip as she clenched and released her walls around his steel-like hard inches.

"You want to be fucked?" Hammer asked, his voice thick with his desire.

She nodded, looking at her reflection in his mirrored shades.

Hammer stepped back, freeing his dick. It glistened with her wetness. "Turn your ass over," he ordered, holding the hem of his T-shirt between his chin and chest.

Jessa did, looking back at him over her shoulder.

He used his knee to spread her shapely legs and pushed her down until the side of her face and her breasts were pressed against the cool top of her desk. He slapped her buttocks with his dick before thrusting it inside her.

She closed her eyes and stretched her arms to grip the edge of the desk as his hard strokes caused his hips to pound against her buttocks and his thighs to slap against the back of hers.

"This is what you want?" Hammer asked, one hand gripping her buttock and the other pressed down upon her back.

"Yes," she cried, rising on the toes of her shoes to line her pussy up with his strokes.

"Shit," he swore, stepping back to pull out his hard and long inches. He tapped his smooth tip against her buttocks.

"Please," Jessa begged in frustration, feeling her climax recede.

Hammer chuckled. "Please what?" he asked, giving her just the thick tip. "Huh? Please what?"

Jessa felt desperate and hated it. "Fuck me," she pleaded in a hot little whisper.

And he did, filling with her with every inch before he double-pumped his hips in between two long and hard strokes.

"Yes, yes, yes," she moaned.

His sex was always so good. So passionate. So electrifying.

He was better than her deceased husband or Eric. Bigger. Harder.

"You're the best," she gasped.

"Damn right I am," Hammer boasted, bending over to press kisses to her cheek. "Let's get this nut."

Jessa loved the warmth of his body pressed down against her back as he continued thrusting inside her. She felt his dick stiffen in those hot moments just before his cum coated her rigid walls.

Her cries of pleasure matched his as she joined him in climaxing, enjoying the heat, the passion, and the tiny explosions deep inside her core.

"Shit," she swore, still working her walls to drain his dick of every last drop.

Hammer gave her cheek a gentle bite before he eased his spent dick out and stepped back from her.

Jessa rushed to pull her skirt down from around her waist as she rose to her full height. "Does it smell like sex?" she asked, considering opening the windows.

He finished zipping and buttoning his cargo pants, shaking his head. "Your pussy is always fresh, baby," he said with a toothy grin.

She smiled at him as she reclaimed her seat and gripped the edge of the desk to pull herself forward. "You're welcome," she quipped with a wink as she raked her crimson nails through her hair.

Hammer sat down in one of the red leather club chairs in front of her desk, propping his ankle on the knee of his other leg. "Now I'm gonna catch hell staying alert all day," he said, pushing his shades atop his head and revealing his grayish blue eyes. "You drained *all* my energy."

She eyed him, loving that he was a slightly older version of Michael Ealy. Chiseled cheeks. Strong jawline. Beautiful eyes in an even more beautiful brown complexion.

He smiled and her heart fluttered.

"You regret it?" she asked, forcing herself to look away from him.

"Hell no."

Jessa had been in love before—not the confused emotions she felt during her lengthy affair with Eric, but real love like that she had for her husband. She knew the signs, and the more time she spent with Hammer having sex, going on dinner dates, or just spending time at her home, the more she had to accept that she cared about more than just his hard dick.

"What do you have planned for today?" she asked, meaning to shift their focus back on work.

"Surveillance on the Richardson and Overbrook accounts," he said.

Knock-knock.

"Could you unlock the door on your way out?" Jessa asked, reaching for the files he gave her before their quickie.

"I feel used," Hammer joked, rising to his feet.

"You weren't the one ass up, in heels, with your face pressed on a desk," she reminded him dryly.

He laughed as he opened the door. "Thanks, Ms. Bell," he said, easing past Charli Cole standing in the doorway.

Jessa waved her in. "Hi, Charli," she said, closing the file as she took in the off-the-shoulder ruffled shirt she wore with torn denims and heels.

"I wanted to—"

Charli stopped, bending down to rise with Jessa's panties hanging from the tip of her pinkie. "Interesting meeting with Hammer?" she asked, dropping the undies atop Jessa's desk.

Jessa hid her alarm well, leaving the panties right where Charli sat them. "Never make assumptions," she said lightly.

The younger woman arched a brow. "I had a feeling he was *your* private dick."

Humph. Let me get this little bitch straight.

Jessa leaned back in her chair, crossed her legs, wished she had gone to the bathroom to clean up after their quickie, and eyed her new employee. "Mistress, Inc., is all about respect for privacy and presentation of facts," she began. "If we relied on assumptions, we would be out of business."

Charli looked pensive as she clasped her hands in front of her where she still stood.

"I hope you are aware of facts versus assumptions because that's the only way you could fit in here," Jessa finished, her tone cold as her eyes bored in to the other woman.

Charli nodded. "My mistake, Ms. Bell," she said, sounding contrite.

"Why are you here anyway?" Jessa asked.

"I wanted to thank you for the bonus in my payment this week."

Jessa nodded, opening the first of the files. "You earned it," she said. She looked up when Charli remained in her office. "If there's nothing else..."

Charli gave her a brief wave and left.

Once the door closed behind her, Jessa reached for the panties and pushed them into the inside pocket of her Balenciaga tote. "Finally." She sighed in satisfaction as she spread the folders atop her desk and tapped each one as she read three of the names.

"Jaime Hall. Aria Livewell. Renee Thorne."

Her three ex-friends from Richmond Hills.

Jessa purposefully blew up their marriages five years ago, and in her continuous struggle to assuage her guilt, she checked on them to ensure they were doing well in the aftermath. It eased the conscience she'd once lacked.

Reverend Dell says I'm invading their privacy.

Jessa reopened the first file.

Well, let's agree to disagree, Rev.

One by one she read Hammer's detailed reports. When she was done with all three, she was stunned. Each had secrets far beyond the ones they'd once shared with her as their friend and confidante. But that wasn't the real kicker.

One is being cheated on.

"Well, damn," Jessa said, not quite sure what to do with *that* information.

Chapter 3

One week later

Jessa parked her red convertible Porsche just beneath a large black sign embossed with "Richmond Hills Subdivision." She pushed her oversized shades atop her head as she eyed the stone pillars flanking the wrought iron security gate. Beyond the entrance was a beautiful collection of stately homes and manicured lawns.

She had once lived among them, happily.

Until her husband, Marc, passed away and her loneliness—her *desperation*—drove her into the arms of a man she considered a friend. A man married to a woman who had become her friend, as well. Foolishly, she thought their sex had become love, and their affair would lead to their marriage.

Nothing but his fucked-up ass lies. Crazy bent-dick bastard.

Her hands clenched the steering wheel as she remembered him in her bed, his face buried between her thighs, feeding her lies in between eating her out...

"Eric, can you believe this is the last night we have to spend apart?" she asked, reaching up to grab the headboard

as his tongue circled her clit before he sucked it between his lips.

"Mmm-hmm," he moaned against her flesh.

She gasped in pleasure, her hips rising off the bed. Her eyelashes fluttered as she panted, reaching down to grasp the back of his head with one hand. "The moving company will be here at seven," she whispered.

Eric lifted his head, his mouth moist from her juices. "I'm going fishing in the morning," he said.

Jessa let her head drop on her pillow before she raised it again to look at him. "We're moving into our new home and you're going fishing?" she asked, raising her knees to trap his head between them.

"Isn't that what the moving company is for?" he asked, raising his hands to press her legs from his head.

Jessa eyed him as he sat up,. "Months ago, you finally agreed to leave Jaime and your bullshit marriage behind," she said, tapping his back with her foot. "Did you change your mind again?"

Eric twisted on the bed to stare at her. "Hell no," he stressed, reaching to tug her bare thighs with his warm hands. "I love only you, Jessa, and you know that."

Their eyes were locked.

"When will you tell her that you're leaving?"

"After I'm gone," he said. "Less drama."

"So you want me to move into the new house while you fish, and then what?" Jessa asked.

Eric bent to press a kiss to her knee. "Wait for me to get home," he said without hesitation. "As soon as I get back from the fishing trip, I'm coming straight to you."

Hope grew in her heart.

"You promise?" she asked, her voice barely above a whisper, revealing her doubt, her need, and her timidity.

"I swear," Eric insisted. "Tomorrow everything changes."

"And tonight?" she asked, uncrossing her legs and spreading them.

He smiled as he lay back down on the bed to lower his head.

She arched her back as he drew his tongue from the divide of her buttocks and up to her plump clit.

"Fucking liar," she muttered, opening her purse to pull out her cigarette case.

The next day while she'd been at the new house awaiting the moving truck, she'd sent that infamous text message. She had truly believed him and gloated, feeling sinful joy that she'd wrecked their marriage.

She remembered it well, even all these years later:

LIFE HAS MANY FORKS IN THE ROAD AND TODAY I'VE DECIDED TO TRAVEL DOWN THE PATH LEADING YOUR HUSBAND STRAIGHT TO MY WAITING AND OPEN ARMS. I CAN'T LIE AND SAY I HAVE REGRETS. I LOVE HIM MORE THAN YOU AND I NEED HIM MORE. YOU SAW HIM FOR THE LAST TIME THIS MORNING. TONIGHT HE COMES HOME TO ME. HE'S MY MAN NOW. THANKS FOR NOT BEING WOMAN ENOUGH 4 HIM.
  XOXO

"Life has many forks in the road," she said sarcastically with an eye roll. "So fucking dramatic. Bunch of bullshit."

And in the end, plain embarrassing.

After his fishing trip with his friends was over, Eric Hall went home to his wife. Although she knew from her friendship with Jaime that their marriage was far from the perfect scenario they portrayed, Eric had looked her dead in the face and lied about leaving her. He had allowed her to sell her home in Richmond Hill and acquire another knowing damn well he was a pathological liar.

Jaime left him that night when he got home from fishing, and he blamed Jessa for that. When she ended things as well, his crazy truly came out, and he stalked her. He harassed her. He threatened her. He sat outside her house for hours on end. He ejaculated on the window of her house. He—

"No," Jessa said forcefully, closing the cigarette case and dropping it onto the passenger seat of her car.

I'm not reliving that crazy shit anymore.

She looked up at her rearview mirror but quickly shifted her eyes away. Her reflection was a bit too hard to stomach when she felt like she'd started the ball rolling—not on his crazy, that was there simmering all the way ready to boil over—but the affair and that message she regretted ever sending was all her.

"All me," Jessa said softly, looking up at the mirror again.

So why am I here?

She released a heavy breath as she checked the side mirror and pulled away from the curb. As she drove around the small New Jersey town she once called home, she had good memories of her life with Marc. Walking to the park, dinner at one of the restaurants, watching him golf at the country club, couples massage at Serenity Spa...

Yes, Serenity Spa. Jessa slowed the Porsche down. "A little pampering is just what I need," she said, checking the rearview mirror before she shifted over to make the right turn past the cupcake bakery on the corner.

Three miles up on the left she made the turn onto the large paved driveway of the renovated 1930s Georgian cottage. She pulled up to the valet stand, leaving the key in the ignition before she exited and smoothed the wide-legs red pants she wore with a black silk halter top. "Thank you," she said to the valet, passing him to enter the spa.

Jessa paused at the entrance. The décor was completely different. Her vibrant clothing clashed with the whitewashed walls. The bleached floor with muted accents and watercolor art were immediately relaxing. The nerves she felt about being back in town receded a little bit as she looked around.

"Welcome to Serenity Day Spa. How may I help you?"

Jessa stiffened her spine and notched her chin higher as she crossed the space to reach the turquoise-tinted glass front desk. "Hello...Barbi," she said to the petite blonde, reading her name tag. "I do not have an appointment, but I am desperate need of a massage and body scrub. Any openings?"

Barbi slid her waist-length Marcia Brady–esque hair behind her ear before she tapped away on the touchscreen computer. "Actually, with it being midweek we're not very busy," she said. "I could fit you in this morning."

"Perfect," Jessa said, pulling out her wallet from her bag.

Barbi swiveled a large tablet around to face Jessa. "If you could just enter your name and all of the services you would like," she said.

That's new as well. Hello 2015.

She booked facial and massage treatments.

"That will be six hundred and fifty-four dollars," Barbi said.

Jessa handed over her Plum American Express card before being led to the row of changing rooms to change into a pale blue woven cotton robe. She hung her clothes in the small cabinet and set her bag on the top shelf before turning the key in the lock and taking it out to slide into the pocket of her robe as she stepped out into the hall.

"Kittie, it was good catching up. Let's do lunch real soon."

Jessa froze. *Kittie. Couldn't be. Better not fucking be.*

Jessa turned. "Shit," she swore with an eye roll that had to show nothing but the whites of her eyes. *Motherfucking Kittie Hall.*

Wife of Eric Hall Senior and mother to Eric Hall Junior. Both men had tried in their own ways to destroy her and Kittie had defended their actions.

Well, those that her dumb ass knows about.

Jessa looked on in amusement as Kittie spotted her down the length of the hall and her eyes widened in shock. Jessa crossed her arms over her chest and leaned against the wall as she watched the older woman look over her shoulder before she made her way toward Jessa. She also was dressed in a Serenity spa robe and flips-flops that made a light slapping noise against the bleached wood floors as she moved.

Here we go. All right, bitch, let's play.

"What the hell are you doing here, you harpy?" Kittie spat in a harsh whisper. "Are you following me?"

Jessa arched a brow. "Listen, I'm trying to avoid my own path straight to hell. I wouldn't dare follow you down yours," she said dryly.

"Oh, hell has your name written on it," Kittie said coldly, forcing a fake smile and smoothing her silver bob with her hand when a spa worker walked past them.

Lunatic.

"And you're married to Satan and bore his spawn," Jessa said, not trying to lower her voice.

Kittie's eyes widened before they filled with tears. "Don't *you* dare speak on my dead son. Not when it's your fault he's dead."

And for a moment, Jessa regretted her words, and then she knew she was changing for the better. Standing before her was a grieving mother, her only child lost to her. In many ways, they were more alike than they were different.

"Your first daughter was saved from you!" Kittie said, her glee at Jessa's loss filling her eyes.

Jessa pushed up off the wall and took a step forward, towering over the short, round woman. Any softness or remorse she had dissipated with ease. She gave her a smile that bordered on wolfish. "I dare you to mention my daughter again," she said, her voice low and threatening, as she fought the urge to snarl.

Kittie gasped a bit and stepped back, clutching at the front of her robe. "You are crazy," she whispered.

"I'm crazy?" Jessa asked in disbelief with a little smile that lasted a millisecond.

She opened her mouth, ready to spill secrets that would humble Kittie Hall. But she couldn't. They were her leverage against her husband, a powerful man, who wanted to punish her by taking her daughter—their grandchild—away from her. Instead, she stepped back, forced herself to relax, and gave up the urge to win the fight. Keeping Eric Hall Sr. at bay and not having to battle for the custody of her daughter was more important than revealing to Kittie that her husband had pursued her for sex.

Jessa smirked.

She had allowed him to press disgusting kisses to her neck just long enough to record him with her teddy bear nanny cam and used the video to blackmail him into dropping the custody battle.

No. I can't give up my leverage. I'm smarter than that.

Instead, Jessa moved past the woman and walked down the hall.

"Scandalous, low-life, trifling, immoral, vile *bitch*," Kittie said from behind her.

Jessa turned. "Your granddaughter is fine, thanks for asking," she said.

Kittie blustered as she kicked off her flip-flop, stopped down to pick it up, and flung at Jessa. It hit against the wall with a *splat*.

Jessa chuckled as Kittie balled her hands into fists in frustration. She looked up at the corner and pointed at the video camera. "I'll be sure to get my attorney to subpoena a copy of their files," she mocked. "I'm sure any judge would love to see how you react in anger."

Kittie was alarmed as she looked up at the round black

glass surrounding surveillance equipment. She pressed her lips into a thin line, sent Jessa one last hateful glance, and then quickly disappeared into her changing room.

Jessa glanced at that bubble again, before making her way back to her own changing room and unlocking her cabinet to remove her iPhone. Quickly, she zipped an email to her attorney, doing just what she'd threatened, and then headed back to her private room to focus on nothing but relaxation for the next three hours.

Kittie was long gone by the time Jessa emerged from the Serenity Spa. Once she was behind the wheel of her Porsche she headed back across town to the Richmond Hills subdivision.

Tell her the truth.

She pulled to a stop just a few feet from the security gate. The guard game out of the stone hutch and looked concerned as he eyed her. Vaguely she noted he wasn't the same guard from when she resided in the upscale community.

But if I tell her, then I have to reveal I have them under surveillance.

She frowned.

Just mind your own business, Jessa Bell.

She eased the car into reverse, finishing a K-turn to turn around and leave the subdivision.

Bzzzzzz.

Jessa dug her iPhone from the side pocket on her tote with her free hand. "Yes, Hammer," she said, coming to a red light and easing to a stop.

"You're not in the office today?" he asked.

"I will be," she said. "I have some errands to run. Why? What's up?"

"Just checking on you. You've had something on your mind all week," he said. "And last night...we just slept."

"Really, Hammer," she said, as her stomach rumbled in her hunger. "One night of dry dick and you hunting me down? What's next? A tracking device?"

He chuckled. "Yeah, I eased one up in you the last time I fingered that pussy," he joked.

"You won't be the first Negro to go crazy over this cha-cha," she countered, slowing down her Porsche and turning onto Fairmount Avenue.

"Nah. No offense, but I'm not crazy and I've had good pussy before," he said, sounding offended.

She pulled into the side parking lot of the Terrace Room restaurant. "Good ain't the same as the best," she said, pulling into a spot before she turned her car off. She let her head fall back against the headrest as she pinched the bridge of her nose with her free hand.

"Come remind me it's the best."

"Horny bastard," she said, her tone playful.

"Come take the pressure off," he countered.

She laughed softly, checking her makeup in the rearview mirror. Her laughter died down as she eyed the three women walking into the restaurant together. Aria. Jaime. Renee. Her heart pounded wildly. *Fate is a mischievous bitch.*

She leaned forward to look up at the clear blue skies. "Or is this your way of telling me to stop stalling, God?" she asked.

"Huh?" Hammer asked, obviously confused.

Jessa shook her head. "Nothing, Hammer, let me call you back," she said before ending the call. Seconds later the phone vibrated in her hand as he called her right back. She turned the ringer on silent and dropped it inside her bag.

I'm trying to do something right, right?

She grabbed the bag and left the car, pushing the door closed before she made her way up the concrete walk to the wood doors. When she entered, she almost felt like she was taken back to 2010. Nothing about the décor had changed. She smiled at the maître d'. "Table for one, please," she said, her eyes already moving past him to look about the restaurant.

He led her to a small table by a large bay window.

"Thank you," she said. "I'm just going over to say hello to some... *friends* first."

"Yes, madam."

Jessa stiffened her back and made her way over to their table. Her façade was cool, but in truth her pulse raced. She knew this was a bold and defiant move.

Jaime looked up from her menu and spotted her first, saying something to Aria on her left and then Renee on her right before all three women looked at her with openly hostile eyes. *Well, here we go...*

All three women rose to their feet.

"Hello, ladies, have a seat? I know I will," Jessa said, setting her bag on the floor and folding her curvy frame into the seat before her. "We need to talk."

"You're six years late to the day you were supposed to meet us here but instead sent that stupid-ass text," Renee said. She was still tall, thick, and toned with her hair cut even shorter and framing her pretty face. *Still dressed like she's forever on her way to a business meeting.*

Jessa frowned a bit and then her face filled with clarity. "Actually, we were supposed to meet at the spa, and I've been there as well today, not even remembering," she said, glancing at each woman as they continued to stand

"What the hell do you want?" Jaime asked, looking less refined and poised than the façade of perfection she used to project as the socialite wife of a wealthy businessman.

"To make amends for what I did to all of you," she admitted, crossing her legs and leaning back in her chair as she looked up at them.

"This bitch," Aria muttered.

It was she that Jessa did not trust. Aria was born and bred

in Newark and loved to remind everyone of that fact by her temperament and her willingness to get physical at the drop of a hat. She would gladly push aside her Ivy League education, her career as a journalist, and her position as the wife of a prominent doctor to go straight Newark "Brick City" New Jersey on anyone who tried it with her. Jessa knew her well. They had been friends since college. In fact, it was she who had encouraged Aria and her husband, Kingston, to move to Richmond Hills.

She eyed the dark-skinned beauty who now wore her thick black hair straight and long. She would always be the ghetto girl who made good but never forgot where she came from. Proudly.

Jessa had cared for these women as friends and then blown up their lives like enemies.

"One of you deserves to know the truth about your relationship," Jessa said.

All three women flung up their hands in disgust.

"Is everything okay, ladies?"

Jessa didn't bother to turn and eye the waiter who came up to the table behind her. Instead she reached in her bag and pulled out a folder, putting it atop the place setting in front of her. It was a dare to be ignored. All three sets of eyes dropped to the folder. *Curiosity always killed the cat.*

"Not *this* bullshit again," Aria snapped.

Renee waved the waiter away.

Jaime was the first to sit.

Jessa's eyes shifted to her. That day Jessa sent the message, Jaime had left Eric. Through her surveillance via Mistress, Inc., Jessa knew all about her six-month relationship with Graham Walker, also known as Pleasure, the man-whore she used to pay for sex. That came to an end two years ago, and the last she'd heard, he was living out of the country, so the fear in Jaime's face confused her.

Jessa had once paid Pleasure for oral sex just to embarrass

Jaime. *Hell, if his dick game is half as good as his tongue game, then she might still be dicknotyzed.*

"Listen, I know I am the last person this info should come from, but I'm here in person with proof, doing the Lord's work," Jessa said plainly, picking up the file.

"Did this bitch say she doing the Lord's work?" Aria said, her voice cold and incredulous as she took a seat.

Jessa paused. "So once again you're doubting me, Aria?" she asked. "Once Marc died, suddenly the best friend who happened to be pretty became the bitch not to be trusted around anyone's husband."

"Are you fucking kidding me right now?" Jaime asked, the words almost running together. "You do remember that you slept with *my* husband—"

"Who eventually stalked and tried to kill me," Jessa inserted.

All three women shook their heads at her, completely dumbfounded.

"And don't forget killed himself and left me to raise his child alone," Jessa added. "I think I've been punished enough. Trust me, I regret fucking with all that crazy."

Renee finally dropped down onto her seat. "Something is seriously wrong with you, Jessa, but you don't even know it," she said, her voice soft.

"No, something is seriously right with me because I am trying to make amends and do what's right," she explained.

"The Lord's work. Right, bitch?" Aria drawled with an exaggerated eye roll.

I thought motherhood would calm her ratchet ass down some.

"Look," Jessa said loudly, holding up her hands. "I'm *trying* to hip one of y'all to getting played by your man...and *no*, I'm not the mistress this time."

"I ain't even got time for this shit. Not again, trick," Aria said, reaching down to grab her Gucci tote. "I'm out."

Jaime reached out to touch her wrist and stop her.

"You're not the one who should leave," she said, giving Jessa a hostile stare.

Renee reached out and scooped up the file, opening it.

"Don't fall for her shit," Jaime said, reaching across the table to grab at it.

"It's me," Renee said solemnly, dropping the file to the table. "Again."

Photos of her husband, Davin, in bed with another woman slid across the table. Jaime and Aria both gasped in shock.

Jessa felt regret. Had she made the right decision to involve herself in the lives of these women again? Renee's last marriage did end with her ex-husband Jackson's affair, and it drove her to drink. Could she even handle another deception? *Shit. This can't be right.*

Renee stared off into space before she closed her eyes, and her shoulders slumped as she released a long heavy breath. "Damn, Davin," she whispered.

Aria shoved the photos back into the file and slammed it closed. "Hell to the no, ho, you *gots* to go," she coldly said, rising to point her finger toward the exit. "Bounce before I bounce you."

Jaime eyed Jessa, taking the file crushed in Aria's fist. "Where did you get this?" she asked.

Uh-oh. I hoped no one would ask that.

Renee now looked at her as well.

The truth shall set you free.

"I've been checking up on all you," she admitted. "Hoping that you weren't still suffering after I sent that message that day."

"You sued me," Jaime stressed.

"For what was owed to my daughter from Eric as her father," Jessa countered.

Aria lunged across the table, sending their glasses of water tumbling. Jaime and Renee jumped to their feet to restrain her.

Jessa didn't move. Not even a flinch.

"My intentions were good," she said slowly and firmly, hoping that would help her words break through to them.

It did not.

She nodded in understanding as she picked up her tote and rose to her feet. All eyes of the patrons of the restaurant were on them. "I promise you I am not getting any pleasure from this, Renee," she said earnestly.

"Go to hell," Renee said, her eyes as chilled as her voice.

Jessa turned and walked away from the table, notching her chin higher as she left the restaurant.

Interlude

I met my bitch of a mother . . . and she didn't even know it.

She couldn't even recognize the child she gave birth to. I saw parts of me I inherited from her, and still she registered nothing of herself in me. Each time I encountered her, I yearned for her eyes to see me—really see me—and claim me and give me the love I had been denied all these years. And each time, I was disappointed.

It hurt.

It was fucked up.

It made me want to get fucked up. But I didn't.

I'd been clean for more than six months, and that was major. That last overdose scared the shit out of me. I checked myself into a thirty-day drug rehab. Plus, revenge was my new high.

A few weeks after I got home from rehab, I was about to enter my building on the Upper West Side when Eric Hall Sr. first entered my life with news of my mother's identity. Jessa Bell. Then for the longest time I would just say her name, seeing how it felt on my lips, trying to evoke some other emotion than rage from the stories he told me of her losing custody of me because of her neglect and abuse.

That day, my world was truly shattered. Up until then I could *fantasize about who she was and why she gave me away. He offered a reality that was painful. I went numb for days. Craved weed and cocaine. Pills. Wanted to get so high that I flew above the pain.*

But I didn't.

My life has been hell at times, growing up in a world where I didn't belong because I was born to a mother who didn't need me to belong to her.

I wanted to know more about her. My mother. My abuser. I had to be sober for that.

I researched her. There was plenty about her online. I knew it all and was ashamed. I understood that high-end life she led and was angry. I learned I had a baby sister that she was raising and was bitter.

I read her book, The Mistress Memoirs, *and then burned it in my fireplace. There was no mention of me. I had been erased from her life and probably her memory. A fucking afterthought. A mistake. A regret.*

I hated Jessa Bell.

I knew nothing of my father, but that didn't matter. Any man can bust a nut, but a woman carries her child inside her for many, many months, and to turn your back on that connection, to injure the child you bore, that was beyond low.

To me, she was as evil as she was beautiful.

I took delight in being near her, in her space, invading her life under the cloak of a false name and identity. Working for her in this ridiculous business that just glorified the mess she'd made of her life. To give me away, and the most she could accomplish was fame for being a whore? A sidepiece?

Humph. That shit pissed me the fuck off.

It's okay, though. I did it. I made it into her world. Although I didn't know just what I would do to wreck her life the way that she wrecked mine, it felt good knowing that, ultimately, I was in control, and with that upper hand, when the shit hit the fan, it would be my way.

That bitch won't even see it coming.

Chapter 4

One month later

"You ready to talk about it now?"

Jessa paused in lightly stroking the soft hairs on Hammer's chest as she lay beside his nude body in the middle of his king-sized bed. "Talk about what?" she asked, knowing it could be a myriad of topics she considered taboo for them.

"Your affair with Eric and everything that happened because of it."

Jessa became pensive. Three years since they first hired him as the investigator for Mistress, Inc., nearly as long since they'd first become lovers, and this was the first he'd asked about her salacious past.

Why the hell didn't he leave it that way?

"Haven't you read my book?" she asked, rolling away from his warm body to rise from the bed. They had spent lunch making love. "It's a *New York Times* best seller."

"Jessa."

"It's available in audiobook if you're not a book reader," she said with a brief glance back at him over her shoulder before walking across his loft-style apartment into his modern glass-walled bathroom. *Not much of a hiding place. Shit.*

She turned to leave, but paused with her hand on the sliding glass door as she watched him stride over to her. Her eyes took in his nudity even as she felt anxious that he would not relent on his line of questioning. She took a step back as he filled the doorway, blocking her exit.

They eyed each other.

"No, Hammer," she said, crossing her arms over her bare chest.

"Yes," he insisted, raising his arm above his head to grip the top of the door frame.

"Why?" she asked in annoyance.

"Because I want to know more about you than how to make you cum," he answered without hesitation.

Her heartbeat sped. She felt light-headed from the intensity of his stare. He was daring to cross a line and wanted her to join him on the journey.

"I have known pain from an early age," she said to him in a whisper, her tears welling at the thought of her daughter Georgia and the cruelty of her creation. "I would like to forget the person I became because of it."

"To forge ahead and be better—do better—I have to tell the truth about my role in this scandal with which everyone is so fascinated. It began before the sending of that message from a mistress to a wife," he said.

Jessa's eyes widened in surprise. It was the first line from her book. "So you did read it," she said, not sure how she felt about that.

He nodded.

"When?" she asked, her heart pounding with the ferocity of a racehorse's hooves across a finish line.

"Before my first interview with you," Hammer admitted. *Humph.*

"Don't you want to know more about me?" he asked, his voice deep.

She shook her head. "To know more is to love you more," she admitted.

He tilted his head to the side, his beautiful eyes squinted, as he lowered his arms and came to stand before her in his charcoal slate bathroom with its bronze hardware. "So, you do love me?" he asked.

Jessa closed her eyes and released a breath. "I meant—"

"Because I love you," Hammer said, leaning down to breathe the words against her lips.

Shit.

Jessa's eyes dropped to his mouth before rising to get lost in his gaze. Her heart was elated. Her head was afraid. She leaned toward him, resting her forehead against his chest. "I been through too much, Hammer, for some bullshit from you," she said.

"And I been through too much to give you bullshit," he said, enfolding her in his strong arms as he pressed kisses to the side of her face.

She leaned back to look up at him. "You swear?" she asked, her fear present and obvious in her eyes and tone.

"I *swear.*"

Jessa rose on her bare toes and pressed her hands to his handsome face, kissing him as she felt the door to her heart open wider to let him in.

Hours later, Jessa parked her Porsche in her spot in the office building lot and climbed from the car to make her way to the elevator. She was running late from lunch and Keegan was blowing up her phone. It wasn't until she had finally left Hammer's apartment that she took her phone off "do not disturb." Only calls from her nanny and mother were allowed.

Ding.

"Hold the elevator, please," Jessa called out just as the door began to close.

The door halted and reopened.

She smiled as the same sexy blond man in the nice suit stuck his head out. He smiled at her as well, flashing perfect white teeth. She couldn't deny he was the epitome of white-boy fine. Like Paul Walker, rest his beautiful soul, or Brad Pitt. *Hell, Paul Newman and Robert Redford in their prime kind of fine. Like, I understand why Lisa Bonet can't get enough of her husband, Jason Momoa, level of sexy.*

"We keep meeting this way," she said, as she stepped on the elevator beside him.

He smiled again. "I would say it's fate if. . ."

"I wasn't married," Jessa finished for him.

"Right," he agreed.

"Right," she copied.

They rode up in silence, and when he reached the twelfth floor, he gave her a respectful nod before striding away. Again, her eyes drifted over the fit of the suit on his fit physique, but she forced her eyes away. "You're with Hammer now," she reminded herself softly, looking up at the ceiling until the door closed and clocked temptation.

I'm with Hammer.

Jessa eyed her reflection displayed on the metal elevator door. She smoothed her hands down the length of the light denim skinny jeans she wore.

Am I really trying my hand at love again?

The elevator came to a stop, and just before the door slid open she saw the doubt in her own eyes. She made her way down the hall to their office. As soon as she pushed the door open, Keegan and Felisha looked up from where they both stood at the reception desk.

"You *have* to see this bullshit," Keegan said.

Felisha nodded, her eyes wide.

Jessa approached them, shifting her Saint Laurent bag to her side. "What is it?"

"Perv alert," Keegan drawled, scratching her scalp with the rubber end of a pencil. "Big-time, honey. This one is two slices of bread short of a sandwich."

Jessa's steps paused. She had been friends with Keegan long enough to still be slightly confused by her Southern sayings but land somewhere in the ballpark of what she was colorfully expressing. "Do I want to see this?"

"*Hell* naw," Keegan admitted. "But get your ass over here anyway."

"Ready?" Felisha asked, looking at Jessa over the rim of her glasses when she reached them.

Jessa gave her a stern look, as if to say, "Little girl, don't play with me."

Felisha restarted the video.

"This is my third time watching it," Keegan admitted. "Listen *carefully*."

Jess gave her an odd look before locking her eyes on the screen.

The video was blurry and shaky at first, but soon it was clear and steady as it focused on a couple sitting at the end of a bar.

"My wife doesn't have the same . . . taste as me."

Jessa bent down to peer at the screen at the familiar background. "Is that the Plaza?" she asked.

"Sure is," Keegan supplied.

The video zoomed in on a tall and handsome redheaded man sitting at the hotel bar with a woman. She could only make out her profile, but it was clear she was beautiful and dressed for business. The woman she didn't know, but the man was a former client. "Warrington Sachs," she said in a surprised whisper.

She fell quiet as he continued to talk.

"I have needs," he said, taking a sip of some brown liquor.

"And I love to please," the woman replied.

"But for what price?"

She smiled and stroked his chin. "Depends on what you need."

Jessa was confused and held up her hand. "Pause it," she demanded, sharing a look with Keegan. "Didn't he hire us to catch his wife?"

Felisha handed her a red file.

Jessa took it from her, quickly reading through Hammer's notes and photographs proving his summation that Mrs. Helen Sachs was a loyal wife with no reason to be suspected.

"I had someone in place to . . . satisfy me, but she relocated a few months ago."

"Slick bastard," Jessa muttered, closing the file.

"Lucky for me," his date said.

"Is she a pro?" Jessa asked.

Keegan shrugged one shoulder. "I think so, because she'd have to be to agree to this crock of shit."

"I want you to defecate on me."

Jessa froze. Jessa frowned. Jessa felt her lunch go in reverse. "HuhSayWhat?" she asked, with a little tilt of her head.

The woman slid her hand from his, and it was clear from the sudden stiffness of her back that his request shocked her as well.

"He wants her to *shit* on him," Keegan said in a loud voice as if Jessa's hearing was failing her.

"I liked it smeared on my chest while you ride my dick."

"No," Jessa said, holding up her hands. "Nope. Nada. Not gone happen. Nah. Never. Hell to the no. No way. Negative."

Felisha stopped the video.

Keegan chuckled. "Hell, you missed the big finale. It was a shit show."

"Summarize it, please," she asked, feeling disgusted.

"Well, he offers her five thousand, and that turns her little frown upside down and then she proceeds to tell him that she just had a big ole dinner," Keegan said, stifling her chuckle and putting on a deadpan expression when Jessa eyed her. "So they head upstairs to a room, and I guess that's when—"

Jessa pointed a finger at her. "Don't you dare," she stressed, knowing Keegan's sense of dry humor.

"The shit really hit the fan," Keegan finished.

"Really?" Jessa asked.

"No shit," she continued.

"Keegan."

"I guess he had a shit-eating grin the whole time," she said, biting her bottom lip and wiggling her eyebrows.

"Fuck you," Jessa sang, turning to walk toward her office.

"Okay, Jessa, I'm sorry," Keegan said, rushing over to grab Jessa's shoulder and turn her around. "I don't mean to be a shit stirrer."

Jessa brushed Keegan's hands away and grimaced as she swatted at Keegan's thigh as if to scold her friend and business partner.

"Okay, I'm done," Keegan promised.

"Where did that video come from?" Jessa asked, opening the file to look at a picture of Mrs. Sachs smiling at a friend over lunch at Barneys. *Just completely lost in the sauce about her perverted husband.*

"Tyler," Keegan offered.

Their agent Tyler Infill was tall, dark, tanned, and handsome. When he wasn't going on casting calls for acting jobs or handling assignments for Mistress, Inc., he was in the gym, and it showed in every hard contour of his body. They used him as bait for Mrs. Sachs—at her daughter's school, the grocery store, her weekly lunch dates with friends. Even church. Not once had she given him anything more than a passing glance.

"We had Tyler baiting another client and he recognized Warrington," Keegan said. "He emailed the video to us."

"Forward me a copy," Jessa told Felisha, who did so with a nod.

Keegan eyed her for a little while before she shook her head. "No. She is not our client, he is."

"He *was*," Jessa corrected.

"Stay out of it," Keegan insisted. "I just wanted you to see it for shits and giggles."

"Really?" Jessa said again.

"That one wasn't on purpose," she said, before clearing her throat.

Felisha raised her hand. "I have a question?" she said.

Jessa and Keegan both eyed her.

"Do you think it messed it up for him if she had corn for dinner?" Felisha asked innocently, pushing her spectacles up on her nose with her thumb.

Jessa chuckled, seeing that Felisha was earnestly awaiting an answer.

"Now *that's* funny to you?" Keegan asked. "I'm insulted. This is a problem."

"Don't start no shit, won't be no shit," Jessa slid in before playfully sticking out her tongue.

All three women howled with laughter.

It's easier being bad.

Jessa's eyes shifted from her rose gold iPhone to her computer, where the video of Warrington Sachs walking into the hotel room with his beautiful prostitute was paused on the screen. There was a time, not long ago, where she would have felt no remorse or given a second thought to the plight of Mrs. Sachs or her marriage. It would have amused her had she allowed it to break through her bubble of self-interest.

Another damn dilemma.

Jessa shivered in revulsion at the thought of Warrington Sachs's perversion. *Like, what the hell does he get out of that shit—no pun intended.*

Her eyes shifted to her computer and her mouth twisted in disgust at the list of sexual perversions. Her curiosity had led her to Google and Wikipedia's pages on paraphilia now leaving her with far too much info on just what turned some people on.

Vomit. Blood. Shit. Death.

The hell?

Jessa closed the internet page, positive she would have nightmares about it all.

Bzzzzzz.

She pressed the intercom button. "Yes, Felisha," she said.

"Renee Thorne is here to see you. Are you available?" her receptionist asked.

Renee?

Jessa drummed her crimson nails against the top of her desk. She was surprised, thinking she'd seen the last of her last month when all three women berated her and sent her on her way.

Fucking embarrassing.

"Ms. Bell?" Felisha said.

It was the oddest moment to remember when she reverted back to her married name. Her agent and book editor had put the kibosh to her show of independence, thinking her notoriety was attached to the name Jessa Bell. *You do realize when you say your name quickly it sounds like jezebel. Try it. JessaBell. JessaBell. JessaBell.* Jessa frowned as her agent's whiny voice echoed around her.

"Ms. Bell? Are you available?" Felisha nudged again via the intercom.

Jessa reached into the bottom side drawer of her desk. In it were the monthly reports about Jaime, Aria, and Renee. She extracted a blue one and set it in the center of her desk. "Send her in," Jessa said, smoothing her hand over her hair as she stood.

She put on a cool façade as Felisha escorted Renee into her office. "Hello, Renee. Care for a refreshment?" she asked, as she waved a hand toward one of the chairs before her desk.

"No," Renee replied, her tone stiff as she took a seat and set her tote on the floor beside it.

Jessa paused in reclaiming her seat, feeling annoyance at Renee's sullen attitude. She looked back at Felisha. "A Bellini for me, please," she requested.

Renee scratched her eyebrow. "Alcohol on the job, huh?" she asked.

Jessa arched a brow. *This bullshit is running out.* "What can I help you with, Renee?" she asked, forcing a fake smile.

Renee eyed her across the desk. "This isn't easy for me," she began.

Knock-knock.

Felisha entered carrying two champagne flutes. She set one on the desk before Renee and handed Jessa the other. "I brought you one in case you changed your mind, Mrs. Thorne," she said, eyeing her over the rim of the glasses.

"I won't," Renee insisted.

"Ms. Thorne doesn't drink . . . any longer," Jessa explained, waving her hand for Renee to remove it.

"Wait," Renee called out.

"And what will that help, Renee?" Jessa asked in a quiet voice. "You've been down that road before, and I believe it led to a DUI charge."

Renee's eyes hardened in anger.

Felisha hurried from the room with the flute in her hand.

Jessa took a sip of her drink, savoring the taste of it before she swallowed. She pointedly checked her diamond watch before leveling her eyes on Renee. "You wish you weren't here. You're uncomfortable. You're embarrassed. You wish I would die—even though it was that white woman he married that was his mistress and not me. Still, you hate me. Blah, blah,

blah. I get it," Jessa said, having another sip of her drink. "What do you want?"

"Who is my husband's mistress?" Renee asked.

She arched a brow. "You didn't *ask* him?"

Renee looked annoyed. "He doesn't know I know," she finally answered.

Ah. Now it all makes sense.

Jessa glanced down at the file on her desk, but she didn't need it. "His new secretary," she said.

Renee snorted in derision. "How fucking cliché," she muttered.

Jessa eyed her, remaining silent, as she tapped one finger atop the file. "Spouses pay me good money for this type of intel," she said.

Renee rolled her eyes heavenward as she picked up her tote. "Fucking figures something was in this for you," she said, pulling out a checkbook with a Gucci cover. "How much?"

Jessa shook her head. "Renee, all I ask is your forgiveness," she said.

Renee looked surprised, and then doubtful. "I'd rather write you the check," she said.

Lord, this bitch is really trying me. I hope you see that.

"You are far too angry for a wife that told me she attempted to cheat on her first husband with her assistant who didn't close the deal because he's gay," Jessa began. "And for the last two weeks, you've been punishing your second husband for cheating by fucking your ex-husband, who is now married, thus making you a mistress. Welcome to the club."

She enjoyed how each word from her mouth seemed to widen Renee's eyes in shock.

"I was a wife who let my grief turn me into a mistress," Jessa said, tilting her head to the side as she eyed her former friend. "It happens, *right*?"

Renee shifted her eyes away from her and looked uncomfortable.

Jessa recognized her guilt. "I'm not looking for friendship, Renee. Not at all," she stressed as she pushed the folder toward her. "Consider my debt to you for sending that silly message paid. That's all I ask."

Renee jumped to her feet and snatched up the file to shove into her tote. She roughly nodded as she moved to the door. "Stop having me followed, Jessa," she ordered, her voice tight.

"Fine," Jessa said with honesty, picking up her flute to finish her drink.

Renee left her office without another word.

The bathroom door eased open and she shifted her eyes in the mirror to see one of her new hires, Lacey Adams, enter. Jessa smoothed her hands down the sides of the short and fitted gold silk halter dress with a plunging neckline she wore. She turned, giving the beautiful woman a polite smile. "Are you enjoying yourself, Lacey?" she asked, quickly sizing her up.

Once every other month, she and Keegan took the entire staff out for dinner. Tonight was that night.

"Yes, the food is so good," Lacy said, licking her lips nervously as she moved past Jessa to set her purse atop the counter.

"Good," Jessa said, picking up her iPhone and clutch from the counter before she moved past the younger woman to the door.

"Ms. Bell, how am I doing?"

Jessa paused with her hand on the door handle and looked back at Lacey over her shoulder. "Just fine, Lacey," she said with truth. "If you weren't, you would have been fired."

And that was the truth. She didn't have the charisma of Charli Cole, but she got the job done. She had the type of innocent, introvert sexy that some men loved, and Jessa used her as a mark for them. No, Charli Cole and other agents snagged men quicker with their confidence and their sex appeal, but Lacey Adams really fucked them up with that "let me take care of you and only you" vibe.

"Do you have a cigarette?" Lacey asked, snapping her own heart-shaped gold clutch closed.

Jessa eyed her before she reached in her clutch and withdrew a platinum cigarette case, pressing the latch with her thumb. It opened in her hand as she extended it to her. "How did you know?" she asked.

Lacey took one. "I smelled it in your office one day," she admitted.

"Something about exhaling the smoke and seeing the small cloud it makes dissipate in the wind soothes me when I'm aggravated," she said, snapping the cigarette case closed and dropping it back inside her clutch.

Lacey nodded. "I'll smoke it outside," she said, before turning to enter one of the stalls.

Jessa paused at the door. "Lacey, just like many other things in life, like it but don't love it," she advised, before leaving the restroom with one last comforting smile.

The door closed behind her and her steps faltered as she spotted Hammer leaning against the wall next to the door to the men's restroom. The dark gray blazer, shirt, and slacks he wore suited him well.

She shook her head at the look he gave her, holding a slender finger to her lips, as she passed by him. The eyes of many men were on her, openly or covertly, as she moved through the dimly lit restaurant to the private dining room in the rear. There was a time she got her inner strength and her esteem from the attention of men. That was in the past.

Soft music was the backdrop to the chatter of the employees of Mistress, Inc,. as she reclaimed her seat at the round table next to Keegan. "Beautiful bunch of people," she whispered to her.

Keegan tossed her hair back as she eyed the three women, sans Lacey, and two men, not including Hammer as the lone detective of the agency. "I still can't believe this idea of yours is working," she said, picking up her flute to sip her champagne.

"Supply and demand, Keegan," Jessa said. "Supply and motherfucking demand."

They toasted to that.

"Oh, and the Lord's work and all that shit, right?" Keegan drawled, her Texas twang thick and the sarcasm present.

Jessa arched a brow and moved her flute away to avoid another toast. "You're going to hell," she said.

Keegan shrugged. "I'll gladly go if he's waiting for me there with a hard-on," she said, lifting her chin toward Hammer entering the room and reclaiming his seat between Charli Cole and her very first agent, Yoni Lee.

Jessa's grip on her glass tightened. "I thought we agreed he was off-limits," she gently reminded her.

"All bets are off in the afterlife, honey," Keegan said, shaking her head in disappointment.

Humph. All bets been off for me.

Jessa remained silent, her eyes locked on Hammer's head bent toward Charli as they talked.

"Looks like we might need a reminder about not fraternizing at work," Keegan said, her eyes on Charli and Hammer as well.

"He's old enough to be her father," Jessa whispered harshly, hating the jealousy that punched her gut and squeezed her heart.

"Honey, *all* men are daddy when they laying the pipe right," Keegan said, chuckling at her own play on words.

Jessa tapped her butter knife against her glass as she rose to her feet. Hammer turned his attention from Charli, and she gave him a long stare that made the smile fade from his face. "Just want to thank you all for your hard work in making Mistress, Inc,. a success. Thank you for your beauty, your smarts, and your loyalty to our vision for this company. I appreciate you all," she said, eyeing each one and finally locking eyes with Hammer as she raised her glass in a toast.

"I love you," he mouthed.

She smiled, giving him a nod, as she felt her heart swell in her chest and seem to burst like fireworks with happiness.

Chapter 5

Two months later

There was a noticeable shift.

Jessa lowered her head into her hands and massaged her temples with her thumbs.

"Are you okay, Mama?"

The sound of her daughter's caring voice tightened her throat with emotion and brought tears to her eyes. With one last shaky breath, she cleared her throat, raised her head, and plastered a fake smile on her face as she looked at the computer screen filled with Delaney's face. "Mama's just fine," she lied.

Delaney's leaned in to press her lips to the screen, leaving a peanut butter and jelly–smeared print that evoked a genuine smile from Jessa.

A smile that broke through the guilt that had plagued her of late.

She would never share the same bond with Georgia that she had with Delaney.

Georgia was on her mind again.

Shit.

If only it could be as simple as a lyric in a song.

Memories came to her more and more over the last few days. Questions. Assumptions. Wishes for the life she wanted for her daughter. For *her* daughter. And Georgia was hers. Nothing could change that fact.

And, of late, as Delaney got older, Jessa was unable to deny the truth herself. *I have two daughters. One I know and love. One I will never know but still love, because she is mine.*

Jessa twirled in her chair, giving the screen her back as she bent over and released a long, shaky breath as a pain that felt visceral raced across her chest. She felt her tears wet her knees. A cry she couldn't contain escaped her lips, and she was barely able to mute the sound.

It seemed every moment she fought so hard to be a good mother to Delaney reminded her that she never fought for the chance to do that for Georgia. Long after she outgrew the pain of having her taken away and went numb about the violation—*the rape*—by her father, she had changed her life. Became successful in spite of it all.

And still, I never searched for her. There were many weeks and months I never even thought of her. I told no one. I treated her as shameful.

"Peek-a-boo, Mama."

Jessa winced at her daughter's voice, realizing she innocently thought they were playing a game. Quickly she swiped away her tears before swiveling again in the chair to face the screen. "I see you," she finished softly, reaching out with a shaking hand to stroke the screen.

Winifrid lifted Delaney onto her hip. "It's time for her nap, Ms. Bell," she said politely.

Jessa was grateful, and not just because she stressed that Winifrid needed to maintain Delaney's schedule. She nodded and waved before lowering her hand to end the Skype session.

"Jessa."

She was startled and sat back when her mother's face suddenly filled the screen. "Yes," she said, rubbing her fingertips against her palm as she fought to beat off her anxiety.

"What's wrong? And don't lie to me. I could see it in your eyes when you were talking to Delaney," Darla said, her tone no-nonsense.

The points of her stiletto nails dug into her flesh as she tightened her grip. "Just a little tired," she lied.

The time had come and gone for her mother to show concern. Jessa had long since learned to live without it, especially after she stood at the window of her grandmother's house and watched her mother walk away and never return.

Men, drugs, and her mental illness had claimed all Darla's attention, leaving her with no time for a little girl who wanted nothing but her mother's love.

The same love Georgia might have wanted from you, hypocrite.

"I should be home before dinner," she said.

"Jessa—"

"Good-bye." She hit the button to end the connection and felt relief when the screen went black.

"Maybe it's PMS," she muttered, hating how her emotions were all over the place. Varied. Scattered. Overwhelming.

Should I find her?

Jessa surprised herself with that thought. Never had she imagined she would ever seriously consider locating Georgia. Never.

And say what?

How are you?

Do you even know you're adopted?

Do you hate me?

Have you wondered about me?

Forgive me.

Please don't ask me who your father is.

"Where is Hammer?" she said aloud suddenly, seeking a diversion from her thoughts.

Mind-blowing sex would definitely do it.

She snatched up her office landline and quickly dialed his cell phone number. She felt anticipation of hearing his voice and desire at the thought of summoning him to come to her and make her cum.

Make me forget.

Bzzzzzz.

She hit the intercom button as she held the receiver between her shoulder and ear. "Yes," she said.

"Your two o'clock appointment is here."

She'd forgotten.

"Hey, baby," Hammer said, his voice echoing in her ear when he answered his cell.

She smiled tenderly. "Hey. Where are you? I need you," she said into the phone, her voice warm and soft.

"I'm right at my desk, Ms. Bell," Felisha said, sounding confused.

"Huh?" Jessa asked, shaking her head. "Not you."

"Not me? Then who?" Hammer asked.

"Ms. Bell, your appointment? Are you prepared to see her?" Felisha asked.

The combo of her rising anxiety, Hammer questioning her in one ear and Felisha whining in the other, pushed her to the edge. She pounded her fist on the desk. "Shut up," she snapped, rotating her head to work the kinks from her neck.

"Shut up?" both Hammer and Felisha said.

"Hold on," Jessa said into the phone before setting the receiver down on the desk.

"Felisha, give me five minutes and then bring her in," she said in to the intercom before ending the connection.

She massaged her temples with her fingertips before picking up the receiver and pressing it to her ear. "Hammer, sorry about that. I was talking to Felisha, not you," she said, easing her fingers beneath the layers of her hair to lightly stroke her scalp.

"That's good to know . . . I think," he mused.

She smiled. "Listen, I have a meeting with a new client but I would really love to *have* you in about an hour," she said, not ashamed of the pleading in her tone.

"Have me?" he asked, his voice deep and warm.

"Yes, on me and in me," Jessa teased.

Hammer chuckled. "Damn, that sounds good."

"Good enough to make it happen?"

"I can't, baby," he said, sounding regretful. "You have me stretched out this week. I'm following a mark as we speak, and I still have to set up surveillance for a couple of setups tonight."

Her disappointment smarted.

"When will I see you again?" she asked.

"We have that meeting with Keegan in the morning."

Jessa rose to look out her office window at the New York landscape. "Not like *that*, Hammer," she said lightly, twisting the phone cord around her finger as she stroked it with her thumb.

"Mistress, Inc., business is booming. I'm pretty slammed all week, baby," he said. "I can stop by your office before the meeting and relieve the pressure."

She smiled a bit at the sight of a man and woman pausing on the street to share a kiss as the fall winds whipped through the towering buildings and surrounded their bodies with a flourish. "No, I need more than a quickie," she said, turning as the couple turned from each other with a wave. "I need to lie in your arms after and sleep."

"Are you admitting that you can't sleep well without me?"

"Yes," she admitted.

"Careful, Jessa Bell, sounds like you might be falling in love," Hammer teased.

Knock-knock.

"Might be?" she asked, looking at her office door as it opened.

He laughed. It was low and soft and seemed to radiate

from some happy place inside him. "We're on the same page, beautiful," he assured her.

"Tomorrow night, then?" she asked, giving a smile to the stylishly dressed brunette Felisha guided into her office.

"Wouldn't miss it," he promised.

Jessa hung up the phone and extended her hand. "Mrs. Montgomery?" she asked, surprised by the fuller-figured middle-aged woman who strode in with a hesitant and nervous smile.

Her Chanel pantsuit was ill-fitting, her nails unpolished, and she wore no jewelry save for a modest wedding ring and eternity band. Her hair was pulled back in a severe ponytail, and she constantly shifted her eyes as if too nervous to meet a stare.

Most women resented coming to her for her services and made it clear in their tone or their expression. Jessa didn't care. She was amused by their hypocrisy all the way to the bank when they paid her hefty fee.

Still, what was most disarming about Mrs. Montgomery was that she was African American.

The majority of the clients of Mistress, Inc., were not.

"What can I help you with?" Jessa asked as she reclaimed her seat behind her desk.

Bella Montgomery smiled as she sat her Chanel handbag on the desk. She fidgeted with her wedding ring and cleared her throat. "I don't know where to begin," she said, her voice soft and uncertain.

"My husband and I have been married for fifteen years. We have always been so close. So in love," she said, smiling a bit as she focused her eyes on her bag on the desk. "I would have never imagined a wealthy and powerful man like Horatio falling for me."

Jessa gave her a polite smile as she waited for the woman to finish her story.

"We had so much in common and we did everything

together and went everywhere together," Bella said with a soft smile as she reveled in the memory. "I remember meeting him for the first time. I was sitting in Central Park reading on a bench in front of a beautiful crepe myrtle bush that was as tall and wide as a small house."

Jessa was acutely aware of the subtle hint of a Southern accent in her voice.

"He was sitting on a bench a little way down from me when I noticed him," she said. "He was tall and dark and fine. I forgot all about that book. He was on his cell phone and suddenly he laughed. His whole face came alive. My heart kinda stopped, you know, and I felt things I had never felt before."

Jessa folded her arms atop her desk. "Love," she said softly, caught up in the woman's story.

"At first sight," the other woman finished.

"I couldn't take my eyes off him. I didn't want to," she said. "And when he grabbed his briefcase and strolled by, I kept on looking at him. Didn't have a care except soaking up as much of him as I could in case I never saw him again. And then . . . he turned and looked back at me."

Jessa envisioned her every word, letting the scene play out in her head.

"We stared at each other and then I smiled," she said, with a soft little laugh. "Could hardly believe I did it. It was the most flirting I ever did in my whole life. Me. Still feeling like that ass-backward little girl from Hawkinsville, Georgia."

So I was right.

"He came back and I stood up. We introduced ourselves in front of that bench that sat in front of the crepe myrtle bush that reminded me of the South," she said, reaching for her purse.

Jessa eyed her as she paused.

"Every day after that, we met at that bench," she said, pulling out a small leather-bound book and opening it to reveal a crepe myrtle flower, once red and bright, now flattened and darkened with age. "When we eventually married he planted crepe myrtle bushes around a bench in our backyard, and every year for any special occasion he would gift me a large bouquet of crepe myrtle flowers. It was like he never wanted to forget that first day we met. And then suddenly last year...no more bushes. No more bouquets. And far too much time when I am left all alone."

Bella's eyes were sad and they filled with tears as she stroked the dried flower with her thumb.

"And you want to know why?" Jessa asked, her voice soft.

She nodded as a tear raced down her cheek. It wet the petals. "I *deserve* to know why," she stressed.

Jessa nodded. "I agree. That is the entire purpose of what we do here. We get to the truth. Our usual turnaround time is about two weeks, sometimes a month. We do use the services of an in-house private detective and decoys, but I want to assure you that no sexual activity is allowed. The fee is twenty-five thousand dollars with fifteen thousand up front. We will be discreet and respectable, and above all, we *will* get to the truth," she assured her.

Bella nodded, reaching inside her purse again for a matching Chanel checkbook cover. She used a gold pen to fill out the check and sign it with flourish. "This is drawn on my personal account," she explained, as she sat the check on the top of the desk and pushed it across the smooth surface.

Jessa blinked and looked up at Bella with a smile as she picked up the check and slid it into her the top drawer of her desk. "I hope that there is some other reason for this shift in your marriage," she said as she stood, signaling the end of the meeting.

With a hesitant smile, Bella rose as well with her Chanel tote on her arm. "I look forward to hearing from you soon," she said, before turning and exiting the office.

Jessa hit the intercom button. "Felisha, get Charli on the

line for me," she said, confident that the sophisticated beauty was just right for their new case.

The light filtered through the stained-glass windows of the church, creating a beautiful mosaic on the polished hardwood floors. Jessa stroked her bottom lip with her thumb as she stared at the colors. It seemed the perfect moment for a choir to sing. *Something slow and heart tugging about loving the Lord—*

"Jessa."

She looked up, focusing her attention on Revered Dell sitting on the edge of the stage. "Yes?" she asked.

He cleared his throat. "You kept your appointment with me, but you've been quiet for the last five minutes," he said.

"I have?" she asked, voicing her surprise.

He nodded.

She nodded as well as she looked about the sanctuary. "Is there a reason why we never meet in your office?" she asked, focusing her eyes back on him.

He crossed his arms over his chest and stretched out one of his legs. "Is that what has been on your mind the last five minutes?" he asked.

"No," she answered truthfully.

He remained quiet.

"Let me recap since our last session," she said. "Business is great. Money is good. My daughter is a good kid—praise God. My mother is on her meds. In my search for more good karma I informed someone—not a client and not a friend—that her husband was cheating—"

"*Not* a friend and *not* a client?" he asked, his brows furrowing. "And praise be to God *not* Jaime, Aria, or Renee. Right?"

Jessa shifted her eyes back to the colorful mosaic on the floor.

"You can't be serious?" he balked.

"What?" she asked innocently.

He frowned. "And how do you know what is going on in the lives of these people?" he asked, his disapproval obvious.

Jessa winced. She opened and closed her mouth several times before releasing a long breath. "Does it matter?"

"If you're the mistress again, then that's a yes."

She arched a brow, finally locking eyes with him. "After all this time, you refuse to acknowledge my growth, Reverend Dell. That's hurtful," she said.

"My apologies," he said.

They fell silent.

"And how do you know about the cheating?" Revered Dell asked.

This will not go well. Wait. I'm grown and I meant well. Why am I ashamed for doing good shit?

"Listen, if I did not have my PI investigating them, then Renee would never know the truth," she said.

His mouth dropped open as he tilted his head to the side and gave her an odd look. "Please consider that you are too caught up in the lives of people who have no desire for you to be in their lives," he explained slowly, as if he thought she was dim-witted.

Jessa smoothed her hair back from her face. "I'm feeling a little judged, Reverend Dell," she complained. "And considering I'm not judging you, it feels really unnecessary."

"Judging me for?" Reverend Dell asked, leaning forward to press his elbows onto his thighs.

She looked around at the sanctuary. "Why don't you have sessions in your office anymore?" she asked. "Or am *I* the only one isolated to the sanctuary?"

"There goes that five minutes," he said.

"Yup," she agreed.

Reverend Dell squinted a bit as he eyed her. "I am more comfortable meeting with you here than in my office. Yes, that's true," he admitted.

"So let me get this straight. Not only am I a reformed mistress who fell off the wagon, now I can't be trusted not to seduce my pastor," she said, her tone sly as she rose with her tote in hand. "Why not douse me with holy water and press a cross to my forehead?"

Revered Dell rose as well. "Jessa—"

"I'll do the work for you and exorcise my evil self out of your church," she said as she walked up the aisle.

"You're not evil, Jessa," he called behind her. "You're on the same path we all are on, to be the best versions of ourselves."

Jessa stopped and turned. "I *have* changed, Rev," she said, her hurt clouding her eyes. "I know I have. I'm not perfect, but I'm trying. And the last thing I need is for a man of God to make me feel like there is no hope for me."

He eased his hands into his pockets as he slowly made his way up the aisle toward her. "Perhaps being around you makes me feel like there is no hope for me, Jessa," he admitted.

"Oh," she said softly in understanding, before nodding as she waved her hand up and down the length of her body. "I am a lot."

He chuckled. "Yes, you are, *but* the Lord is even more, and my focus and dedication is to Him. No temptation will sway me from doing his work."

"That's good to know, Reverend Dell," she said, as she turned to leave. "*Very* good to know."

Jessa pulled her car to a stop before her house. She looked up at the soft glow of light filling each window. It was all beautiful and inviting. A home. Not her first by far, but definitely the one she had the most peace and happiness in. *In the words of Martha Stewart, that's a good thing.*

"But why is the entire house lit up?" Jessa murmured as she climbed from the car. "Some of my mother's bullshit."

She locked her car and activated the alarm but remained standing by the vehicle. The fall wind was chilly, but she tilted her head back and took a deep inhale of the air, letting it fill her lungs as she looked up at the moon. *Life ain't bad at all.*

"Jessa, what you see up there?"

Oh hell.

She closed her eyes as the sound of slippers dragging across the concrete echoed into the quiet of the night as her mother came to stand beside her. When she opened her eyes and saw her mother frowning as she too looked up at the sky, Jessa couldn't help but smile. "How are you, Mama?" she asked.

"Confused as hell," she said.

Jessa reached for her wrist and squeezed it gently, drawing her gaze. "No, how *are* you?" she asked again.

"I get so bored sometimes, Jessa," Darla said, raising her arms in her colorful silk caftan and doing a semiturn. "This is a long way from Harlem, where you can just sit on the stoop and see all kind of shit and a store was just down the street."

"And have plenty of men around to tell you what you should already know—that you're beautiful," Jessa said. "By now you should have learned a man doesn't need to pay you compliments."

Darla arched a brow. "Don't be a hypocrite," she snarked.

Jessa eyed her. "I'm not a hypocrite."

"Bullshit," Darla drawled with emphasis. "Those are dick strokes Hammer is paying you, not compliments, little girl."

Jessa averted her eyes and bit back a smile. "What I'm *saying* is," she stressed, giving her mother a serious face.

Darla reached out and pressed her fingertips to her daughter's lip.

Jessa's eyes widened and she sputtered as she jerked her head back from her mother's touch.

"What *I'm* saying is that I am still hot to trot and open to some male companionship, and until you either become celibate or become addicted to a dildo, don't tell me how I am supposed to be happy with a dickless life," Darla said. "*Comprende?*"

Her mother's sudden usage of Spanish threw her a little, but she nodded.

Darla's eyes softened and this time she pressed her hands to Jessa's cheeks. Her smile was wide and genuine. "Listen, I know more than probably anyone what all you have faced in this lifetime—the shit done to you and the shit you did to others. And I know my role in it and thank you for forgiving me," she said, stroking Jessa's chin with her thumb.

Jessa felt the urge to step out of her mother's embrace again, but she didn't. She stood there, wanting to connect with the woman who bore her. Not wanting to have an undercurrent of resentment pulse between them. She blinked rapidly at the emotions that rose up.

"I see you happy, my Jessa, and that makes me so happy for you," Darla said, her voice filled with pleasure. "I don't care what anyone says, I know that you deserve it after everything you have been through."

Jessa closed her eyes, hating that she was taken back to *that* moment in her childhood.

"Nope. Don't you do it," Darla said, lightly tapping her cheeks. "Don't go back there, Jessa Bell."

The memory disappeared.

"*Choose* to be happy," Darla said, with one final press of her hands to her cheeks before she dropped them.

"I want to, Mama," she admitted, her smile hesitant.

Darla winked at her as she took one of Jessa's hands and walked toward the gate leading to the backyard.

"Where are we going?" Jessa asked.

"Just come on."

Jessa followed behind her reluctantly. She was never 100 percent sure her mother was all together and wrapped tight.

They passed through the open gate. The lights from the paved walkway lit their path.

Pop!

"What the hell was that?" Jessa asked, jerking her hand free and stopping in her tracks. "Was that gunshots? Where is *my* baby?"

"Gunshots? In this hood? Girl, please." Darla turned and sucked air between her teeth. "You always were a chicken. Come on."

Jessa shook her head. "Mama, tell me what you're up to," she snapped, pointing her finger.

Darla swiped her hand dismissively before turning and rushing up the rest of the path with the tails of her caftan lifting up into the air behind her.

Damn nut. She turned to head back toward the front of the house.

"Where you going?"

Jessa froze and turned.

Hammer stood there in a tuxedo, his hands in his pockets and the walkway lighting seeming to give him that *The Last Dragon* glow.

She smiled as she walked up to him standing at the end of the path. "Hello," she said, reaching to lightly wrap her hands around his lower arms.

"Surprised?" Hammer asked, bending his tall frame to press a kiss to her forehead, both cheeks, chin, and finally, her mouth.

"Considering you said you were working? Yes, I am," she said, with a hint of flirtation. "And the tux is a nice touch."

He chuckled, his eyes crinkling at the corners. "Perfect," he said. "Ready?"

"For?" she asked, feeling coquettish as she tilted her head to the side and bit her bottom lip.

"Let's go see," Hammer said.

She removed her hands with reluctance, but then slid one into his when he turned.

They walked around the house to the backyard.

Jessa inhaled deeply in surprise and then released the breath slowly as she took in the large pergola over the lit concrete fire pit. It was adorned with bright red roses, twinkling white lights, lit candles, and a gold bucket with an open bottle of champagne. There were dozens of round bouquets of roses hanging from the tree limbs above it.

"It's beautiful," she said, her heart pounding.

She looked around with the wonder of a child at all the effort he put into her surprise. When they came to stand beneath the structure, the scent of the roses was heavy and the warmth of the fire pit welcomed in the slightly chilly air of a fall night. "Are we having dinner out here, because I am starving," she said, looking down at the champagne bottle and realizing the removal of the cork caused the noise that scared her earlier.

At his continued silence, Jessa turned to find Hammer down on one knee with an open ring box in his hand. She covered her now gaping mouth with her hand. "Seriously?" she asked softly, tears brimming in her eyes with far too much ease.

Hammer nodded. "Very seriously," he assured her.

Jessa stepped forward to stand before him, reaching out to stroke his chin and look down into the beauty of his eyes. "Me?" she asked, her tone more high-pitched than she liked.

He chuckled and reached for her left hand with his free one.

She trembled as he stroked her pulse point with his thumb.

"I want to spend the rest of my life loving you, making love to you, protecting you, and cherishing you," he began. "You excite me, please me, calm me, and center me. We have become far more than I thought we would be when I first complimented you on the fit of that skirt."

"The red leather one," she added, remembering the moment well.

"Exactly."

They shared a laugh.

"Jessa Bell, will you spend the rest of your life with me and make me a part of your family?" he asked, squeezing her hand.

Can I really have it all? Jessa tilted her head back and looked up at the stars in the inky sky.

"Choose to be happy," her mother had said.

Could she finally leave all of her past behind and moved forward with Hammer? The unexpected death of her husband, abandonment by her mother, the rape, the loss of Georgia, the affair with Eric, the betrayal of her friends, that damned childish message, Eric's death, and so much more.

She looked down at him patiently waiting; neither his gaze nor the touch of his hand ever wavered.

Jessa nodded, looking at him moving the three-carat solitaire ring up her finger.

Hammer rose and slowly wrapped his arms around her to pull her close as he kissed her.

Deeply.

Slowly.

Lovingly.

"Yes," she sighed into his open mouth just before he gently sucked the tip of her tongue.

"Congratulations!"

With reluctance, they ended their kiss. Jessa turned to see her mother, daughter, and nanny dressed in tuxedos as well. "Okay, that's too cute," she said.

"I look good," Delaney said, freeing herself from Winifrid's hand to run over to Jessa and Hammer.

Darla and Winifrid followed behind.

"Welcome to the family," Darla said, beaming happily before she embraced him.

"Congratulations, Ms. Bell," Winifrid said, before stepping back to lift the digital camera she held. "Smile, everyone."

They all faced her.

"Cheese, Miss Winifrid!" Delaney said before smiling so hard that her cheeks rose and caused her eyes to squint.

They all laughed and Winifrid caught just that moment.

Chapter 6

"Hold the elevator."

Jessa stopped scrolling through Louis Vuitton's Instagram page to reach out and press the button to hold the doors open. She could hear the hard bottom of the shoes beating against the concrete. A fast pace, but not a run.

Soon, her sexy white stranger stepped onto the lift beside her, just as handsome, stylish, and impressive as ever.

She gave him a polite smile.

His was wider and warmer. "We *have* to stop meeting like this," he said, his voice deep.

Jessa glanced up at him, thinking his frame was more suited to sports than business.

"I think it's fate," he said, leaning his tall, muscular frame back against the wall as he checked the time on his watch.

"I think my husband would disagree," she said, her tone amused.

He snapped his tanned fingers. "I was just about to add *if* you weren't married," he joked.

Jessa arched a brow. "Somehow I don't believe that."

"You're smart."

"Most definitely," she assured him, dimming the light of her smile back down to politeness.

As the elevator quietly ascended she shifted her eyes from his and watched the numbers on the display above the doors light up as they passed each floor. When his cell phone vibrated loudly, she inadvertently looked over at him again. She was surprised to find his eyes resting on her before he pulled his iPhone from the pocket of his coat.

She couldn't deny his attention warmed her. *It's still good to know I can get it if I wanted it—which I don't.*

He sent his call to voice mail.

She looked on as he slid the phone back into his pocket. "It'll just be bad reception anyway," he explained.

"True," she agreed.

They fell silent again.

She turned her attention back to the numbers.

"I thought of you the other day," he said.

This time she turned and leaned against the wall opposite him. She said nothing and just tilted her head to the side as she gripped the handle of her tote with both hands.

"Right in the middle of an important meeting, I suddenly wondered if you smelled as good as you look," he admitted, his eyes dipping down for a moment to her neck.

Jessa shifted in her stance. "How did your meeting turn out?" she asked, purposefully trying to refocus his train of thought.

He accepted the diversion with a chuckle. "Very well... once I stopped wondering if a beautiful brown neck was scented with something sweet."

Not bad. I love perfume with fruity notes.

"Congratulations," she said.

He nodded in welcome.

The elevator smoothly slid to a halt. With another broad

smile, he stepped off when the doors slid open. "Have a good day, stranger," he said.

He took a few steps down the hall.

Feeling mischievous, Jessa called out, "Hey, stranger."

He stopped and turned.

"I do," she assured him with an impish wink.

His chuckles reached her just before the doors closed.

She had to admit their little banter amused her, and she smiled at his buoyant chuckles as the elevator continued its ascent. Her own iPhone vibrated loudly just as the lift stopped and the door slid open. She pulled it from the outside pocket of her tote as she stepped off. "Lydia," she read the Caller ID.

Her literary agent.

Jessa's finger hovered over the button to end the call, but her curiosity won out. *Shit.* "Hello, Lydia," she said, walking down the hall, past the frosted glass door of the Mistress, Inc., offices, and to the end where the long, narrow window displayed the New York landscape.

"How have you been, Jessa?" she asked, her Italian accent thick.

What do you want?

"I'm well," Jessa replied, hoping to get past the amiabilities. "I have some news—"

"Good or bad?" she asked with an arch of her brow as she focused on her reflection in the glass. She plucked a small piece of lint from the rose gold coat she wore over a cream top and wide-leg pants.

"Depends," Lydia offered. "A prominent production company out of Hollywood wants to option your book to be made into a film."

Jessa frowned, turning to lean back against the windowsill. Her eyes landed on the door to her offices.

There was a time when her life—her sins—had been on display. With the help of a publicist she made her scandal her platform. Fame and notoriety had been hers, and she'd craved the limelight.

But not anymore.

The name of her company wasn't on the door and she didn't advertise. She had long since cut ties with her PR and turned down a substantial offer to do a second book with her publisher. She craved the shadows that now protected her to some degree. A film and its publicity would mean rehashing every sordid detail.

Why would I want to stir in that shit again?

She hitched her tote up onto the bend in her arm and reached inside with her free hand to pull her engagement ring from its hiding place inside the zipped inner pocket. "Things are good right now, Lydia," she said, stroking the band with her thumb. "I refuse to worry about the birds in the bush."

"I've been around long enough to know that sometimes these options work and most times they don't," Lydia said, filling the silence. "But just having the option on the table gives us extra leverage to up the advance for a second book."

"No, no, no," Jessa said, her voice low but firm. "No book. No movie."

"Why don't you take a few days and think about it," Lydia advised, her soft tone intended to soothe and encourage. "The last thing I want is for a rash decision to lead to regrets."

Jessa laughed gently as she began to retrace her steps down the hall. "Oh, Lydia," she sighed in amusement. "I already have a lifetime's worth of regrets. One more won't break me."

"But—"

"Talk to you soon," Jessa lied, ending the call before there was any more of Lydia's soothing and encouraging.

★ ★ ★

Mrs. Robert Hammer Young? Mrs. Jessa Young? Mrs. Hammer?

Jessa had whittled away the entire morning with such thoughts. She held her hand up to the light cascading through the window, loving how it made the solitaire diamond sparkle brightly. She wanted nothing more than to walk into Keegan's office and share her good news with her, but she didn't allow herself to do it. She'd decided that morning when she rose in Hammer's arms, still sex drunk and high off love, that she just wanted to have an enjoyable day. No drama. No stress. No worries.

Just one fucking day.

"Felisha, call the police!"

Jessa frowned and sat up straight at the commotion in the outer office. Quickly she rose and rushed across the short divide to snatch the door open. She gasped in shock at Warrington Sachs standing in the foyer naked, his trench coat down around his pale ankles and the brown boots he wore.

I am absolutely not in the mood for this shit.

She glanced over at Keegan standing in the doorway of her own office and Felisha still sitting at the reception desk with her phone in hand. "Felisha, put the phone down," Jessa said, as she walked toward the man.

"*You* ruined my fucking life," Warrington roared, pointing at Jessa.

"Your life was ruined when God gave you just four inches, my love," she drawled calmly with a pointed look at his genitals.

"You bitch!" he said, covering his dick and balls with his hands.

"Jessa!" Keegan snapped in annoyance, coming to stand beside her.

She eyed her. "You're the queen of snappy one liners, but in this moment, *I'm* wrong?" she asked.

"Your interference in my marriage is going to make me

lose *everything*—even the clothes on my fucking back," Warren said, his eyes wild and darting over the room. "I hired you. You had no right sending that video to my wife..."

"Oh hell," Keegan drawled behind her.

"So obviously you wanted me naked and in your fucking face or you would've stayed out of my business," he spat, his mouth twisted in anger as he freed his genitals and then wiggled his dick at her.

"Not today, Mr. Sachs," Jessa said with a shake of her head as she came to stand before him.

He paused, looking down at her in confusion.

"Maybe *any* other day, but not today," she insisted.

"Who the fuck are you to meddle in my life?" he asked.

Quicker than a flash of lightning during a rain storm, Jessa reached out and grabbed his balls. She roughly jerked on them as she gritted her teeth and bored into him with her angry eyes. "I'm the bitch with your balls in my hand, you sick, perverted son of a bitch," she growled low in her throat as he released a high-pitched squeal like a pinned pig. "Now, knowing you, you're probably turned on right now, you demented fuck, but I promise you if you don't gather what little sense you have left, put your coat back on, and get *the fuck* out of here, I will make you a eunuch."

"Oh Lord," Keegan sighed.

Jessa twisted the fleshy sacs clockwise. His knees gave out beneath him and his body sank downward. "If you ever bring your shit-loving weirdo ass in here again, then I will send you out of here without *these* small motherfuckers," she warned, bending with him to keep his balls in her grasp.

Hanging out with Aria rubbed off on me more than I thought.

She jerked them again.

Tears filled his eyes.

"I told your wife about your dirty little secret, and you have offended me with the sight of your small dick," she said, enjoying the sweat that dampened his brow and quivering upper lip. "So we're even. Right?"

He nodded vigorously.

Jessa released him and he dropped to the floor, drawing his knees to his chest as he writhed in pain. She pressed her hands to her hips, her breathing jagged, as she fought the urge to kick him. "Get out," she said, her voice soft as her heart pounded from her exertion.

She started to wipe her face with her hand but caught herself, the smell of his musky privates still clinging to her hand. "*Please*," she stressed.

Warrington struggled to his feet, his trench coat already clenched in his free hand and his other softly cupping his genitalia. He too released rapid, shallow breaths as he pulled on his coat and tied it as he eyed her with open hostility. "I hate you," he said.

"There's a quite a few of you who do," she countered with ease. "Form a club, have monthly meetings to whine, and then get the fuck over it, Mr. Sachs."

Moments later he gave them all one last antagonistic look before he left the office, leaving the door open wide.

Jessa reached to turn the lock on the knob and then kicked the door close.

Wham!

She turned.

Felisha was still at her desk, her eyes wide with what could only be shock. Keegan stood there gawking at her, her expression incredulous. "I thought we agreed not to contact Mrs. Sachs, Jessa?" she asked, her arms crossed over her chest as she massaged her elbows, an obvious attempt of comforting herself.

Here the fuck we go . . .

"If you would like to talk to me, I'm headed to wash my hands and then I'll be in my office," she replied, turning to stride across the space to their restroom.

It wasn't until she waved her hand beneath the touchless faucet to turn on the water that she remembered she still wore her engagement ring. Quickly she cleansed it and her hands of the sweat of Warrington's balls before drying her hands and slipping the ring inside her sheer brassiere. It pressed against her flesh.

She eyed her reflection as she smoothed any flyaway hairs from the melee. She couldn't lie. The last few minutes all seemed like a horrible dream.

I had his damn nuts in my hand.

Her frown was deep and filled with her distaste. "Shit, shit, shit," she swore, pressing her damp palms to her neck as she forced herself not to completely lose her wits.

In truth, she was just as rattled as Keegan.

"Fuuuuuuuck!"

She allowed herself a twenty count before she finally opened the restroom door and made her way back across the reception area. Keegan and Felisha's conversation came to an abrupt end when she passed by them.

She rolled her eyes as she entered her office, standing by the door with her hand on the knob, knowing Keegan was headed in right behind her.

"How the hell are you so calm like this all couldn't have gone very differently?" Keegan asked.

Jessa closed the door behind her. "I'm calm because this was an oddity. And I handled it," she said, watching Keegan pace behind the club chairs positioned in front of her desk.

"You intentionally lied to me and went and did what you wanted to anyway," Keegan said, pausing to give Jessa wide-eyed stare.

"There are two of us, Keegan, so you don't have final say either," Jessa said. "I never agreed but refuse to argue with you about it."

"So you lied?" Keegan inserted.

"No, I let you have a one-sided conversation about a topic I was done with," Jessa said, very matter-of-factly.

Keegan's expression became incredulous. "Please don't pull on your big bitch boots about this, Jessa," she said.

"What the hell does *that* mean?" she asked.

Keegan leaned back against the wall. "Sometimes you can be a bit of a bitch, darling."

"Says pot to kettle, *darling*."

They fell quiet.

Jessa was the first to break the silence. "Keegan, you knew going in that my intent was to help those who are being betrayed by their spouse—mostly women, but sometimes men, too. Mrs. Sachs was not a client, but she was not only betrayed by having her health put at risk because the man I assume she screws sans condom likes to rub his dick in shit to get off. So, *Keegan*, I'm *so* sorry if you're not in agreement with hipping his wife to his freaky side-life, but I felt I had no choice."

Keegan began pacing again, pausing at times to look at Jessa with her mouth open as if she wanted to speak but couldn't.

Jessa crossed her arms over her chest and watched her.

"So just fuck the consequences," she finally said.

Jessa applauded. "Good job. I really thought you went mute."

"Bitch boots," Keegan reminded her.

Jessa sighed, trying to keep down her steadily rising level of annoyance. "When you insisted on joining in on this business, I assumed it meant we had the same goals in mind," she began, moving to lean against the front edge of her desk. "Now, if it isn't what you want and you're doing some heroic shit here, then I'd rather buy you out and continue on alone. But I won't be judged or treated like a child because your opinion differs from mine."

"What Jessa wants, Jessa gets, huh?" Keegan asked, her voice tinged with sarcasm.

She thought of the child she'd never raised and the one she was currently raising alone.

"Not always," she said.

Keegan walked over to the window behind Jessa's desk. Jessa glanced over her shoulder at her before facing forward and lifting her hand to lightly press against her ring in her brassiere. *My good day was just shot to hell.*

She closed her eyes and tilted her head back, trying to transport herself to the night before when Hammer proposed and then to when Hammer undressed her in her bedroom, planting kisses all over her body until he settled his head between her thighs and kissed her clit until her back and buttocks arched off the bed and she cried out in hot release.

"I have to admit that for the last year or so, it has felt like this is all one big powder keg waiting to blow."

Reluctantly, with the bud nestled between the lips of her core throbbing to life, Jessa pushed away her sultry memories. She sat down on the desk and shifted around enough to eye Keegan as she crossed one leg over the other. "So, you don't think this is about helping people anymore?" she asked. "Hell, did you ever?"

"Honestly?" Keegan asked, looking back over her shoulder. "Sometimes it makes me go home and take a bath in steaming hot water, trying to clean away the filth we encounter when we watch those videos. Some of the things these husbands say to women who are complete strangers are total mind-fucks. Some of them are nasty and sick in the head. I mean, who *really* offers to eat a woman's cha-cha on the first night. Like *hel-lo.*"

Jessa smiled in spite of herself. "For one, you're snooping and dipping into shit that doesn't concern the numbers and the fiscal management of Mistress, Inc."

"True, but it's like watching *Maury Povich*," Keegan wailed, throwing up her hands. "You just can't look away. You feel like you have to know if that guy is the kid's father or not."

"But it's not like that for me, Keegan," Jessa stressed, her tone intended to be serious. "I really am just trying to help people. I'm trying to get into heaven. Fix the bad karma I put out in the universe. Do some good because I did so much fucked-up shit. I really am. Maybe that's the difference between us, but I need you to understand that."

Keegan focused her gaze back out the window. "It looks like rain," she said, looking up at the gray, shadowy clouds dominating the sky.

Jessa nodded as she rose and moved around the desk to take her seat. "Yes, the weatherman called for rain," she said, hiding her annoyance at their politeness as she retrieved her tube of matte nude lipstick and compact to touch up her mouth.

"Did you really say heroic?" Keegan asked as she came back around to stand in front of the desk.

Jessa cut her eyes up to her as she put the lid back on the tube. "Yes, my name is...um...Captain Catch a Hoe," she said, with a wink, smoothing stray flyaway hairs as she looked at her reflection.

"Wait a hot donkey-shit minute," Keegan said, squinting as she pointed at Jessa's hand.

Uh-oh.

"You had a ring on. I noticed it when you were milking the weirdo, but then I forgot," she said. "Now it's gone, and it just kicked in that I saw it. What happened to that big diamond?"

Her perfectly wonderful day was over. Traffic on her commute into the city? *Bearable. It was the same as any other day.* The mild flirtation with the stranger on the elevator? *Amusing.* Warren Sachs's mental breakdown in his birthday suit? *A pure shit show—pun intended.* Tackling Keegan about the engagement? *This blows, and not in a good way.*

She glanced at the time on her phone. It was just noon. *What else, Lord? What else?*

"There *is* something I wanted to share with you," Jessa began. "Last night...Hammer asked me to marry him, and I accepted."

Keegan's range of emotion played out on her face. Surprise. Doubt. Suspicion. Hurt. Doubt again. Envy. Sardonic amusement. And finally, anger.

Jessa missed not one bit of it.

She grabbed one of the club chairs to jerk it back and drop down onto its seat. "I guess you both got a nut and a good laugh behind my back," she said, both her tone and eyes hard and unrelenting.

Jessa unintentionally licked away some of the lipstick she'd just applied as she looked down at her desk and released a sigh. "The nut? Definitely," she admitted. "The laugh at your expense? Never, Keegan."

"And just how long has this been going on right under my nose?" she asked.

Jessa met her eyes with her own. "Long enough to know that I love him," was her reply.

Keegan flung her head back and released a lengthy laugh filled with sarcasm. "Long enough to make sure he took his boots off beside your bed and not mine," she said.

Bitch, please.

Jessa pressed her teeth softly into her bottom lip to keep those words from slipping off her tongue. "Keegan, I apologize for lying to you and breaking the promise we made to each other to keep it nothing but business with Hammer."

"And speaking of business, where does this leave me? Am I booted off the island because you two have an alliance?" she quipped.

"Nothing about me and Hammer affects you, just like always," Jessa said.

"Except now I know."

"Right."

"Probably were in heat right in this office," she mumbled under her breath.

"Sometimes," Jessa admitted smoothly.

Keegan jumped up onto her feet and looked down to study the chair.

"Now you're just being an ass," Jessa said, leaning back in her chair. "Besides, I never wasted a drop."

Keegan rolled her eyes. "Good one," she admitted begrudgingly, resuming her earlier pacing.

"You know, I made apologies for it all," Jessa began. "Regardless, I am a woman who has been through some shit. Some you know about. A lot of it you have no clue."

She held up her hand when Keegan opened her mouth to speak.

"See, I am in love. I am at peace. I am happy," Jessa stressed, her eyes filled with her emotions. "And I also need my friend who just figured out I'm getting married to be happy for me. I've been wanting to tell you all morning, but I didn't want *this* to ruin my day."

Keegan eyes were wide and filled with exasperation as she walked to the door. "You are the high priestess of guilt trips, and I am not falling for your shit today, Jessa," she said over her shoulder before she jerked it open and stormed out.

Jessa rested her chin in her hand and looked upward. *Lord, she tested me, but I did good. Right?*

Keegan came to stand in the doorway again, leaning against the doorjamb. In the distance behind her, Jessa could see Felisha peering at them over the red rim of her spectacles from her seat at her desk. She gave her a wide-eyed stare and then chuckled when the young woman literally jumped in her seat before lowering her head, pretending to be busy reading something on her computer screen.

Jessa now shifted her eyes up to Keegan's face.

She stepped farther into the room and closed the door securely. "I have two more things to get off this big chest of mine," she said, moving to stand before Jessa's desk.

Her annoyance stiffened her spine. She spread a smile across her face.

"This hurt me more than anything," Keegan admitted. "Being sneaky like this just made me wonder if what everyone used to say about you was right."

Jessa frowned.

"Oh, come on now. Don't get your britches in a twist over something you already knew," Keegan said. "But I didn't listen to the warnings to stay clear of you. I went on my own gut and the changes I saw you make. But this slick shit here made me wonder if I wasn't the one wrong, instead of everybody else."

Jessa opened her mouth but remained silent when Keegan raised her hand.

"One more thing," she said.

Jessa arched a brow. "Just one? You promise?" she said unable to contain the hint of sarcasm.

Keegan gave her a withering look before sitting down.

"Sorry. Go ahead," she said, with a long, drawn-out sigh.

Keegan extended her hand. "Let me see the rock," she said, with a begrudging smile.

That surprised Jessa as she genuinely smiled as well. She pulled it from inside her brassiere and slid it back on her left ring finger before extending her hand to set it inside Keegan's.

"Not bad at all," she admitted, looking up at Jessa as she rubbed the back of her hand with her thumb.

Jessa softened. Her stance in her seat. Her eyes. Her annoyance.

"I'm really starting to believe I have my happily-ever-after, Keegan," she said, her voice soft.

"Finally," Keegan stressed.

Jessa nodded, shifting her ring back and forth on her finger as she looked down at it and let everything it stood for swell in her chest.

Finally.

Interlude

I guess I should be grateful to my adoptive parents.

They didn't have to choose me, but they did. That already made them better than the bitch who bore me and the man who fucked her to make me—whoever the hell he was. They gave me a good life and they were nice people. Good people. They loved me the best they could.

I was the one unable to properly receive it.

I was the one fucked up.

I sat parked in front of my family home. My life lately had been all about pausing and reflecting on shit a lot. The two-story brick colonial was the epitome of upper-middle-class Connecticut. Beautiful. Grand. Prominent.

My grip on the bottom arc of my steering wheel tightened a bit.

Like a fool, I would placate myself into thinking my mother had to be struggling with a low-income job and gave me up so that I could have a better life. Jessa Bell's house was more beautiful and prominent than this. Her life was golden. Her and Delaney. There was no room for me.

There was no excuse for there not to be room for me.

I climbed from my car and made my way up the stairs to unlock the double doors.

"Hello," I called out. "Mom, Dad, I'm here."

I paused, waiting for my mom to come from whatever room she was in to hug me and kiss my brow or my father to yell out for me to come to him in his man cave and hug him before sitting to watch sports with him.

Neither happened.

I closed the front door and made my way into the kitchen to open the side door leading into the three-car garage. Both of their vehicles were gone, leaving just my father's speedboat.

I felt relief.

The all-too familiar façade of pretending to love them as I knew they loved me went away.

None of it mattered to me anymore—and maybe never did. Even with their love, their money, and the good life they provided, they still were unable to fill the deep well of inadequacy within me.

My need to reflect led me back out to the hall where the family photos were arranged on the wall. And with every step I touched a photo of myself, trying to connect with the sad little lost girl putting on such a good front to cover up the fucked-up thoughts in my head. Thoughts I began to have from the first time they sat me down and explained to me that I was so special that they chose me to be their little girl. That was at four or five, and even then, I skipped over the good of being special and went to the question of why I wasn't special enough for my real mommy and daddy.

After that conversation, everything changed for me. I didn't know it then, but it was a defining moment in my life. They didn't mean it to, but the truth fucked me right on up.

I began to feel unwanted even with all of the love and affection they gave me.

"Fraud," I whispered to the pictures capturing the moments of my life.

Every year in private school up until my graduation, posing in my uniforms for chess, fencing, debate, and swimming. Behind the wheel of my first car at sixteen—a brand-new cherry red Toyota

Solara. In designer gowns at all of my school formals. Posed in front of international monuments from my summers abroad.

Even with all of their love and attention, they still didn't see me.

I started getting high at the age of thirteen, foolishly trying to fit in with the rich and privileged kids. They smoked weed, I smoked it, too. They laced their blunts. Me too. They snorted powder. I fell right in line.

And not once did my adoptive parents catch on. They were still clueless that I overdosed and almost died. Hiding shit from them was so damn easy.

I stroked my neck, feeling the familiar urge to get high. Even a blunt would do me good right now. I fought off the urge, though, like ignoring hunger when there was no food to eat.

I pulled my iPhone from the back pocket of my jeans. Swiping through the photos, I enlarged the one of Jessa sitting at her desk at the office, gazing out the window with a faraway look. She never even saw me standing there. Never noticed me watching her.

Nothing new.

One day she would see me. She wouldn't have a choice. I was just sitting, taking notes, and making plans. It wasn't quite time. Not yet.

I swiped again.

Another photo of my mother and her chosen daughter. Delaney, I think is her name.

I was at the office when her nanny brought her by to visit our mother.

It doesn't matter. Fuck 'em both.

The front door opened.

I erased the lines of anger on my face with a welcoming smile as my parents entered. My mother with her blond hair and cobalt blue eyes. My father, tall and broad with brown hair and hazel-green eyes. They were nothing like my mother and they looked nothing like her—or me, for that matter. The root of my feelings of not belonging. Not fitting in. Wanting to belong.

It wasn't their fault at all.

This was all about Jessa Bell, and I was going to make her pay.

Chapter 7

Two months later

"Your engagement ring is beautiful, Ms. Bell."

Jessa paused in writing notes on her iPad, her stylus pen in hand, as she cut her eyes up to look across her desk at Charli. The young woman smiled at her before shifting her gaze back to the jewelry. Jessa did the same, raising her hand from where it lightly rested against the desktop. "Thank you, Charli," she said with a polite smile that was forced, before turning her attention back to her iPad.

"I guess congratulations are in order?"

Jessa looked at her again, looking beautiful as ever in a bright red leather peacoat. Her skin was blemish free, her makeup perfection—and not overdone. Sleek hair. Stylish diamond jewelry.

A fucking mini-me. And in the seven months since she joined the firm she's now my top agent. Of course.

"Thank you," Jessa told her.

"Hammer, right?" she asked.

"As a matter of fact, yes, Hammer and I are getting married. We are happy as hell. The date is all set. And none of that has anything to do with why you are sitting in my office right now," she said, raising her brow and giving her yet another forced smile.

Charli's eyes dulled and she licked her lips before clenching her jaw.

"So, it's nearing the end of the year, and I like to meet with all of our agents and make sure we have all open cases closed out and to see if you have any insight on a particular case or suggestions for how we can improve things here at Mistress, Inc.," Jessa said, ignoring the woman's obvious hurt feelings. She looked back down at her iPad. "Any insight?"

Charli shifted in the seat before crossing her legs as she looked contemplative. "I really like the work, the hours are great, and the pay is decent."

Decent?

Jessa remained silent.

"I really think it's helping me with my acting," Charli added.

Jessa nodded in understanding. "Any suggestions?" she asked, making notes on Charli's digital file on the tablet.

"I think the agents need to spend more time with you, Ms. Bell," she said frankly.

Jessa looked up at her in surprise. "With me?"

Charli nodded. "I think you are the epitome of what most men want, and the female agents could learn a lot from how you carry yourself."

Looking contemplative, Jessa set the pen down again and leaned back in her chair to study her. "Thank you. I haven't always used my wiles for the greater good, but, um...I do admit I seem to have a way with men—whether I want to or not," she admitted. "But I hired you on the spot because I see that spark in you, Charli. So the last thing you need is to be me or hang around me or emulate me. Trust me. Just keep being you. It's working."

Charli looked pleased. "Then we have a lot in common."

Jessa gave her another polite smile before picking up her pen and turning her attention back to the tablet. "Let's finish up. I have some more agents coming in today as well," she said. "Now, I think your last open case for the year is Mrs. Bella Montgomery, and I understand that he was not receptive to you at all."

Charli turned her crimson lips downward. "Nothing. I did a couple of stroll-bys, forced an eye contact, tried to start a conversation. Laid out the cleavage. Offered to buy him a drink. Sucked on the cherry in my soda because we're not allowed to drink on a case. Sexy leg cross in a clinging wrap dress. The works. I don't know, maybe I'm just not his cup of tea, maybe he just loves his wife or he already has a side chick lined up because he kept calling someone on his phone and was aggravated when they didn't answer. So I don't know," she said, with a one-shoulder shrug.

Jessa made notes. "Okay. Thank you," she said, reaching into her side drawer to remove a bright red envelope with "Mistress, Inc." embossed in gold lettering. She slid it across the desk to Charli.

She picked it up and opened it on the spot, her eyes widening in surprise.

"Your Christmas bonus. Good work, Charli, and I hope you decide to remain with us next year," Jessa said, having enjoyed each and every moment she slid one of those vibrant envelopes to one of her employees that day.

"My plan wasn't really long term," Charli said, rising to her feet. "Can I let you know after the new year?"

"Of course," Jessa said, swiping her finger across the tablet's screen to pull up a new file.

Charli extended her hand.

Jessa momentarily shifted her gaze to it before looking up at Charli again as she reached to shake her hand.

Charli squeezed down.

Jessa withdrew. "Have a good day, Charli," she said firmly. "And ask Lacey to come in on your way out."

The fuck?

As Charli took her leave, Lacey Adams entered and took the seat in front of Jessa's desk.

The intercom buzzed. Jessa pressed the button. "Yes?" she said, waving a hand for Lacey to take a seat.

"You have a call from Aria Livewell," Felisha said.

Jessa frowned. *First a visit from Renee, now a call from Aria. What's next? Lunch with Jaime?*

"Take her number and I will call her back," she said, releasing the intercom button.

Her curiosity was piqued.

She gave the beautiful woman sitting across the desk from her a welcoming smile but was unable to focus her attention at first. Usually observant, she barely noted the striking black ensemble she wore or her topknot and natural makeup that gave her that fresh-faced beauty that a lot of men favored.

"Ms. Bell."

Jessa looked up at Lacey, shaking her head for clarity. "Yes, Lacey, I'm sorry. Just have a lot on my mind, and you are my last appointment for the day, so I'm a little tired," she explained.

She smiled with an understanding nod. "No problem. I can understand that," she said.

"Good, so let's get to it and then we both can head home," Jessa said, picking up her stylus pen.

It's beginning to look a lot like Christmas.

And Jessa loved every bit of it as she drove up the drive leading to her home. The white lights entwined atop bushes and wrapped around posts twinkled brightly against the darkness of night. She reached for her iPhone and shook it. "Siri, call Hammer."

"Calling Hammer."

It rang just once.

"What's up, baby?"

"Where are you?" she asked as she pulled to a stop before her house, taking in the same white lights adorning the trim of the eaves and the windows.

"Looking at you from your living room window."

Her eyes shifted to the left as she climbed from her vehicle. She could see his silhouette outlined against the sheer curtains. She rushed inside and was welcomed by Hammer pulling her into his embrace in the foyer. "I haven't seen you all day," she complained, as she pressed her mouth to his cheek and left a print of her kiss.

Hammer leaned back to look down at her. "My boss is hell," he joked, feigning seriousness.

"Aw, poor you," she said, pouting as she lightly stroked one of his earlobes.

Quickly he tasted her mouth before he reached for her hand and pulled her behind him toward the living room.

She resisted just long enough to kick off her heels and set her tote on the table in the center of the sizable vestibule. As soon as they reached the arched entryway, her eyes went to the towering unlit tree, trimmed in gold decorations, but quickly shifted to her mother holding Delaney on her hip.

"Welcome home, Mama," Delaney said, already dressed in her teddy bear pajamas.

Jessa knew that meant Winifrid had already bathed her for the night.

"Yes, she is," Darla said.

Jessa eyes squinted as she thought she heard a slur in her mother's voice.

"We wanted to surprise you with the tree," Hammer said. "We did the tree ourselves. Right, Delaney?"

"Yup," she agreed with him.

Jessa eased from the light embrace of Hammer's hand on her hip as she quickly walked over to them and eased her daughter onto her own hip. She pressed kisses to her cheek before setting her down on her feet as she looked over at her mother and sniffed the air. "Are you drunk?" she asked, her tone hard.

"What?" Darla asked, nearly stumbling on the hem of her tiger print caftan. "I ain't had nothing to drink but some eggnog. This is just good vibes, baby girl. Get into it. Pull the stick out your butt."

"I'm ready for my presents from Santa and he got plenty of room under the tree," Delaney said.

"Light it up, Ham-mer!" Darla said at the top of her voice, snapping her fingers and clapping her hands as she two-stepped.

She's drunk. She. Is. Drunk.

Jessa frowned, turning to look on as her fiancé lowered the lights in the room with its twenty-foot ceilings and then plugged in the tree. "Where's Winifrid?" she asked him, as her daughter clapped in delight.

"We did a good job, y'all," Delaney sighed.

Jessa ignored her cuteness. *Focus, bitch. Focus.*

The brightness of Hammer's toothy grin dimmed a bit. "I sent her home early, baby," he said, rubbing circles on her back as he looked down at her. "What's wrong?"

"Oh, Christmas tree…Oh, Christmas tree," Darla sang, swaying with her arms splayed and her legs spread wide, causing the lights from the tree to show she was naked beneath the thin material.

"Oh," Hammer said, averting his eyes.

"Honey, there is a lot we need to talk about before we get married and merge households," Jessa said, turning her back on her mother. "Uppermost is never, ever, ever, never, ever, ever let Winifrid leave early. Okay? Okay."

Hammer turned his back on Darla as well, and they now both faced the entrance. Delaney came around to stand there and look up at Hammer and then at Jessa.

"My mother is not to be left alone with Delaney," Jessa said under her breath, turning her daughter's head so that she wasn't staring directly into her mouth.

"And never give my mother anything to drink—whether straight up or spiked in eggnog," she hissed.

Hammer looked contrite. "I didn't know," he said. "I made the eggnog and I put a little brandy in it."

Jessa closed her eyes and dropped her head. "She's in recovery, and it doesn't interact well with her meds—"

"Hi, Gramma!"

Jessa and Hammer froze before they both turned to find Darla now standing directly behind them. Her eyes were bright.

"The only child in this house is Delaney, Jessa Bell," she said. "Respect me always. I am your mother."

Jessa tried her best not to roll her eyes. "I think you should sleep it off," she said gently. "Let me help you upstairs."

"I am not drunk!" Darla bellowed, knocking away the hand Jessa rested on her elbow.

Jessa wiped away the spittle that sprayed against her chin and throat. "You did not mean to get drunk, but your behind is drunk and you being sloppy with it. If you had fallen with my daughter—"

Hammer moved quickly in between them and scooped Delaney up into his arms. He carried her over to the Christmas tree, and she immediately began reaching out to touch the large gold balls with the tip of her finger.

Jessa's anger dissipated. She was grateful for his intervention, but felt ashamed that she had to have anyone else remind her that she was behaving badly in front of her child.

She released a heavy sigh as she left the living room and took the small hall into the den on through to the kitchen. She located the bowl of spiked eggnog and dumped all of it into the sink, using the spray to rinse the splatter down the drain. "Damn," she swore, turning to bend over the island and press her forehead to its cool top.

She released rapid, shallow breaths that pressed down against the marble and then rebounded to warm her lips. She felt as if she was losing a fight to anxiety. She wanted nothing more than peace in her home. In her life.

"Lord, please help me," she prayed, her words landing on the countertop, as she fought to reclaim her inner peace. "Please guide my steps."

The sound of Nat King Cole singing "The Christmas Song" drifted in from the living room.

Jessa allowed herself one last deep breath before she stood tall and made her way back to the living room. At the entry she paused, smiling at the picturesque sight of the illuminated tree, the fireplace now lit, her mother sitting on the couch with her head tilted back as she snored softly in her sleep, and Hammer sitting on the floor with Delaney in his lap as he rocked her to sleep.

She walked into the room, mouthing the words to the Christmas carol as she softly touched her mother's hair when she passed her to reach Hammer. She stooped beside him, wrapping an arm around his broad shoulders as she pressed a kiss to his temple. "You are my salvation, my peace, and my spot to fall," she whispered near his ear.

He turned his head to kiss her mouth. "There's nothing I wouldn't do for you," he breathed against her still moist lips. "Absolutely nothing."

They stared at one another, the brown depths highlighted by the lighting in the room.

"Time for bed," she said, taking Delaney into her arms and resting her head on her right shoulder before she rose to her feet.

"It's still early," he said, unfolding his legs and rising as well. "It's just like seven or so. We haven't had dinner, and I am *starving*."

Jessa paused at the entrance to look back at him. "I'm hungry, too," she said with a pointed look below his belt.

Hammer looked down and then up. He gave her a wolfish grin. "I can feed you. Whatever you want off the menu is available," he said.

Jessa chuckled and continued out of the living room. "Throw a cover on my drunk-ass mama," she said, rubbing Delaney's back when she stirred in her sleep.

"Mama," she whispered softly.

Jessa's heart tugged as she climbed the stairs. She hummed Delaney's favorite lullaby near her ear, soothing her back into deep slumber.

Hammer came up behind her. "Gonna take a shower," he said as he passed, taking the steps two at a time.

Jessa continued up to the second floor and made her way to Delaney's room. The scent of baby powder from the plug-ins sweetly scented the air, and she inhaled it as she turned on the night-lights on either side of the bed. She continued to lightly hum as she laid Delaney down and pulled her lightweight pink blanket up around her stomach.

"What would I do without you?" she asked her softly.

Same thing you did without Georgia. Get over it in time.

Jessa closed her eyes, hating her inner thoughts and how she was her own worst critic. "Good night, Delaney," she whispered.

She turned on the video baby monitor before making her way to the door adjoining the room to the master suite.

Now that she was to be wed, and with Delaney eventually getting older, she knew the time would come to move her daughter to a room farther down the hall. *I do not need a kid listening to our sexcapades.*

The room was softly lit and Hammer was still in the shower. She turned on the television and switched the channel to the local news as she undressed. When the next few minutes were filled with reports on murder and mayhem, she switched to a music channel. Soon the sound of Luther Vandross and Cheryl Lynn singing "If This World Were Mine" filled the air.

She sang along as she lit candles and dimmed the lights before heading to the bathroom when she heard the shower turn off. Hammer walked out with a plush towel wrapped around his waist, swatting one of Jessa's buttocks as she passed him.

"Hurry up," he said.

She glanced back over her shoulder to see his erection now tenting the cloth.

"Matter of fact, fuck it," Hammer said, flinging the towel away and striding over to easily swing Jessa's nude body up over his shoulder.

She laughed, reaching down to swat at his bare buttocks.

He flipped her down onto the bed. She squealed in surprise. "We're going to wake Delaney," she said.

He lay down beside her on his side, his head propped on his hand as he looked down at her. He smiled as he trailed his hand from her knees and up her thighs.

"I need to bathe, Hammer," she insisted, gasping softly as she buried her head against his neck at the feel of strong fingers opening the lips of her core and stroking her clit.

Hammer bent over to kiss her shoulder before rising again to watch the pleasure on her face as he eased his middle finger deep inside her.

Jessa cried out as her hips involuntarily arched up off the bed and she spread her knees. "Shit," she swore softly, pursing her lips and releasing a long stream of breath.

He reached for one of her hands and guided it to his dick.

She found him stiff and curving. Ready for her. Hard for her. She tightened her grip.

He grunted and hissed in pleasure.

"I could cum just watching you," he said softly.

She looked up at him. His eyes were on her. Intently.

Watching and gauging the pleasure he gave her as he stroked her walls with his finger and teased her clit with light circles. She felt embarrassed and hid her face against him. "Don't watch me," she pleaded, releasing him to cover her face with both of her hands.

"Look at me," Hammer demanded, lifting one of her legs over his before he smoothly slid another finger into her before circling both fingers against her rigid walls.

She grimaced in pleasure, her mouth gaped and her heart pounding.

"*Look* at me."

Jessa did.

Hammer bit his bottom lip as he quickened the pace of his finger strokes. "So tight and wet," he moaned.

Her eyes locked with his as she panted, her nipples hard and pointed upward as she arched her back. "Hammer," she sighed, rolling her hips against his hand.

His eyes darted down to take in the movement of her body, and he shook his head in wonder. "You're so damn beautiful," he said.

She raised her head from the pillow to suck his mouth into hers.

Hammer deepened the kiss, lightly drawing the tip of her tongue into his mouth to suck before stroking it with his. He broke away with one final crush of his mouth against hers. "I don't know what I want more—to make you cum with my hand or my dick."

Jessa trembled, reaching out until she felt his hardness again in her hand. She caressed the length of him. Gently, she dragged her thumb across the smooth tip and then stroked him downward until she felt the strong and hard root of it. "I prefer this," she said, tilting her chin up and hotly licking at his bottom lip.

He hardened in her hand. She felt it. Her clit throbbed with renewed life beneath his touch.

"Your hand ain't hard, thick, nor long as your dick. It doesn't cum with me," she whispered, lost in his eyes. "It doesn't get hot inside me when you cum."

Hammer withdrew his fingers from her before he lay down atop her, spreading her legs with his knees and positioning his dick at her warm and moist opening.

She shook her head. "Let me ride that dick," she demanded.

He turned over onto his back, bringing her body with his. She sat up straight, her thighs pressed against his narrow hips as she arched her back and reached between their bodies to guide his hardness inside her.

"Ah," they cried out.

Jessa's head fell back and she brought her hands up above her head as she closed her eyes and enjoyed the feel of him inside her, pressing against her walls, filling her completely. With a grunt followed by a hiss, she began rolling her hips in tight little circles, enjoying how the base of his dick stroked her clit every time she completed one full circle. Her nipples ached and she cupped one full breast, teasing her own hard nipples as she rode him.

"Jessa," Hammer moaned as his hands dug deep pockets into the soft flesh of her buttocks.

She smiled and pouted her lips as she looked down at him, biting her bottom lip softly.

"That's right, baby, fuck me," he begged, lifting his hips up off the bed to thrust upward. "Fuck me."

She cried out her. Her heart raced. Her clit throbbed. Her nipples ached. It felt glorious. "Yes, yes, yes," she sighed, bending down and dangling her sweet globes above his face.

He buried his head between them, turning first left and then right to suck the side of each.

"Lick 'em," she begged in a hot whisper as she arched her back over and over to bring her core up to the tip of his dick to squeeze with her walls before the next downstroke.

And he did, his tongue flickering against one nipple and

then the other, back and forth. Each lick more delicious than the last.

She loved that and he knew it.

She got wetter. The sounds of the sex play echoed in the room.

Her entire body tingled with passion, satisfaction, and anticipation.

"Suck my nipples," she ordered softly.

He did.

She arched her back higher and higher, feeling a bit of his release leave the line and coat her walls. Her moves on him were easier. Less friction. The glide of the base of his dick against her clit slickened.

She freed her breast from his mouth. "Look at me," she ordered into the heat between them as she sat up, taking his hands into hers to draw up her body to her breasts.

The candlelight was beautiful against their brown skins and illuminated in their eyes. The mood was sultry. The music serenaded. The connection between them intense and electrifying.

"I'm coming," she whispered to him, her eyes locked on his as she looked down at him.

"I know," he panted, his chest rising and falling beneath her hands. "I feel it."

She smiled and lightly bit her bottom lip. "Join me," she requested.

He grunted and thrust his hips upward, clenching his teeth. "I...I...am."

They never looked away from each as their thrusts and glides quickened in pace and deepened as they climaxed in unison.

She felt his heart pound against her palm, matching her own. Their bodies swung between trembles and going stiff. Sweat coated their bodies. The temperature of the room elevated. The headboard lightly knocked against the wall.

They cried out roughly.

In that moment, as she felt her release coat his inches, she didn't care. Not one bit.

Hammer sat up and wrapped his arms around her, one hand gripping the roots of her hair and the other clutching one cheek of her soft buttocks. He buried his face against her neck and sucked the spot where her pulse thumped as he filled her with his seed.

Jessa was weak, but she continued to ride him, helping to push him over the edge as she held him close and lightly bit his muscled shoulder. "Fill it up," she begged him.

Hammer's body went stiff. "Jessa, your mama!" he roared.

She looked to the door.

Her eyes widened in shock at Darla standing in the doorway with her hand still on the knob as she watched them.

Hammer slid from under her and rolled off the bed onto the floor to hide his nudity from her mother's eyes.

Darla began to cackle, loud and erratic, her eyes and her mouth wide.

"What is wrong with you?" Jessa screeched, rising from the bed to rush across the room, grab her mother's shoulders, and push her back out of the room before she stepped back in alone and closed the door.

"How long was she standing there?" Jessa asked as she crossed the room and came around the bed to look down at Hammer sitting on the floor with his legs bent and his arms stretched out over his knees.

Hammer shrugged. "I opened my eyes and she was standing there," he said, his voice annoyed.

Jessa grabbed her housecoat from the door of the closet, twirling it around her body to slide it on. "How much liquor was in that damn eggnog?" she asked as she jerked the edges closed and tied it with hard movements.

Hammer rose with ease and began blowing out the candles,

his dick now limp and spent. "Not much, but you don't have to worry about it. After tonight, liquor is banned from the whole house."

"Even my locked wine cellar for which only *I* have the key?" she asked as she walked over to the door.

Hammer shook his head. "Ask me again when we're not a few minutes fresh off your mother watching us fuck," he said.

"Deal," Jessa agreed. "I'll be back."

Beyond the door, after she closed it, Jessa gave herself a moment to lean against it. She didn't know if she was more embarrassed or angry or a mix of both. With a deep breath, she walked down the hall to her mother's suite. She knocked softly on the door twice before turning the knob and pushing it open. It was her turn to stand in the open doorway and stare at her. Darla sat in the custom La-Z-Boy next to her bed with the footrest up high and her mouth again open in her sleep as she snored.

"I don't believe you're really sleeping, Mama," she said. "Hell, you probably weren't really knocked out downstairs either."

Jessa walked into the room and opened the drawer holding the medicine caddy. All the appropriate slots were empty. "These psych pills better be down your throat and not tossed away," she warned, closing the drawer and sitting down on the edge of the bed.

Darla's snores continued like a low-key chain saw.

"But I'll say this right now and then again in the morning," Jessa told her. "You have one more time to drink even a thimble of alcohol and I am done. So I'd advise you not to put lips to nothing else unless you poured it yourself from an unopened soda, water, or juice bottle."

More snores.

Jessa rose and made her way back to the door. "Like I said,

we will go over this in the morning," she said over her shoulder before reaching for the knob and closing the door behind her as she left.

She pinched the bridge of her nose with her fingers, hating that in her mind's eye, parts of her life were truly unraveling.

Chapter 8

*T*he water of the lake was still. The only ripples were caused by the gentle motion of the boat. The rays from the sun broke up its darkness, and the sound of nature echoed with beauty.

The scene was surreal.

On the middle seat of the rowboat, Jessa turned to her left and smiled at her daughter Delaney. She reached over and squeezed her hand. "I am so thankful to have both of you in my life," she said, turning to look at Georgia sitting on the other end of the boat, nearly her twin and in her mid-twenties.

Jessa reached for her hand as well. "Both my daughters," she said with pleasure. "Now my life is complete."

Suddenly the sun disappeared beneath gray clouds.

"We better go home," Jessa said, taking the oars in her hands and beginning to row backward.

Thunder and lightning erupted, momentarily breaking up the darkness. The rain came moments later, heavy and *steady. Cold winds stirred, causing waves and rocking their small boat.*

"Shit," *Jessa swore, looking around and seeing the vast amount of water as a threat. Through the veil of rain, the shore seemed too far in the distance to reach.*

She rowed harder, feeling the strain in her shoulders, arms, and back. She didn't care. She had to save them. It rested on her shoulders. Her daughters depended on her. "Hold on, girls," *she shouted, some of the rain entering her open mouth.*

The wind whipped around them, pushing and rocking them.

A scream rang out.

Jessa turned just as Delaney fell into the water, her arms and legs flailing. "Noooooo," *she roared, reaching out to grab her wrist.*

"Mama, save me. Please don't let me go," *Delaney said before a wave rose and covered her head.*

Jessa desperately clung to her wrist with both of her hands as she pressed her sneakered feet to the side of the boat for leverage.

Another scream.

Jessa's eyes were wide as she looked back over her shoulder as Georgia tipped over the side and into the dark depths of the water as well. "Please, God," *she prayed, futilely shaking her head to divert the rain obscuring her vision.*

She freed one hand to reach and grab one of Georgia's thrashing limbs.

With a grunt, she leaned backward, trying her best to pull them above the depths. "Lord, help me. Please help me save my daughters," *she begged, her desperation giving rise to tears that blended with the rain showers.*

"Mama, save me," *they cried out in unison.*

She looked from one to the other.

Panic clawed at her. She had never felt so hopeless. So useless . . .

Jessa awakened with a start, sitting straight up in bed. She covered her face with her hands as she released short, rapid breaths that caused her chest to rise and fall. She couldn't stop the rise of tears as all of the emotions from her dream clung to her reality. "Oh God," she whispered, her shoulders shaking as she cried.

The loss felt all too real.

She knew the implications. She understood the symbolism. *I can't have it all.*

Mindful of Hammer's body in the bed beside her, Jessa eased her knees to her chest and buried her face in the small space between them to release a silent scream, wishing she could truly let out a yell of frustration. She felt alone with nothing but her thoughts, fears, and guilt to surround her.

She flung back the covers and rose from her bed, pulling on her red satin robe, to make her way across the room and through the door to Delaney's bedroom. She stood by her bed and took comfort in her restfully sleeping, trying not to feel foolish for carefully watching for the rise and fall of her belly to ensure she was breathing.

Did Georgia ever have someone love her and watch over her in her sleep?

Did she have a good nanny and a professionally designed nursery? High-end clothing? A trust fund?

Safety? Security?

Is she still alive? Healthy?

Does she know she was adopted?

Does she ever wonder about me? Her father?

Jessa grimaced, feeling her stomach revolt at the truth of Georgia's parentage. She turned and walked back into her bedroom. She paused to find Hammer sitting up in bed. He reached to bathe the room in soft light from the lamp on the bedside table.

"You ready to talk?" he asked, his voice deep and warm.

Maybe I should tell him the truth? Tell him about my father? Tell him about Georgia?

"Talk about what?" she said with feigned nonchalance as she made her way back to her side of the bed and removed her robe.

"Whatever it is you're hiding from me," he countered, even as his brown eyes dipped to take in her nudity.

She sat down on the edge and faked an elaborate yawn, with an arm stretch and all, before lying down as she pulled the sheet and duvet up around her shoulders. "I just got up to check on Delaney," she lied. "Go back to sleep."

He became quiet.

Jessa tried her best to relax as she waited for the movement of the bed signaling he had he lain down as well.

It never came.

"You know, I think it's bullshit that you're willing to share your life with the world and not with me," he said, breaking the silence.

Damn.

Jessa grimaced.

"Yes, this is an old argument between us, but I think it's time we finished it," Hammer said.

She turned over to face him, easing her hand across his thigh to stroke his dick. "Let me help put you back to sleep," she said, leaning forward to take him into her mouth.

He pressed a palm to her forehead to stop her. "Not gonna work," he insisted.

She flopped onto her back on her side of the bed. "Robert, please," she begged, reverting to his given name in hopes he would understand that she was serious about not divulging her past.

"Robert?" he balked. "Now I *know* you're hiding some shit."

Her anger sparked like a lit flame. "This is not what you want, Hammer, so *leave* me be," she warned, turning her scarf-covered head on the pillow to give him a hard stare.

"What the hell does *that* mean?" he asked.

She sat up and the covers dropped to her waist. "Okay, 'Mr. Open and Aboveboard at All Times,'" she snapped. "Why haven't I met anyone in your family or any of your friends? Your mother in California? Your son in Paris? Your friends? Not a one. What are *your* secrets? Maybe you have a few of your own so your ass is so sure I have some *because* the only difference between us sneaking and fucking and now is a ring. Nothing else. Not a damn thing else, Hammer."

Jessa felt triumphant when his face became perplexed. *Take that, motherfucker. Now back up off me.*

"This desire to know more about me *just* hit you?" he asked, now looking disbelieving.

"No," she said.

But that was somewhat of a lie. It had crossed her mind in the week since their engagement, but the idea of introducing new people into her inner circle hadn't appealed to her. She had decided not to push the issue until she just slapped it on the figurative card table as her trump card.

"I just figured you would meet everyone at the wedding in three months, but it's easy to fix," Hammer said. "No problem. Whatever you want."

Backfired big-time. Shit!

"It never crossed my mind to arrange a meet-up before then because I'm a fully grown man who doesn't need anyone's approval to marry the woman I love."

Jessa shifted her eyes away from him.

"What's crazy is I could've just researched your background—"

Her eyes darted to him.

"But I didn't," he said. "I want you to tell me. I want you to share your life with me. I want to be able to trust you."

"You don't trust me?" she asked.

"Fully? How can I when my gut tells me you're keeping something from me?"

"It's not another lover," Jessa admitted.

Hammer smiled, reaching out to playfully tweak one of her nipples. "*That* I know," he said.

She glanced away from him, to the door leading to the outside hall. Her mind flashed back to the night her mother had stood there and watched them having sex. She closed her eyes and shook her head as if to free it of the memory forever.

No such luck.

"You're wrong to assume I shared everything about my life in the book," she began, pulling up the sheet to cover her breasts. "There is so much more."

Hammer pressed a warm hand to her bare back.

"Delaney is not my only child," Jessa confessed, keeping her face averted from his.

The hand disappeared.

She pressed her eyes closed and told him her secrets, hating that clear and vivid images of every bit of it replayed as she talked. She felt it all as if it was happening to her right in that moments instead of over twenty years ago. And when she was done relaying the horror, the loss, the shame, and the continuing guilt, the breath she released was shaky.

"Jessa," Hammer said softly, settling his hand on her shoulder and pulling her toward him. "Thank you for sharing that with me. I am so sorry I pressed you."

Jessa nodded. "It was for the best. Now there are no secrets between us," she said, settling her body back against the strength of his.

"And your father?" he asked, his voice hesitant.

She winced.

The rape she never forgot. The moment he slit his own throat when he awakened from his drunken stupor and realized that he had violated his daughter? That she normally repressed. "He's dead," was all that she replied.

"And your child?"

"I never saw her after her birth."

"She?" he asked.

Jessa nodded. "A girl."

"We could find her," Hammer offered.

With both hands, Jessa tightly gripped the arm he had wrapped around her. "No," she insisted. "I think it's better she never meets me or knows the truth...about...about..."

She shook her head, unable to say the words or relive the torturous moments again.

"Do you wonder about her?"

"Of course. More so since I had Delaney," she admitted, feeling her tension about sharing the truth ease.

"Listen, give me some info—which I noticed you withheld—and let me check on her," Hammer offered, pressing a kiss to her temple.

"No."

"We don't have to reach out to her or speak to her. We're just checking that she's okay," he pressed.

"No," Jessa snapped. She felt instant remorse and sat up to turn on the bed and face him. "This is for the best, Hammer."

He opened his mouth.

She covered his lips with her fingertips. "I've changed, and for my own good I have to move forward," she said. "I have to because her family has done enough disservice to her and I can't risk the truth fucking her up in any way. Can you imagine finding out your grandfather is also your father?"

Hammer kissed her fingertips before removing them from his mouth. "I don't agree, but I respect your decision."

Jessa felt relieved.

"I just want a quiet, normal life. No drama," she said. "That's why I turned down an offer to write another book or have the first one made into a movie."

Hammer smiled. "Thank God," he agreed. "No regrets?"

"Not a one," she said truthfully.

"You want me to make you a cup of tea or something?" Hammer offered.

"No, I really just want lay my head on your chest and try to sleep," she said.

He reached back and turned off the lamp before lying down and pulling her body with him. "You have led one helluva life, Jessa," he said.

"Yes, but I think this is the best part of it," she said, stroking the hard contours of his chest. "At least I hope it is. I can't take too much more."

"This is the best part. I promise you that," he said, gently massaging her lower back.

They fell silent. Soon the sounds of Hammer's snores echoed against her ear. Sleep didn't come to her as easily. Fear of another nightmare centered on her daughters kept her awake long into the night.

"Mama, save me."

"Jessa."

She blinked, putting aside dark visions of drowning daughters, as she met the eyes of Keegan from across the table in their favorite upscale soul food lunch spot. "Yes?" she said.

"What do you want to order?" Keegan asked, glancing up at the waiter with a polite smile.

Jessa looked up at the tall, bald man in his black polo and black pants. "I'm sorry," she said. "I'll have my usual smothered chicken and mashed potatoes," she said, handing him the leather-bound menu.

"I'll be back with your drinks," he said, quickly turning and heading toward the bar.

Jessa sat up a bit in her chair and raised her hand to get his attention. "I didn't order a drink yet—"

"Peach Tea Fizz," Keegan supplied.

Jessa relaxed back against her chair, already looking forward to the peach tea and champagne concoction. "Thanks," she said.

She fell silent as the in-house jazz band began a soulful rendition of "Baby, It's Cold Outside." Christmas was just a week away and the music set the mood for the upcoming festivities.

The waiter came up to their table, setting Keegan's glass of red wine and Jessa's drink before them. "Your food should be ready in another few minutes." he said before retreating.

Keegan followed him with her eyes. "I think I would like to fa-la-la-la-la all over him," she drawled as she took a sip of her beverage.

Jessa smiled. "You have a Christmas present for him, huh?" she asked with amusement.

"Humph, it's the gift that *keeps* on giving, darlin'," Keegan sighed.

They toasted to that.

"Have you started thinking about your wedding plans?" Keegan asked.

Bzzzzzzzzz.

Jessa picked up her vibrating iPhone from where she'd laid it facedown on the table.

"It's the office," she said before answering. "Hello."

"I'm sorry to interrupt you, Ms. Bell, but Aria Livewell threatened to come to the office and plant her foot in my behind—not the way she said—if I didn't call and have you return her call. She said ASAP."

Jessa frowned. She was done with trying to make amends

with Renee, Aria, or Jaime. She'd offered them the truth, honestly trying to protect them, and still they ridiculed her?

"What's wrong?" Keegan asked, her face filled with concern.

Jessa put the phone on mute. "An old friend reached out to me via the office and left a number," she said, and then realized she wasn't lying.

Keegan relaxed.

Jessa rose to her feet. "I'm going to step outside and return the call. Please excuse me," she said, dropping the linen napkin onto her vacated chair. She unmuted the phone as she made her way through the restaurant to the ornate but small vestibule. "Felisha, send me the number," she said, grasping that short of a restraining order, there was only one way to be free of Aria Livewell.

"I can transfer you," Felisha offered.

So you can eavesdrop? No, ma'am.

"No, just text it," she requested.

She ended the call and moments later she received the text. Once she put the call through, it rang just once.

"Yeah."

Jessa rolled her eyes heavenward at Aria's rudeness.

"I'm shocked you would want me to have your new number," Jessa said, moving out of the way in the small vestibule as a couple entered.

The winter chill blew in with them, and she shivered as it surrounded her.

"I didn't. This is a burner phone. Last thing I need is you calling Kingston on the low-low."

Jessa flung her head back and laughed. "Me? Call Kingston? For what? To be bored to death?" she asked. "I barely kept awake listening to his boring ass talk during dinner parties."

"No the fuck you didn't!" Aria snapped.

"Oh yes, I did," Jessa volleyed back. "And I meant it."

"I guess a lunatic murderer does seem more your speed,

right?" Aria asked snidely. "Was it exciting getting choked out before you watched another woman's husband kill himself, huh?"

Lord, give me strength.

"What do you want, Aria?" Jessa asked, ready to move on from their childish banter.

"I'm calling in that favor," she said, her Newark accent still heavy even though she had long since left behind more humble beginnings for a life in the upper-middle-class gated community of Richmond Hills.

"And that would be for?" Jessa asked, truly confused.

"Trying to ruin my marriage with that lying message you sent."

"How could I forget it?" Jessa asked.

Lord, is this a test?

"I want to know whatever you know about my husband."

Humph.

Jessa forced herself not to gloat at Aria turning to her for help. "Fine. I do owe you one for that message," she said.

"Just like that?" Aria asked, sounding disbelieving and suspicious.

"I'm busy and I don't have the time nor the desire to keep going back and forth with you."

"But—"

"I'll call you when the report is ready," Jessa said, meaning to interrupt her.

She hung up on her for good measure, knowing it would send her into a tirade.

That was spiteful.

Jessa paused with her hand on the brass knob of the door leading back inside the restaurant. She paused and looked upward. "Forgive me," she mouthed, before opening the door and welcoming the warmth as she entered.

Her steps faltered a bit when she spotted her blond

stranger from the elevator at a round table with several other suit-clad men. She moved toward them and he glanced up just as she neared their table. His surprise quickly shifted to that same appreciation of her he never hid. He smiled and nodded at her with warm humor in his eyes at yet another coincidental meeting between them.

She gave him a smile, never breaking stride on her way back to her table. As she reclaimed her seat, she looked back to find his eyes were still on her. "Sorry about that," she said, focusing her attention on her steaming plate of food.

"Everything okay?" Keegan asked as she shook pepper on her shrimp and gravy on cheese grits.

"Yes," she said instantly before pausing. "Although things could be better."

Keegan took a bite of her food and did a little shimmy with her shoulders. "How's that?"

Jessa set her fork on her plate, hating that she felt unsure. "I invited you here not just to celebrate our last day of work before we closed for the holidays," she began, taking a sip of her drink—and then another—before she continued, "but to also ask you to plan my wedding."

Keegan nearly choked on a bite of shrimp. She coughed, causing several patrons to stare at her. Jessa rose to come around the table and slap on her back.

Keegan brushed her hands away and took several long sips of water. "I'm fine," she said, still sounding a little strangled.

Jessa retook her seat, giving those who still stared an apologetic smile.

"Excuse me ladies."

They both looked up at a different server standing by their table holding an unopened pink-gold bottle of Ace of Spaces pink champagne and a note. The dark-haired man handed the latter to Jessa. She knew without a doubt it was her stranger.

An early Christmas gift from one stranger to another. Just promise you will share it with your lunch companion and not take it to your lucky husband.
Enjoy!

Jessa tapped the folded card against her chin as she glanced over at his table. He raised his own glass of brown liquor to her in a silent toast. She smiled.

Class act.

"Thank you," she said, looking up at the waiter.

He sat the ornate bottle on the table. "I'll ask your server to bring flutes and open it if you wish," he said, before taking his leave.

Keegan picked up the metallic bottle. "Armand de Brignac Rosé," she said, sounding impressed.

Jessa tucked the note into the side pocket of her tote sitting on an empty chair at their table.

"Who sent it?" Keegan asked.

Jessa hesitated and then shrugged. "A stranger on his way out. The note said Merry Christmas and for us to enjoy it," she said.

And that was all she was willing to divulge. She would love to fill Keegan in on her harmless flirtations with the sexy blond stranger, but she'd learned during her days as friends with the ladies from Richmond Hills to never supply another woman with the ammo to take you out when friends turned to enemies.

Their waiter appeared with two modern-looking champagne flutes and a hand towel folded over his arm. They looked on as he effortlessly opened the bottle with the towel wrapped around the cork and neck as he twisted it. There was nothing more than a dull pop to sound its opening.

"You seem very good with your hands," Keegan said, giving him a long stare filled with her appreciation.

His neck reddened in embarrassment.

Jessa concealed her amusement behind her hand and Keegan continued to openly stare, enjoying that she made the young man uncomfortable. She gave him credit for his steady hand as he poured the pink champagne into their glasses.

With Keegan's attention diverted, Jessa chanced another look over at the stranger. He was gone. *Oh well.*

She turned her attention back to Keegan as the waiter left the bottle chilling on ice in a bucket on the table. "Back to my wedding," she said, tapping her crimson fingernails on the base of the flute.

Keegan settled back in her seat and eyed her, saying nothing.

"I don't want to make the mistake of thinking I can plan it myself because it's small."

Keegan's face revealed nothing.

What more does this bitch want?

Jessa fought not to roll her eyes. "I know you still take a lot of decorating jobs, and you're the most stylish, most organized—"

"You're really shoveling that bullshit, darling," Keegan drawled.

"Stop making me spread it so wide," Jessa countered.

Keegan shook her head. "I have a problem, friend o' mine."

Jessa couldn't hide her exasperation.

Keegan reached into her oversized crocodile tote sitting on the floor beside her feet and withdrew a wrapped present that was the size of a hardcover book. She set it on the table next to her plate. "Do I give you this gift or take on the headache of planning your wedding?" she asked. "And this is a *good* gift, too."

"You could give me both."

"No, ma'am. Just one."

"The wedding it is," Jessa said.

"Then my mama's gonna love this Hermès scarf," Keegan drawled, leaning over to drop it back into her bag.

"Will she even know what it really is? No shade," Jessa asked as she picked up her flute.

Keegan laughed. "Of course not. She'll probably use it to wrap her hair when she gets a fresh permanent."

"Thank you, Keegan," she said earnestly.

"No problem," she said, raising her flute as well.

The two friends toasted.

Bzzzzzz.

Jessa checked her phone. "It's Hammer," she said, rising. "I need to take this."

She reached the chilly vestibule again. "Hey, Hammer. I was going to call you when Keegan and I finished lunch," she said.

"What's up?" he asked.

"I know we're done for holidays, but I need a quick favor."

"Go."

She smiled. "The Livewells. What's up with them?" she asked.

"I thought you were done with those Richmond Hill ladies?"

"I was. Aria called me."

"A'ight. Let me check my notes."

Jessa moved closer to the outside door and looked out the full-length glass panel at the dirty snow piled high on the edge of the sidewalk.

"He's faithful. It's the money where he's fucking up."

That surprised her. She turned from the door.

"He sank a lot of money into opening a new medical practice. A lot of money. I'm not sure, but I don't think it's panning out and their funds are low."

"Does she know?"

"I doubt it."

"Oh yeah, I almost forgot. Mrs. Montgomery called me earlier to check on her case. Are we ready to close it?"

"Not yet. Waiting on some background checks to come in."

"Okay, thanks, baby. I'll see you tonight."

"Jessa," he said gently.

"Huh?"

"I called you," Hammer reminded her.

She grimaced. "You sure did. What can I do for you?"

"I thought about what you said the other night about not meeting my family..."

Jessa stiffened. *No.*

"My moms is..."

Jessa frowned. *He.*

"Coming for Christmas."

Jessa pinched the space between her brows. *Didn't.*

"And she's going to stay with me until the wedding."

Is this what a foot in your mouth tastes like?

"Oh, baby, that's great," she lied, forcing joviality into her tone when she really wanted to take her iPhone and punt it like a football over the dirty piles of snow and into the busy Manhattan traffic.

Later that night, Jessa enjoyed a long, jasmine-scented bath as she sipped on the remaining pink champagne gifted to her. She left the water behind once it cooled and enjoyed pampering her body with her favorite lotion and taking care of her skin with a facial. She left her en suite bathroom draped in her favorite crimson sheer robe with her half-filled flute in her hand.

The hour was late. She was alone.

Delaney was in bed. Winifrid was gone for the night. Her mother was in her room watching 70s sitcoms on television. Hammer was spending his mother's first night with her at his loft apartment.

Jessa was clearheaded and contemplative.

Something wasn't right.

She set her flute on one of the coasters on her nightstand as she sat on the bed with one leg tucked beneath her bottom.

First things first.

Jessa pulled up her old texts from Felisha and found the one with Aria's number. She dialed it and then studied her manicured feet as she awaited an answer. It eventually went to voice mail.

Perfect.

"Aria, this Is Jessa. Kingston passed the test. He's as faithful as ever to you," she said, pausing, and then deciding not to divulge their financial straits. "Listen, this will be the last time I speak to you, so I'm gonna give you some advice. Something I learned during my time operating Mistress, Inc. You can take it or leave it. You're playing a dangerous game waiting for the other shoe to drop concerning Kingston cheating. You got a faithful man. Have more faith in yourself before you push him away with your paranoia. I've finally found love again. In fact, I'm getting married. If after everything that has happened I can trust someone, there is no reason for you not to believe in Kingston more than you do. Anyway, just my nickel. Have a good life, Aria. God bless."

Jessa ended the call, took another sip of her champagne, and then opened the Montgomery file. "What are we missing?" she asked as she opened all the files Hammer had sent her into different windows. "Something is not right."

It wasn't the first case they'd had where the man wasn't proven to be a cheat—Aria was fresh evidence of that—but Mrs. Bella kept insisting and wouldn't accept that he was devoted to her.

She tried to increase the image of the surveillance videos, but it just overlapped over other windows. She wanted to be able to see everything all at once.

The screen on the laptop wasn't large enough.

She grabbed the goblet and Delaney's video monitor and

slipped on red satin ballerina slippers before she left her bedroom suite and walked down the hall. She paused at her mother's open bedroom and looked inside. The bedroom was empty but light shone from beneath the closed door of her adjoining bathroom. The laugh track from one of her mother's beloved sitcoms blared inside the room suddenly.

Her eyes landed on the teacup sitting on the bedside table.

She walked softly into the room, her eyes darting to the door, as she picked up the cup and sniffed its contents. It was free of the smell of liquor. *Thank you, Lord, for that.*

The commode flushing echoed from the bathroom.

Jessa turned and eased her way back out of her mother's room to the hall. She was worried the eggnog incident would make her crave liquor again. Although they kept all alcohol under lock and key, her mother was an addict from Harlem and would figure out a way to get what she wanted when she wanted it.

In the darkness that was only broken up by the subtle light from the sconces lining the wall, Jessa made her way down the left side of the double staircase and to the right hall leading to her private office. She turned the switch to raise the lights. Here was more of Keegan's design aesthetic on display with clean lines and pops of red color on a shiny linen backdrop.

Soon she had the Montgomery files on display on the seventy-inch television monitor She leaned against the front of the desk and gently stroked her neck as she tilted her head this way and that as she surveyed the first surveillance video of Charli trying to catch the attention of Mr. Montgomery while he sat at the bar of a well-known eatery.

Bzzzzzz ... bzzzzzz ...

She looked down at her phone sitting face up on the desk. An unsaved number. *Aria.*

Jessa ignored it as she continued to study the scene. She

walked closer as Montgomery pulled his phone from the back pocket of his khakis.

"He's dressed more for golfing then screwing a sidechick," she murmured. "Not that it matters."

Eric had claimed to spend many a day golfing or fishing, but instead lay in bed with me all day while his wife was none the wiser.

"Lesson learned." Jessa stood close to the screen, and it cast her face and upper body with the lights from the high-def display.

Ba-doop.

"Fuck your voice mail, Aria," she said, turning to swipe the remote and turn up the volume.

She watched the video until the end and then watched it again. And then once more, closing her eyes and tilting her head to the side as she focused in on the moment right after he made his first phone call.

Brrrnnngggg...

She opened her eyes and paused the video. "It could be a coincidence *or...*"

Jessa picked up her iPhone from the desk. The new voice mail notification was on the screen.

Maybe she called to say thank you.

She placed the phone on speaker, her mind really still focused on what *might* be an infinitesimal breakthrough in the Montgomery case.

"Who the hell are you, Jessa 'Slick Ass' Bell, to give me marriage advice?"

"No thanks, then," she drawled, shaking her head.

"You think being a pro at stealing husbands and breaking up marriages gives you the authority on saving marriages? You delusional backstabber. Don't let that bullshit business, and a book that has completely skewed my view on the publishing industry confuse you into thinking that's true redemption for your dirty deeds. Jaime is good—too good—because I would have left my size nines in your—"

Jessa pressed a button. "Bullshit business? But you called me for help though?"

Message deleted.

"Stay mad, child," she said, already bored by it.

She dialed Hammer's number.

"What's up, baby?"

"I hate to bother you," she began, walking back up to the frozen image on the television screen. "But I got a theory on the Montgomerys, and it's a long shot."

"Go ahead."

"I think it's possible his mistress was there in the bar," she said. "He called someone and I heard a phone ring. The ringing suddenly stops at the same moment his call ends."

"That could be a coincidence," he said doubtfully.

"*Or* his mistress was there," she said. "Maybe they were on to us. I want some more surveillance on him. His wife insists he's different. There's a reason, and I want to tell her what it is."

"Okay. No problem. And I'll take another look at the video myself."

"Thank you."

"What are you wearing?" he asked.

Jessa smiled. "The red robe," she said, her voice husky.

"My mama's sleeping."

"And?" Jessa asked, as she turned off the light and left the office.

"*And* I can sneak out for an hour—or two."

"Sneak out?" she asked, teasingly, as she climbed the stairs.

"You want me to come or not?"

"Yes, come on so that you can cum *in*...me."

They shared a laugh before they ended the call.

Chapter 9

Three months later

"All chickens come home to roost."

Jessa stared at her reflection, barely taking in the beautiful organza Berta gown and veil she wore. She shifted her eyes over to take in Hammer's mother standing behind her in the open doorway to her master suite. Their eyes locked in the reflection.

She took in her lilac church suit and wide-brimmed hat, the tightly gripped pearl clutch. She looked every bit of her eighty years of age, and there was no denying the judgment in her eyes as she stared at her soon-to-be daughter-in-law.

She hates me.

Jessa let her mind drift to their first meeting...

"I'm nervous, Hammer," Jessa said as they rode the elevator up to his loft-style apartment.

He soundly slapped her buttocks in the sequined jumpsuit she wore beneath a black ostrich jacket. "For what? It's just my mama, LuBell Young from Fresno, California. Sweetest woman you ever wanna meet," he said.

The elevator came to a stop and began to open.

Jessa grabbed his arm and looked up at him. "And if she doesn't like me?"

Will you?

Hammer bent down toward her. "There is nothing that will be said or done that will make me leave you alone," he promised, pressing a kiss to her lips.

They stepped off the elevator. The scent of food surrounded them, and Jessa had to admit it smelled good. It reminded her of the type of food her grandmother used to cook. Hammer unlocked the door and they entered.

LuBell Young came around the corner, wiping her hands on a towel before she flung it over her shoulder. She was a petite woman with bright eyes and dark skin that was still tight and free of makeup. Her hair was dyed black and still curled like she just took foam rollers out of her hair. She wore a long jean skirt and a T-shirt with a graphic of raised hands with the logo "Hands Up, Don't Shoot."

And over the rim of her glasses, she gave Jessa's outfit a once-over. "Where you going in that frock?" she asked, frowning.

Jessa stopped in her tracks. Hammer tried to pull her forward. She resisted.

"Mama, this is my fiancée, Jessa Bell," he said, moving forward alone to wrap his arm around his mother's shoulders. He tried to nudge her forward.

LuBell shook her head and pointed her finger down at the floor.

She meant for Jessa to come to her, not the other way around. It was respect, and Jessa recognized it well.

Oh hell.

LuBell Young was a no-nonsense woman who did not come to play.

Jessa's smile was nervous and hesitant as she moved forward. "It's nice to finally meet you, Mrs. Young," she said, awkwardly bending to hug her.

LuBell instantly began coughing.

Jessa shut one eye and froze as a light spray of spittle hit her neck and shoulder. She stepped back.

"I can't take all that strong perfume," LuBell said. "I don't wear nothing but baby powder and a little Avon Timeless on special occasions."

"Mama," Hammer said, his voice scolding.

"What, Robbie?" she asked innocently.

Jessa covertly used the inside lining of her coat to wipe her neck. "Robbie?" she asked, glancing at him.

He shrugged.

"I made some stewed chicken feet and dry white rice, Robbie," she said, reaching up to pat his cheek before she cut her eyes over to Jessa. "I hope that's okay with you?"

Chicken feet? She only cooked it to test me. Wrong one, you old bitch.

"That's fine," Jessa said, busying herself removing her coat and hanging it up in the armoire Hammer kept by the front door.

"She real comfortable, huh?" LuBell asked Hammer before walking into the kitchen.

Jessa turned to face him.

Hammer held his hands up and then pressed them together as if praying.

"Your mama fucking with me, you know?" she muttered to him as she passed.

He reached out and grabbed her arm. "Jessa."

She gave him a "Negro, what" look.

"That's my mama," he reminded her.

"Let's see if your mama can take it like she dish it," she said, snatching her arm away from him and walking into the kitchen.

Jessa walked right up to the stove and went in LuBell's pot. She grabbed a teaspoon and tasted the broth off the stew. "Not bad, Mrs. Young, but my grandmama would add some sliced fat back or pork jowls to hers to give it more flavor," she said, putting the lid back on the pot.

"Well, ain't that about a damn nerve," LuBell said, looking completely offended.

"Okay, stop it," Hammer said. "Let's eat."

Jessa moved over to the dining area and took a seat at the table as Hammer carried the tureen that now held the stewed chicken feet. He set it on the table, giving Jessa a stern look, as he took the seat at the head of the table. LuBell sat across from Jessa.

"Mrs. Young, I truly love your son and I'm not sure what I have done to offend you," Jessa said.

Hammer groaned.

"You're the reason my boy ain't been back to Fresno to see me," LuBell said.

"That's on me, I should have brought Jessa out to meet you," Hammer said. "We've been busy, that's all."

"Doing what? From my understanding, what she's known for don't take but a few minutes," LuBell said, with a "so there" expression. "What she got to do for the rest of the day?"

Hammer took Jessa's hand atop the table into his and squeezed it tightly. "Mama, you always taught me respect is given where it is earned, and since Jessa arrived you have been nothing but disrespectful to her," he said, his voice firm. "I've never seen you act like this, and it's not worthy of who I know you to be."

LuBell's mouth became a thin line.

Jessa stroked his palm with her thumb.

"I wouldn't want to do anything to upset you, Robbie," LuBell said.

"And?" he prompted.

"And that's it," she stressed.

This is not my first rodeo with a jealous woman.

"I'm sure Mrs. Young just needs a chance to get to know me," Jessa said, giving his hand one last squeeze before she freed it.

Jessa reached for the salt shaker and cut Mrs. Young a look as she sprinkled it liberally onto her food.

His mother's mouth flattened again and her eyes were hostile, but she said nothing.

Jessa turned on the padded wooden bench that sat before her makeup table. This was the first they had been entirely alone in the last three months. Hammer had made sure of that. "Ma'am?" she said to Mrs. Young.

"You heard me," LuBell said, before looking around the room. "Miss High and Mighty."

"I guess that means you like my bedroom," Jessa said, trying so hard to keep her patience.

She had sent her mother, Delaney, Keegan, and her beauty squad from the room to allow for a few moments of peace and quiet before the wedding began downstairs in her backyard.

"You just remember that when your time comes, Jezebel," LuBell said, pointing a gloved finger at her. "And it's coming. It always does."

Jessa looked and felt unsure. Was there truth to her words?

LuBell saw her fear and cackled as she turned to walk away.

The fuck?

She turned on the seat to look at her reflection.

You can't have it all.

All chickens come home to roost.

You can't have it all.

Her anxiety made her itch, and Jessa scratched at her neck as she began to pant. She rose from the bench and walked over to the closed patio doors. She could see all their guests milling about with cocktails already in hand. Hammer was with his friends and his son, Robert Jr., all of whom had been kind and funny and welcoming of her into their lives. LuBell walked up to them. "Fucking little mean-ass gremlin," Jessa muttered, shifting her gaze around the crowd until it landed on Revered Dell.

"I need to speak to his behind," she said, her breath fanning against the glass. "ASAP."

She eased the door open a crack. "Revered Dell," she hollered.

She heard nothing but the upbeat music of the deejay.

"Fuck!" she screeched, jerking the door shut.

She walked across the room to where her iPhone was plugged into the wall behind the tall dresser. "Shit," she swore, when she spotted Keegan's own iPhone with the camo OtterBox sitting there as well.

Jessa spotted one of Keegan's walkie-talkies. "Okay, not as stupid as I first thought," she said, picking it up from where she left it earlier.

"Keegan," she said into the device as she moved toward the patio doors again.

Nothing.

"Keegan," she repeated, looking for her in the crowd.

She was talking to the deejay. "DJ Loud Ass Music," she snapped. "DJ Turn It the Fuck Down. DJ Your Ass Is Fired."

"Keegan!" Jessa roared as soon as she moved away from the deejay both.

She and several people near her jumped in surprise.

Jessa looked on as Keegan took the walkie-talkie from the hip of her jean and race-walked up the middle of the aisle.

"Go ahead, Jessa."

"Bring me Reverend Dell," she said.

Keegan stopped and turned look back down the length of the aisle. "Something wrong?" she asked.

Jessa turned the walkie-talkie off and tossed it over her shoulder onto the middle of her bed. "That's a dumbass question. Why would I ask for him if everything was right?"

You can't have it all.

All chickens come home to roost.

Jessa paced like a fanatic, unable to shake the feeling of foreboding.

"Jessa, here he is."

She turned to the open doorway and felt relief at the sight of Reverend Bell coming to stand in the doorway behind Keegan. "Okay, you out," she said, pointing to her friend. She turned her finger to the reverend. "And you in. Let's go, Rev."

"Alone? In here?" he asked, leaning his head in to look around with obvious disapproval.

"Oh yeah, I forgot," she said, remembering him basically admitting that she was Eve tempting him with the forbidden fruit.

Keegan looked from Jessa to Reverend Dell.

"Could you go get dressed?" Jessa asked her, pointedly looking at the jeans and T-shirt she still wore.

"Right," Keegan said, easing past the minister to leave the room.

Jessa stepped into the hall and closed her bedroom door behind her before she made her way down the hall to the closed door of the guest room she'd assigned Keegan. Quickly she turned the knob and opened the door at the same time.

"Ow!" Keegan cried out as the door slammed into her.

Jessa stepped inside and looked down at her on the floor rubbing a spot on her forehead. "Predictable. That's what you are," she sang to the tune of Nat King Cole's "Unforgettable."

"I'm going. I'm going," Keegan said rising to her feet and crossing the room to the adjoining bath.

Jessa stepped out into the hall and eyed the Rev giving her a disapproving look. Her shoulders dropped before she stuck her head inside. "Sorry, Keegan," she said, sounding more like an insolent child than a woman ten minutes from being wed.

"Better?" she asked Revered Dell as she neared him.

"Yes, *if* you meant the apology."

She reclaimed her spot in front of her closed bedroom door.

Reverend Dell stepped back from her.

She looked down at her feet and then up at him. "Are you good now?" she asked, perturbed.

He looked at her as he nodded. "You really are a beautiful bride, Jessa," he told her.

"Thanks, Rev," she said her annoyance softening. "Listen, I need you to tell me that everything is going to be fine."

"I can't promise you that," he said. "You both completed the premarital counseling I required to perform the wedding ceremony and I think you're well-suited, but I can't promise that everything will be perfect. Remember, we discussed that marriage will never be perfect."

"Yes, but will I?" she asked, her tone soft and vulnerable as she allowed her body to slump back against the door. She looked up at him as tears swelled. "I am so messed up, and I'm trying, I really am, but there is something testing me. Always somebody pushing me. This is a lot of work, and the old me, to be honest, was just easier, Rev, so what does that say about me?"

Reverend Dell leaned back against the wall and gave her that look fathers give to their daughters—loving and admonishing all at once. "No one's walk with God is the same, and we all are tested. We all have to make a conscious effort to do the right thing, and that's all that matters. Not that initial thought or action but your deliberate thought and your deliberate action. It is your intent that matters. And you are trying when we both know there was a time you clung to what made you feel better regardless of who got hurt."

Jessa looked down at her engagement ring. "It honestly feels like I don't deserve it," she admitted.

Reverend reached for her hand.

She looked up at him, comforted by the warmth in his brown eyes.

"You are far harder on yourself than the Lord is on you, that I can promise you," he said.

You can't have it all.

"Do you love him? Do you want to marry him? Do you want to continue the work to be the best you can be, Jessa?" Reverend Dell asked her.

"Yes," she said softly with a nod.

He gave her hand one last squeeze before he released it. "Then let's get you married."

"Okay," she agreed, feeling hopeful and calm under his guidance. "Thank you."

He gave her one last comforting smile before he turned and made his way down the hall and then the steps.

Jessa slowly walked down the white burlap aisle runner adorned with blush and violet rose petals. She moved in sync with the melody to "You and I (We Can Conquer the World)" by Stevie Wonder. From beneath her veil she locked her eyes on Hammer standing at the white pergola awaiting her in a beautifully tailored charcoal gray tuxedo.

She heard the whispered compliments of their wedding guests, but her mind was focused on the classic R&B song that was an ode to love and togetherness.

"In my mind, we can conquer the world . . ."

When she reached him, he smiled and extended his hand to her. She took it and kept her eyes locked on him even as she handed her bouquet to Keegan, serving as her lone bridesmaid in a strapless embroidered gray gown.

The song ended and together they turned to face Reverend Dell.

"Ma-ma!" Delaney shouted. "Get me, Ma-ma."

Everyone laughed or happily sighed.

"Shhhhh." Jessa turned to hold her finger in front of her mouth as she eyed Delaney in a beautiful charcoal linen dress with a sequined cat headband that matched her Mary Jane shoes.

Darla tried in vain to settle her down.

Hammer quickly eased past her.

Jessa looked on as he reached for Delaney, and she gladly allowed him to pick her up. He came back to stand beside her as Delaney looked over his broad shoulder and waved to everyone in their seats.

"You ready to lock in for the rest of our lives?" Hammer asked her.

Jessa nodded, aware of Revered Dell's eyes on them. "For forever and a day," she promised him truthfully.

"This is beautiful and just what I needed."

From behind her oversized black shades, Jessa looked out at the picturesque landscape of Antigua as they sailed the Caribbean Sea aboard a yacht.

"Nice surprise?"

She leaned up from his chest as they lounged together on the aft deck. She turned and kissed her husband. "Fabulous surprise. Thanks for booking this excursion," she said, taking in how bronzed and handsome he looked shirtless with his dark aviator shades on.

Jessa settled back against him.

Their honeymoon at the Sandals Resort was just the disconnect from the world that they needed. She was loving the warm climate, beautiful scenery, and food so good they happily overindulged. The five-hour cruise with seafood and champagne lunch was the right outing after being holed up in their private villa enjoying being pampered by their butler, ordering from room service, and making love until they both were sore.

Once the boat docked they enjoyed a walk together on the beach. She didn't know if anything felt quite as good as her feet pressing down into the warm sand.

"Good thing I'm not jealous," he said.

"Why?"

"All eyes are on you," he said, sounding amused.

The wrap she wore around her hips was sheer and did little to shield the white thong of her strapless one-piece bathing suit.

The wind blew and Jessa reached up to hold her large woven hat atop her head. "Not all," she insisted.

"Enough," he said, reaching behind to slap her buttocks and then looking down to enjoy the sight of it jiggling in response.

Jessa came to a stop and looked up at him through her shades. "I want you inside me when you slap it," she said.

"And when is that?" he asked, looking down at her.

"As soon as we get back to our villa," she said stroking his chest. "Honeymoon rules."

"Shit, you ain't said nothing," he told her, before picking her up and headed up toward the resort.

They had agreed on the plane ride to Antigua that sex on demand was the first rule.

Hammer didn't set her down on her feet until they were inside the villa.

"You had everybody looking like I broke a foot or something," she told him.

"Did you want me to put you down?" he asked.

"Hell no. Not ever."

Hammer grabbed her hips. "Let's stay in for the rest of the day."

"What about horseback riding on the beach at sunset?" Jessa asked.

He dipped his hands around her to tightly grip her buttocks. "I got enough to ride right here," he said.

"I know that's right," she agreed, turning in his embrace to press her behind against him.

She felt him harden against her and she bent over. Her hat fell from her head onto the floor.

He pulled the thong of her strapless bathing suit to the side and entered her. He was hard and hot. His fingers dug into her flesh. The feel of the soft hairs surrounding his shaft tickled her. His deep and fast strokes made her moan. He brought his hands around her waist to press one beneath her suit to massage her clit and the other to cup her breast.

That made them both cum.

It was fast, hot and electrifying.

Hammer stepped back, freeing his dick from her. Jessa dropped down on all fours as she struggled to reclaim the strength in her legs and the air in her lungs.

Good sex. Good man. Good love. Is this all real?

"Give me a quick sec, baby, and I'll get you up from there," Hammer said, sounding breathless. "*Shit*, I gotta myself together first."

And she laughed. "I'm good," she said, rising to her feet with aid of the nearby chair in front of the desk.

Hammer laughed when her legs wobbled. "We're not spring chickens," he reminded her.

"I'm not an old rooster either, though," she said.

"Let's shower before we hit the bed," he offered.

Jessa nodded in agreement, dropping a beach towel from their bag onto the chair before she sat down on it. "I'm coming. I wanna check on Delaney again."

She opened her laptop to Skype back home. She was grateful that Winifrid had agreed to live in while they were out of the country, but she still liked to lay eyes on Delaney twice a day—sometimes more. She smiled when the nanny's face filled the screen. "Hello there, Winifrid. Where's my baby?" she asked, her eyes shifting to the background of the bedroom.

"I'm sorry, Ms. Bell—"

"Mrs. Young," Jessa reminded her, stroking the diamond wedding band she wore along with her engagement ring.

"Sorry, Mrs. Young, she's down for her nap," Winifrid smiled.

Jessa checked the clock. "I forgot the time," she said, offering her an apologetic smile.

"That's okay."

"And your other charge?" Jessa asked.

"She went walking around the block."

Jessa did a double tale. "Say what now?" she asked.

Winifrid chuckled and held up both of her hands.

What the hell is that old woman up to now?

The morning after their wedding when she and Hammer went to the airport for their flight, they had also taken Mrs. LuBell Young to her terminal and made sure she was on her flight back to the West Coast.

Why can't I be so lucky?

"Winifrid, do me a favor and let me know when she gets back safe, please?" Jessa ran her hands through her hair and shook her head.

"No problem."

She gave the nanny a perfunctory smile and ended the connection. "What is my mother up to now?" she asked herself aloud, already feeling herself worry.

There goes honeymoon rule number three.

She closed the laptop.

Bzzzzzz . . . bzzzzzz . . . bzzzzzz . . .

Jessa released a long yawn as she eyed her beach bag. Her cell phone was vibrating loudly.

She looked at the door to the bathroom in the mirror hanging above the dresser.

"Honeymoon rule number two," Hammer said, coming to lean in the open doorway.

He has the fucking ears of a dog.

"No business calls," she said softly, rising to accept the hand he extended to her.

Together they walked into the bathroom just as the steam escaped to swirl and cover them.

Interlude

*S*ometimes I just wanted to forget.

Other times the thought of my mother's demise at my own hands gave me purpose.

Still, those swings back and forth between my reality and this zone of revenge I concocted was maddening. It was crazy what I was doing, and I had enough sense to know it. Still, I continued. Feigning friendships with these other silly people who allowed themselves to be called "agents." Trying to trap doggish men into revealing their hidden sins and desires.

Every bit of it was a façade on top of another façade.

My friends have long since stop calling to invite me out to party.

I was barely holding on to my job as the personal assistant to a celebrity party planner because of Mistress, Inc.

My own life was fading. I never thought I'd be undercover in her life for this long. Almost ten months. Far too much dwelling in the middle place, this shade of gray.

"Georgia," I said aloud just to hear it as I stared at my reflection in the mirror over the sink in my bathroom.

My life was a mess, and I couldn't take it much more. The

pleasure I received from secretly being in Jessa's orbit was beginning to fade. As was my desire to crush her world like a thin piece of paper in my hand.

I have done things that are not Georgia. Not me.

How much was I willing to lose of myself to gain this control over the life of a woman who didn't even recognize me as the child she bore?

Accepting her invite to her wedding had been a mistake.

Being in her home and around her family—my sister and my grandmother—and being introduced with the same obligatory politeness as the rest of her employees had stung as if I'd been pierced by a knife whose blade had been resting in fire. They had all been accepted into her life while I was outside her bubble like a leech.

And she was beautiful. I couldn't deny that.

That moment right after Hammer picked Delaney up from Jessa's mother's arms and they stood at the altar like a little family, I could have retched in disgust and hatred and jealousy. Instead I had to plant a smile and force joy at what looked to be the happiness of her life.

Did he even know that little precious Delaney was not her one and only child?

During the reception I snuck away the first chance I could. I knew her bedroom was on the second floor because I spotted her at the patio doors before the wedding. Once I was in her room, I walked around and touched everything. I lay across her bed. Sat in her closet with the door closed. Stepped in her shoes. Rummaged through her drawers and envied her expensive lingerie. Tried on her diamond jewelry. Sprayed every last one of her dozen or more perfumes on my inner thighs. Peed in her toilet. Pressed my face into her towels. Laughed bitterly at discovering the nursery adjoined her bedroom. Cried at the beauty of Delaney's room.

"I was here," I remembered whispering into the air just before I finally took my leave, as if leaving an imprint that couldn't be erased whether she knew I'd been there or not.

I would never forget it and took a memento to make sure I didn't.

I looked down at her red ballet slippers I wore.

I didn't have the courage to take anything more noticeable or expensive.

"Are you and Hammer going to have a baby together?"

The memory of that question being asked made me lift my head to stare at my reflection again.

"I doubt it," Jessa had said. "One is enough for me."

Pain that was sharp and aching clutched at me, bringing up tears that wet my eyes. I turned from my mirror image just as my hot tears raced down my cheeks.

This had to end. These glimpses into her life were hurting me. Opening up doors in me. Insecurity. Doubt. Self-loathing. Normally, getting high was my escape. That's all I've known all my life.

My sobriety was in jeopardy.

I don't know how much more I can take.

Chapter 10

Two weeks later

"**W**hat the *hell?*"

Jessa dropped the covers of her bed and rose from her knees with the flashlight on her iPhone still beaming. She turned off the feature and pressed her hands onto her hips as she looked around their spacious bedroom suite. Everything was organized and its rightful place.

"So, where the hell are my red slippers?" she asked, flinging her phone on the bed and walking over to her closet to have her third search of the night.

She turned on the overhead lights and walked up and down the length of the closet that now held all of her possessions and Hammer's. "Fuck it," she said, giving up.

She'd spent more time in the last hour looking for them than they were worth. Hammer thought she had taken them to Antigua and left them behind by mistake. *What other explanation could there be?*

"I'll just order another pair," she said, raising her arms to run both of her hands through her hair.

Her eyes fell on her Louis Vuitton luggage in the corner

of the far end of the closet. *I just don't remember packing those slippers.*

She'd just discovered them gone. For a moment she pondered theft, but those fifty-dollar sandals were nothing compared to the jewelry and high-end accessories that were right where she left them. And she'd checked.

Jessa lightly bit down on her bottom lip as she left the closet and checked Delaney's video monitor. She was already bathed and dressed in her pajamas watching Peppa Pig videos on YouTube via her iPad. She smiled when she yawned and stretched her arms high above her head. *Sleep, little girl.*

Jessa left her bedroom and walked down the hall. Her mother's door was closed. She knocked twice. "Ma?"

"Come in."

She opened the door, surprised to find her in bed with the lights dimmed and the volume on the television almost too low to hear. "You not feeling well?" she asked, coming to stand by her mother's bedside.

"I *was* trying to sleep," Darla said, her back to her daughter.

"Sorry, Mama," she said, looking down at the empty teacup on the bedside table. "I'll leave you be. Good night."

Jessa turned.

"I think it's time I go back to my apartment."

Jessa turned again. "Why?" she asked.

Darla lay on her back, her hair covered with a black satin bonnet. "You and Hammer are married and sharing this house," she said. "I feel out of place."

Jessa stepped closer to the bed.

Her mother covered her mouth as she started a coughing fit.

"Mama, you all right?" she asked, pausing in her steps.

Darla gave her a side-eye and twist of her lips before she nodded. "Yeah, just a cold."

"I don't want you to feel out of place. Hammer moving in doesn't change a thing," Jessa insisted.

"It does so," Darla said. "I know you think I'm crazier

than two left shoes on two right feet, but let this old woman teach you something if I ain't never taught you nothing else."

"Mama—"

Darla slashed her hand through her air to silence her. "A man *has* to be a man in his house," she said. "And nothing makes him feel more like a visitor instead of the king of the castle than not being able to walk around his home in his drawers when he gets ready."

Jessa chuckled.

Darla shot her a stern stare before lying back down on her side. "You can take it or leave it, but never forget it," she said. "Now you have a good night."

"Mama, have you seen some red bedroom slippers around the house?"

"Nope."

"Night, Mama."

"We *ain't* done talking 'bout Harlem, Jessa."

She heard her clearly, but Jessa continued out of the room, knowing she couldn't let her mother live alone again. She had the power of attorney on her care, and the final decision was up to her. She closed the door, going to Delaney's bedroom to find her asleep with her thumb in her mouth and the sounds of the video still echoing.

The night air of spring could get chilly, so she draped a blanket over her lightly before powering down the tablet and setting it on her bedside table before dimming the lights and walking to her bedroom through their adjoining door. She checked her gold watch. *Just a little past eight.*

Her eyes shifted to the bed. She missed him already and wished he was there watching mindless television with her or bathing her in the shower or sexing her on the floor...

Bzzzzzz...bzzzzzz...bzzzzzz...

Pushing away her sexy wishes, Jessa lay across the bed and picked up her phone as she rolled over onto her back. She frowned, not recognizing the number. "Hello."

"Mrs. Bell—I mean Young—this is Amanda. I'm sorry to call you, but I didn't know what else to do."

Jessa's arched brows dipped as she sat up on the middle of the bed. "Amanda? Weren't you back on the Montgomery case tonight?" she asked, her heart already beginning to pound. "Did something happen?"

"I'm okay. It's just..."

"It's just what, Amanda?" Jessa asked, being sure to keep her voice calm.

"Mrs. Montgomery was here—"

Jessa's back stiffened. "Say what, say who?"

"Yes, she came up to me before I even entered the restaurant and offered me, like, twenty-five thousand dollars to sleep with her husband and record it," the young woman said, her words rushed and almost running together as she spoke.

Jessa was speechless and licked the dryness from her lips as she tried to come to grips with the news she had just been given. "Why would she do that? What the fuck is going on?" she asked, speaking aloud to herself.

"I thought you should know."

Yes, the fuck I should.

"Where are you now?" Jessa asked, rising from the bed to pace the floor as she massaged her forehead.

"Still outside the restaurant."

"And Bella Montgomery?" she asked, before grinding her teeth.

"She left and paid me a thousand dollars not to tell you."

Jessa paused. "You should have asked for double."

"I did. She offered five hundred."

Jessa arched a brow. "Go home. Don't worry about the husband."

"Mission aborted."

Jessa ended the call. "Fuck! Fuck! Fuck!" she roared, her tone having risen with each obscenity.

"Mama?" Delaney called out, slumber still heavy in her voice.

Jessa winced and froze in place with her hands balled into fists tight enough for her nails to dig into the soft flesh of her palms. She said a silent prayer that Delaney would self-soothe herself and fall sweetly back to sleep.

"Mama!" Delaney cried.

"Shit," Jessa swore, shoving her phone into the side pocket of the linen pants she wore before she walked into the bedroom.

Delaney sat up in her bed, clutching one of her many stuffed animals with one hand and wiping her own tears with the back of the other. "Awww, Mama's sorry," she said, walking over to pick her up. "Did I scare you?"

She carried her to the ivory chaise lounge by the arched window and sat down, massaging her back as Delaney continued to whimper. She forced herself to calm down, worried that Delaney picked up on her tension and was feeding off it.

Jessa looked out the window at the night sky as she breathed deeply, soothing her daughter and herself. It didn't take long for Delaney to succumb to sleep, but she remained holding on to her because the calm and the quiet gave her time to think clearly.

Bella Montgomery is full of shit. For the last four months, that woman has been like a thorn in my ass about her damn crepe myrtle bouquets and her cheating husband. I closed her case months ago and then she calls pleading with us that something still is not right in her marriage. I assign a new agent and she pulls this stunt?

She wants her husband to cheat? She wants him caught? She wants proof?

The question is why?

Why, bitch, why?

Carefully she rose from the chaise with Delaney sleeping in her arms. She gently laid her back down on her bed and pulled her iPhone out, dialing Hammer as she made her way to her bedroom.

She dialed him twice. No answer.

Jessa made her way down the stairs to her office.

She called him again. Still no answer. "Hammer, I need you to switch surveillance to Bella Montgomery. Call me."

Should I call her? And say what? You chose the wrong bitch to use? No. Not yet.

Jessa pulled up the Montgomery files. Everything. Even the financial reports Hammer collected. Everything was about the husband. Nothing on the wife.

Major fuckup.

Warrington Sachs and his shit-loving perversion had exploited a loophole in their services. He used them to try to set up his wife. Jessa knew it and she'd put nothing in place to make sure no one else did the same thing.

Love had softened and blinded her.

And Bella Montgomery came right in and used me.

She hated that.

"Fuck," she said through clenched teeth.

The question still remained: Why?

What did she have to gain?

Money. What else?

Jessa called Hammer again to no avail. She leaned back in her chair, trying not to let her annoyance with Bella Montgomery ruin her night. *Or my fucking business.*

She started to call Keegan but quickly pushed that thought away, not chancing an "I told you so" type conversation. *To hell with that.*

Jessa released a long breath.

Dear Lord, give me patience not to get in my car and go snatch this fraud by her throat and make her tell me what in the entire fuck—

She clenched her fist and pressed it to her mouth as she searched for control over the anger rising in her.

Bella Montgomery wanted to pay one of my agents twenty-five thousand dollars to sleep with her husband and record it.

"She wants out of the marriage and she wants control of it," Jessa said aloud, talking herself through it. "It could give her leverage to press him to make a financial settlement that she wants. New York isn't a community-property state."

Slick bitch.

The desire for revenge was stuck in her throat.

And then she thought of the Bible verse Reverend Dell had told her about during the early days of her counseling sessions with him.

"And when you stand praying, if you hold anything against anyone, forgive them, so that your father in heaven may forgive you your sins," she recited.

It is hard, but necessary.

"Lord help me," she prayed, feeling overwhelmed.

Her hand trembled as she turned the phone over and dialed Hammer's number again with her thumb.

This time he answered.

"Hammer, I need you—"

Jessa stopped abruptly as the soft moan of a woman echoed into her ear. Her heart pounded just that quickly, seeming to want to beat its way out of her chest. "Hello?" she said, before checking the phone to make sure she dialed the right number.

She had.

"The fuck?" she snapped gripping the phone so tightly she was sure she would snap it in half.

Another moan. Then a purr.

Her reflection in the glass of the windows blurred as tears filled her eyes and silently raced down her cheeks, seemingly filled with the shattering pieces of her heart.

It can't be.

It better not be.

There has to be an explanation.

"Please, God," Jessa said softly, feeling her nerves and her fears cause her body to tremble.

As the sound of another woman enjoying pleasure continued to echo into the phone, she fought for control. Her emotions turbulently swung back and forth between the desire to lie on the floor in a ball while wailing and a fiery anger ready to be channeled into punches and kicks.

With shaky hands she swiped away her tears and put the phone on mute before she opened the Find a Friend app to show his location.

His apartment.

Time seemed to slow down around her. She felt as if she spun where she stood. She released a small shrill cry that only hinted at the torture she felt. Each breath she released was shaky and uneven. Even as the soft moans continued, she didn't want to believe it.

"It can't be," she whispered, shaking her head.

She dropped to her knees. "Heavenly Father, help. Give me strength and clarity. Guide my steps. Ease my pain. Make me calm. Please, dear Lord, let this all be a mistake," she prayed with intensity. "Amen."

She rose, wiping the sweat and the tears from her face before pushing her hair back. She breathed through her open mouth, welcoming the oncoming numbness. At least it offered a reprieve from the pain.

Slowly, with a deceptive calm, she began recording the phone call, leaving it behind on her desk as she picked up Delaney's monitor and left her office to climb the stairs. She reached her mother's room and opened the door. "Mama," she said, her voice sounding almost monotone.

"Huh?" Darla said, turning over in her bed. "Say what now?"

"Listen out for Delaney for me," she said. "I'll be right back."

"Jessa—"

She turned and left the room, feeling as if she was in a dream state.

"Jessa!"

She continued down the stairs.

"You hear me?"

She hadn't.

Jessa turned and looked up the stairs. "Ma'am?" she said, sounding more like a young girl than a full-grown woman.

Darla eyes widened in surprise as they took her in before she squinted. "What the hell going on?" she asked.

"Nothing, Mama."

"What he do?" Darla asked.

"Same shit they all do, Mama," she admitted, fresh tears rising.

"Don't you go. You don't need no man you got to chase. There ain't been a man born to make you act a fool in the street," she said, her words slurring a bit. "You hear me?"

Jessa closed her eyes just as a fresh tear raced down her cheek. "I'll be right back, Mama," she said, turning to walk across the foyer to grab her keys and leave the house.

One she was behind the wheel of her red sports car, Jessa used every bit of her inner strength to remain calm and focused as she drove the twenty minutes to reach his loft apartment in Connecticut.

It can't be.

But what else could it be?

She bit her bottom lip and shook her head, pressing her foot on the accelerator to speed up Interstate 84. Her grip was so tight on the steering wheel that her fingers and wrist began to throb. She switched lanes to exit, and the driver of the car coming up behind her laid on the horn.

There ain't been a man born to make you act a fool in the street.

"It can't be?" she said aloud in a whisper.

And she kept thinking and saying it as she drove to his

apartment. Even as she laid eyes on his vehicle in the drive, she still hoped that it just couldn't be. She rode the elevator up, with her back pressed to the wall and her reflection in the mirror looking nothing like her normal cool composure. When she came to stand at his door, she pressed her hand to the steel and lowered her head to rest lightly against it.

"Dear God, please don't let it be," she begged.

Jessa unlocked the door and pushed it opened wide, looking straight across the distance at her husband furiously pumping away inside another woman, who was on her knees in the middle of the bed.

It could be and it was.

She would never forget that exact moment that something inside her that she had fought so hard to reclaim withered and died.

Something inside her snapped.

Hammer looked over his shoulder just as Jessa came barreling across the loft at full speed, knocking down everything in her path to reach them. His eyes widened and he pulled out of his lover to jump off the bed and stretch his hands toward her.

"You bastard!" she roared as she unexpectedly raised her foot and swung it into his side.

Hammer grunted as he took the kick and still stepped forward to wrap his arms around her body like bands of steel. "I'm sorry, Jessa. I swear I'm sorry," he kept saying.

In the midst of the crazy, she took note that in the space of so little time his touch now repulsed her. "Get the fuck off me!" she roared, futilely fighting against his strength. "Who is she?"

Mocking laughter filled the charged air around them.

Jessa froze and Hammer shook his head as he dropped it.

There ain't been a man born to make you act a fool in the street.

Jessa relaxed her body. "Let me go, Hammer," she said calmly, looking up at him.

She leaned to the left and then the right, trying to see the face of his lover. He blocked her.

She knew then his mistress was someone she knew.

"I'm so sorry. I lost my head," he said, his eyes remorseful.

"Yes, I know you did, right inside her," Jessa said, welcoming the coldness within her.

The look in his face changed. He saw the warmth fade from her eyes. "Jessa—"

She licked her lips and gave him a bitter smile. "Why would you want me to stay here?" she asked. "Do I deserve not only to be cheated on but forced to stay in the presence of you and your mistress? I am *done* here."

Slowly he moved his arms.

Jessa smoothed her clothing and raked her fingers through her hair as she stepped back to turn.

"Bye, *boss.*"

She stopped, closing her eyes. *Double betrayal.*

Recollections came to her in a flash with the same speed as a train zooming past on the tracks.

Hammer and Charli always seeming to be in each other's space whenever there was a company meeting.

Keegan had noticed it as well at one of their company dinners.

Looks like we might need a reminder about not fraternizing at work.

Charli questioning her about her relationship with Hammer.

I had a feeling he was your *private dick.*

Charli giving out unnecessary compliments that may have been covertly mocking: *I think you are the epitome of what most men want, and the female agents could learn a lot from how you carry yourself.*

"I guess you were right, *Charli,* we do seem to have something in common," Jessa said as she slowly pivoted.

Hammer's lover stepped from behind him, just as nude as he. "Try again."

Jessa couldn't hide her surprise. "Lacey?"

Hammer released a heavy breath as he retrieved his discarded jeans and pulled them on. "Don't do that," he said.

The woman laughed again, giving Hammer a withering up and down before looking back at Jessa. "I'm so glad you *finally* caught on so I don't have to put up with fucking his old ass no more," she said, boldly walking up to her.

Jessa's eyes widened at the red ballerina slippers she wore. "When did you steal those?" she asked. "I guess you truly did want to walk in my shoes."

She shook her head. "Never," she said vehemently.

Jessa was confused by Lacey's anger and the joy she seemed to be gaining from ruining her life. There was a wildness in her eyes. As if to dare. Provoke. This was an enemy. Jessa stood her ground.

"My biggest disappointment is that my husband—Hammer—was too big a fool to realize he was used in this pathetic war you seem to have against me." She spared him a withering look before locking eyes with her again.

"Do you see me?" she asked. "Do you finally see *me*?"

The light in her eyes changed from anger to hurt. *I barely know her. Is she crazy?*

Jessa held up a hand. "I'm done with this. You're fired. Stay away from me. Have Hammer. Get help," she said, turning as she felt her despair rise again.

She refused to cry or break down in front of these traitors. *Not one damn tear.*

"I'm Georgia, *Mother*. Don't you *see* me?"

Jessa had just opened the front door to the apartment. She whirled as she eyed the woman across the loft. Her face was filled with both hate and glee. Jessa studied her, looking for any clue that what she said was true. *Is she my Georgia?*

"Liar," Jessa spat, pointing her finger at her. "Who paid you to destroy me? Who sent you after me? *Who are you?*"

Georgia's expression became bitter. Her eyes filled with tears. "The daughter you threw away like trash," she snarled. "The one who wasn't good enough. The one you didn't want. I owe you this and so much more for everything you did to me by the very fact that you gave me away."

She leaned back against the door, searching for strength but feeling weakened to her core. There was no denying the trueness of the anger nor the hatred she exhibited.

"Don't lie about that. Don't you dare lie about that," Jessa said in a harsh whisper, pain clutching her chest as she felt her legs giving out beneath her. Her head spun. She felt faint.

"Shit," Hammer swore, jumping up to gather Georgia's clothing and press it to her body as he steered her toward the bathroom. "Get dressed."

"I better listen. I wouldn't want my stepfather to spank me . . . *again*," she said, gloating.

Hammer pushed her in and shut the door.

"I can't do this," Jessa whimpered, completely overwhelmed. "Oh God, I can't do this."

Lacey was Georgia?

The child she was forced to give up hated her and plotted to destroy her.

Hammer cheated.

Her husband's mistress was her very own daughter.

Their love was over.

She dropped to her knees, her forehead and palms pressed to the floor as she felt her world spin off its axis. She felt Hammer kneel beside her. The first feel of his hands at her side trying to help her pushed her over the edge. She released a soul-wrenching cry that pierced the air and she didn't stop until her throat was strained and she nearly strangled on her own saliva.

"Don't worry. Neither one of you will ever see me again."

Jessa looked up from the floor, shoving Hammer's hands from her body as she looked at this woman standing there. Gone was the sweet Lacey. She grabbed at Georgia's wrist. "Are you my daughter?"

"I stopped being yours the moment you gave me away," she said.

"I never gave away my daughter. I never gave away my daughter," Jessa said, releasing her hand, as her body wrenched with renewed tears. "I never gave away my daughter. That's a lie. That's a lie. That's a *lie!*"

Georgia looked down at her with disgust in her eyes. "You the lie," she said, before turning and walking out the apartment.

Why, Lord? Why?

Jessa tried to rise to her feet to go behind her, but as soon as she stood she felt dizzy. "Georgia," she whispered, as her body went slack just before she fainted into the darkness.

Jessa awakened.

She knew she was in Hammer's arms. Through half-opened eyes she recognized her home and that he was carrying up the stairs. She didn't have the will to fight him. Nothing was the same anymore and never would be again.

She had no will. Her body felt as if she had no strength. Her heart was broken, her soul weary.

She let her eyes drift back closed.

"What happened, Hammer?" she heard Darla ask, her tone alarmed.

"She fainted," he answered.

"Fainted?" Darla asked in disbelief.

"Have you been drinking?" he asked.

Yes, Mama, have you?

"Have you been out fucking? Don't worry about me," Darla shot back.

That was a yes. More shit on my plate to eat and swallow. But not now. I can't.

When he laid Jessa down on the bed, she immediately rolled away, escaping his touch.

"Jessa."

She felt the weight of his body on the bed. "Bring me Delaney," she said, keeping her eyes closed. "I want Delaney."

Images replayed. Things she wished she could forget forever.

A small hand patted her thigh. "What's wrong?" Darla whispered.

She smelt the liquor on her breath and was thankful when she stepped back.

"Here's Delaney," Hammer said.

Jessa opened her eyes, quickly shifting them from Hammer's face, unable to take the very sight of him. She welcomed her sleeping daughter into her arms and pressed soft kisses to her brow. She was the only thing in the world she trusted.

"Good-bye, Hammer," she said when he remained standing there looking down at her.

"I want to talk to you, Jessa."

She looked at him. Their eyes met. Her heart broke a little more. "Please," she begged. "Don't."

He turned away.

Jessa closed her eyes again, welcoming the darkness, comforted by the steady up-and-down movement of her daughter's chest in her sleep.

"Listen, just go, Hammer. I don't know what happened. But she don't want you here, and until she is ready to deal with it, you wasting your time," Darla said.

Her mother championing her, even while inebriated, broke something in her. With her world crashing in around her, she longed for nothing more than to be a child with harmless worries who knew her mother would handle the hard stuff.

But that wasn't her reality.

"Good-bye, Jessa," Hammer said.

She shook her head before pressing the side of her face deeper into the pillow.

The room went dark. The door was shut. There were no distractions from her misery. Her mind was free to wander.

How could she not remember the words of Hammer's mother in that quiet moment filled with her tumultuous thoughts. She was a woman who once relished the affair she had with the husband of a friend, and now she was the wife who was betrayed.

It's possible the daughter she gave up for adoption had found her and hated her with a vengeance.

All chickens come home to roost.

Chapter 11

One day.

That was all the time she allowed to wallow in pity and despair. And then no more.

"Good morning, Ms. Young—"

Jessa gave Winifrid a sharp look that caused the rest of the nanny's words to fade away. Her reaction was instinctual. A marriage of less than a month didn't warrant such respect. She forced a stiff smile. "Call me...Mrs. Bell again," she said, deciding not to go back to her maiden name of Jordan.

Jessa Jordan had been a victim. Jessa Bell had been—and still was—a victor.

"Yes, ma'am."

Jessa gave Delaney one last kiss to her brow. "Please keep her away from my mother today," she ordered. "Take her outside or to the park if you have to."

Winifrid nodded and offered her a smile filled with her sadness and her hope for better days for her.

Jessa turned her back, stiffening her back to the pity

offered her as she left the bedroom and walked down the hall to her mother's suite. It was empty. She continued down the hall and to the stairs, descending them.

The front door opened and her part-time cleaning woman, Valeria, entered wearing her black uniform of T-shirt and khakis.

Jessa eyed the elderly Dominican woman with soft wavy hair worn in a French braid that reached her lower back. "Thank you for coming in at the last minute, Valeria," she said. "Please pack all of Mr. Young's things and sit them here by the door. *Comprendes?*" she asked, as she came to stand by the round table in the center of the foyer.

"*Sí, Señorita* Young," she said, her face stoic.

Jessa left the house, turning to give it one last look before she climbed in her car and drove away. *No more happy home.*

She rode in silence during her commute, going through the motions, at times reaching a red light and coming to a stop but wondering how she had even made it there from the last one. When she finally turned in to the underground parking garage and pulled into her reserved spot, she was relieved to not have to focus on driving anymore.

It's just another day, Jessa, just like any other day.

She had to keep telling herself that lie as she made her way over to the elevator.

Images of the hatred in the eyes of the woman claiming to be Georgia swapped places with those of her pure enjoyment at hurting Jessa through Hammer. *He* was her weakest link. Never had she felt like such a fool. She didn't even know where to begin. Her world had become a kaleidoscope of shock and betrayal. She was still processing it all.

The door opened and she stepped on the elevator, dropping her head to her chin as she turned.

"Hold the elevator, please."

Jessa did before she glanced at her watch. *Right on time. Something normal and familiar.*

The sexy stranger stepped on. He already wore a smile as he nodded at her in greeting. "How are you?" he asked, turning to face the closing doors.

"I'm well," she lied, as she hit the button for the twelfth floor. "And you?"

"Still disappointed," he said, giving her a playful wink as he pulled out his iPhone, giving his attention to the screen as he scrolled through it with the steady stroke of this thumb.

Jessa just offered him the same polite smile as always.

The elevator eventually slid to a stop on his floor.

"Have a good day, stranger," he said, before stepping off.

Jessa stepped off behind him.

He looked at her in surprise. "Can I help you?" he asked.

"Yes, take me to your office," she said.

He looked confused. "For business?" he asked.

"No," she replied, her gaze steady as she watched. "Not at all."

Her stranger was still perplexed, but he led her through the hall to wide double glass doors with "Halston Architecture" on them. He opened and held one door for her. She nodded her thanks, barely looking around or caring about the modern décor and the bustle of activities of the company's employees.

"Good morning, Mr. Halston," the receptionist said, rising to hand him a cup of coffee.

He's the boss.

She knew the deference well.

"Thank you, Gracie," he said, stopping to look back at Jessa. "Would you like a drink?"

"No, thank you," she said, aware of the curious eyes of the receptionist on her.

"I'll be in a meeting. No interruptions," he said, before continuing to the right of her glass desk to a black wooden door that was surprising amongst the glass and metal of the contemporary design.

They walked past a large conference room to a set of

matching double doors that opened into his large corner office. She entered before him, already undoing the belt of the lightweight black trench she wore as he closed the door.

"Lock it," she demanded over her shoulder.

He did.

"What is this about, stranger?" he said.

"Well, today is your day," she began, turning to him as she opened her jacket to reveal the sheer black teddy she wore beneath it.

He did a double take as he dropped his phone.

She smiled, although it never reached her eyes. "Last night I discovered my husband didn't ignore his urges like I did with you," she said, trailing her pointed crimson-painted fingernail down her cleavage. "My heart is broken, and I would like for you to help me forget him, if only for a little while."

He stooped to pick up his phone, his eyes trailing up her body as he stood.

"You are the only reason I left my bed today," she said, being honest. "I woke up thinking what can make me *feel* better, and I thought of you."

He stepped closer to her. "He's a fool."

She smelled his warm cologne and saw the desire he had for her in his eyes. "Yes, he is. So, can you help me with that, stranger?" she asked, feeling brazen and dangerous. Reckless, yes, she knew was being that, too. She didn't care.

I need to be desired. Touched. Made to forget. Be selfish.

Jessa took the step that closed the small gap between them, reaching up to grasp his face as she rose on the tips of her toes in the heels she wore. She paused, looking at this man who was a stranger to her.

He tossed his briefcase and phone onto the sofa along the wall before he brought his hands up to ease beneath her coat, gripping her buttocks and pressing her hips forward to feel that he was hard for her. "I'm been dreaming of this," he whispered against her panting mouth.

"I know you have," she said, reclaiming some of the cockiness she'd lost over the years.

He lowered his head and claimed her mouth with his.

She closed her eyes. His lips were smooth and pleasurable, but not familiar.

Hammer was imprinted on her life. Her body knew nothing but that liar's touch.

No more.

She opened her mouth at the first feel of his tongue and she moaned in pleasure as he slowly kissed her. She kissed him back, bringing her hands from his face to the lapels of his suit jacket to work it over his broad shoulders and down his arms, breaking his hold on her derriere. But only for a moment. Lightly he tapped her cheeks before grabbing a handful as he broke their kiss to press his mouth to her neck.

She had to force herself not to jolt at first. Not to remember Hammer.

Soon, she paid attention to his skill. The feel of his lips was soft but not moist. He knew the right spots to kiss and lick. His touch brought her goose bumps.

When he brought his hands to her waist to pick her up, Jessa wrapped her arms around him and buried her face against his neck, inhaling the scent of his cologne and pleased with the fresh taste of his skin. He set her on the couch and then dropped to his knees between her open legs.

He took in the sight of her breasts and nipples pressed against the nearly invisible material before moving down to the thong of her teddy now nestled between the lips of her core. He licked his lips.

She watched him, surprised at the quickening of her pulse in anticipation. *Would he?*

He pulled her teddy to the side and lowered his head to suck her clit between her lips.

Jessa's back arched from the couch as if hit with electricity.

She entwined her fingers in his hair and balled her hands into soft fists as he feasted on her.

He's good. Damn good.

His tongue was soft, feather light and the perfect speed.

Shit.

She felt her thighs tremble. She spread her legs wider and pushed her hips forward. "Good?" she whispered to him.

He nodded, cutting his eyes up to her as he released his tongue and flickered the tip against her quivering bud.

She gasped hotly, rolling her hips against his mouth. "Yes," she sighed, tilting her head against the back of the sofa as she brought her hands up to tease her own nipples through the almost invisible material.

He sucked her again. Deeper. Slightly quicker. Pushing her over the edge. He wanted to please her. He wanted her to cum in his mouth. He wanted to taste it. Lick it.

Jessa panted, her lips pursed, as she felt her core heat and quiver with the rise of her climax.

He dug his hands beneath the weight of her body to lift her buttocks off the sofa as he sucked her to a slow explosion.

Her entire body quivered as she bit her bottom lip to stifle a cry of passion as she enjoyed the waves of her explosive climax. "Hammer," she cried out.

She gasped and then winced, memories of his betrayal with a woman who could very well be her daughter blended with her ecstasy. The release also opened the door to her sadness. Her tears were inevitable and burned as they raced from her eyes. "Shit," she swore. "Shit."

"Look at me," her stranger demanded.

She opened her eyes to find him looking down at her.

"It's not him," he said, his eyes understanding.

She sat up, wiping her tears as she set her feet on the floor on either side of him. She locked her eyes with his as she undid his belt and then his zipper before jerking his pants and black boxers down around his hips. The waistband got caught on his erection, and she gripped his inches to free it, giving him a soft half-smile at his width.

Damn white boy.

He hissed and pumped his hips forward as she stroked him from the root to the tip.

He was long and thick. Heavy. No curve. Just straight ahead, but that was fine. Every man was different, and they knew how to work what they were given.

She looked down at him.

Thank God.

She worried it would be pink or reddish. His was a shade darker than his tanned skin and all one beautiful color.

As she lightly massaged the tip, causing him to shiver, she reached in the pocket of her trench and removed a condom. After tearing the foil with her teeth and removing it, she slid the condom down the length of him before steering his hardness inside her.

He's so hard. So. Hard. Shit.

His lips shaped into a circle at the first feel of her. Her heat. Her wetness. Her tightness.

He took over, wrapping one arm around her back and the other across her buttocks to press her body against his as he pumped his hips, sending his steel deeper and deeper inside her.

She pressed her face against the pulse racing at the base of his neck.

He shook his head.

"Look at me," he demanded of her again.

She gasped as he circled his hips, sending his inches around her core before stroking her hard and deep twice.

Damn, white boy getting it.

"Look at me," he said again, stopping his thrusts.

She did.

"Don't pretend I'm him," he said, his eyes dipping to take

in her panting mouth before rising back up to her half-closed eyes.

Jessa clenched and released her muscles against him as she met his stare.

His eyes widened a little in surprise and then deepened in pleasure.

She released him to grip the edges of the sofa and lift her buttocks up off the cushions as she took over, slowly working her hips back and forth, ending each pump with a grind of her hips.

He shook his head in wonder. "He's a fucking fool," he said, kissing her.

"Yes the fuck he is," she agreed, offering him the tip of her tongue to suck.

"Let me give you some more room to work," he said, rising to turn and sit with Jessa now straddling him.

She dropped the trench to their feet and slipped off the straps of her teddy to free her breasts before guiding his head against her cleavage. He latched onto a throbbing, hard nipple as she gripped her hips while she rode him. She cried out in pleasure.

His tongue is a blessing.

"Are you married?" she asked suddenly, leaning back to meet his gaze as she continued to rotate her hips, bringing her core against the base of his hardness.

She saw the truth in his eyes before he even nodded.

Jessa ran her fingers through his hair and gripped the strands as she rode him harder.

Oh well. Once a mistress, always a mistress.

"Forgive me, Father Dell, for I have sinned."

He looked up from the notepad on which he was writing at his desk. "Jessa," he said in surprise. "I wasn't expecting to see you today."

"Yes, I know you were not," she said, looking around his office as she entered. "But I figured since I just cheated on my husband after catching him cheating on me last night that it called for an emergency session."

"Father Dell?"

They both looked to the door to find Sister Runyon, his church secretary. "I wasn't aware you had an appointment?" she said, glancing at Jessa and then back at the minister.

"No, I didn't, but it's fine. Thank you, Sister Runyon," he said. "We have a counseling session, so if you'll close the door."

"In here?" she asked, frowning in disapproval.

Jessa walked over to the door with a stiff smile.

"Sister Young," he stressed in warning, rising to his feet.

"You're worrying about what's going on in here and you need to teach your husband, the deacon, that his seat in that pulpit is not for looking under the skirts of whatever woman is silly enough to try that front pew during church. *Okay?*"

Jessa closed the door in the woman's shocked face before claiming one of the leather chairs in front of his desk.

Reverend Dell rushed across the room and reopened it. "Sister Runyon, please come in," he said, steering her by her elbow. "Sister Young, I think you owe her an apology."

Jessa gave her a mocking glance over her shoulder before waving her hand dismissively. "I'm tired of her husband trying to eyeball my panties," she said, feeling spiteful and petty.

Sister Runyon gasped in shock.

"Taking your burdens out on others is a selfish and ugly act, Jessa," the reverend said from behind her.

Jessa sighed as if bored. "Go make some lap scarves to give out. That *might* help," she said with an arch of her brow.

"I told you we shouldn't have ever accepted her membership in this church. A zebra don't changes its stripes, Reverend," the woman said.

"Sister Runyon, please, judge not," he said.

"He that is without sin among you, let him first cast a stone," the woman said, quoting the Bible. "What about *that*, Reverend Dell?"

The Bible. Jessa felt a pang in her gut. She thought it carried all the answers to having a better life.

Fool.

"Those who consider themselves religious and yet do not keep a tight rein on their tongues deceive themselves, and their religion is worthless," Jessa quoted in retort over her shoulder. "You're not the only one can bring scripture. So that means nothing."

"Okay, ladies, that's enough of using the Lord's word to battle each other," Reverend Dell said sternly. "Sister Runyon, please leave us alone."

"Humph."

Moments later the door closed and Reverend Dell came around his desk to reclaim his seat. "I think we should start this session with prayer, Jessa," he said.

She gave him a bitter smile as she shook her head. "My days of listening to you and your God are over," she said, her voice low and acerbic.

He leaned back in his chair as if to put distance between them. "I see hell in you," he said.

"Do you, Rev?" she asked, mocking him.

He bowed his head and Jessa knew he was praying for her.

"I did everything right. I begged forgiveness from those I wronged. I went to church. I sought counsel. I paid my tithes. I read the Bible. I did good things with my business. I fought to better my life for my blessings to flow," she said, her anger seeming to pierce every word. "That's what you said the Lord says, you and the Bible, right? Do good unto others and all of that bullshit, right?"

"Jessa!" he exclaimed in shock.

"What? Where are my blessings? Where's my good karma?

Huh? I ain't catching nothing but pure d-damn hell, so if you see it in me, please explain *how* when I have done what was requested of me in the name of the Lord."

He reached onto his desk and pressed his hand down atop his Bible.

She eyed the move before shifting her view back to him. "So now *I'm* the devil?" she asked.

"No, but there is a change in you."

"Is there now?" she asked, crossing her legs.

His eyes dipped down to take in the move before he looked away.

She laughed. "I see there's been no change in you and your desire of me," Jessa said. "Don't worry, Rev. I just had some good dick."

He shook his head in shame, his mouth silently moving.

"I was wife and then a mistress, a wife again and a mistress once more...but I'm not a whore, so I'm not looking to tackle two dicks in one day," she said. "You're good."

"I'm sorry that you have been betrayed and it has made you turn your back on the one who will never forsake you," Revered Dell said.

"Didn't he, though?" she asked, trying to chuckle away her tears and failing. "Didn't he bring me this far and leave me?"

"It is in your darkest hours that you turn to him and not against him."

Jessa rushed to her feet, accidentally knocking the tie of her trench, causing it to open and display her scandalous lingerie. She didn't bother to close it as she turned and walked to the door. "Good-bye, Rev," she said, glancing back over her shoulder. "If your prayers for me over the years have led my life to this...then take me off your damn roll."

With that she took her leave, swearing never to darken the church's doorstep again.

★   ★   ★

Jessa drove her car up the drive, shaking her head at the sight of Hammer's black Tahoe parked in front of her house. She shook her head and released a heavy breath. *I'm not in the mood for this bullshit.*

As soon as she parked and climbed from her vehicle, he exited his as well. "Jessa, your mother won't let me in the house," he said.

She nodded. "That's because you no longer live here, Hammer," she said plainly, barely sparing him a glance as she climbed the stairs.

He rushed up the stairs to stand in front of the door, blocking her.

Jessa sighed.

"I'm sorry. I am so sorry, Jessa. We have to talk about this," he urged, reaching for her hands.

She looked up at him. Studying his face. Taking him in. Looking for the man she thought he was. "You are a stranger to me," she said. "I don't know you. I don't think you know yourself, you too busy pretending to be whatever you need to be to get what you want."

"She set me up. Can't you see that?" Hammer asked.

She pulled her hands from his. "No. Nope. Hell no," she stressed.

He reached behind himself to pull a rolled-up file from his back pocket. "Yes," he said, handing the file to her. "I've been looking into her all morning, Jessa, Lacey Adams *is* Georgia."

Sharp pain radiated across her chest as she eyed the folder. *My Georgia.*

She hoped it wasn't true.

"So not only did you cheat, you fucked my daughter," she said, her eyes glazing over with her tears. "And you really think we can come back from *that*?"

He reached for her again and she held up a hand to stop him as she shook her head and gave him a sad smile. "I had the most glorious sex just now," she told him, moaning a bit as she bit her bottom lip and gave him an exaggerated shiver.

His face crumpled before it hardened. His jaw clenched. His hands balled into tight fists at his sides.

"It wasn't the same passion we had when I thought I loved you, but it was good," she gloated. "I came twice. Once in his mouth and then again when I was riding him."

"Who?" Hammer ground out.

"Who?" she mocked before laughing. "Someone who wouldn't have gotten this pussy in a million years if you didn't fuck up what I thought was a happy home. *You* gave him the pussy."

Hammer reached out and gripped her throat, his thumb pressing against her windpipe.

"He *loved* it," she whispered to him with a smile.

The pressure increased against her throat.

"And so did I," she continued, wanting to hurt him the way that he hurt her. "It was so hard. Like a steel bat. He was younger than you, so it was harder than your dick will *ever* be again—even with a pill."

It was a struggle to swallow as his grip tightened.

"I hate you," he said, his lips curled with the emotion.

She brought her hands up to grip his wrist. "You're late to that party," she told him with effort, her voice strained.

They stared at each other. Hated each other. The chemistry that once was love and passion now fueled hatred and disgust.

The moment was miserable.

She thought of how Eric had once choked her, and for a second fear filled her eyes.

Hammer released her, as if he too remembered that she had almost lost her life in the same fashion. "Jessa, I'm sorry," he begged, his eyes filled with his hurt and regret.

Jessa gasped for breath and smoothed her fingers against her sore neck. She knew marks would come. She unlocked and opened the front door. Her mother sat on the steps, no doubt listening in. Her eyes were glassy.

Jessa ignored her as she began to move the suitcases and plastic containers holding his belongings onto the porch.

"Jessa, we can fix this," Hammer said. "We're even. We can forgive each other and move on."

She shook her head. "Last night I met my daughter for the first time, and she hates me. And I saw you for who you really are, and I hate you," she said, bending to pick up a container to set atop another. "So I am not the person you knew anymore. She's dead. You killed her. And that is not a good thing, because what rose from her ashes will ensure that I will *never* get hurt like she did."

Hammer stepped forward.

She recoiled from him.

His shoulders slumped.

"Good-bye, Hammer," she said, setting the last bag on the porch before she entered the house and closed the door, locking it.

She slumped against it, still gripping the knob, as she fought back the tears that welled up. *How long before it doesn't hurt anymore?*

"A lot of shit going down around here."

Jessa looked over at her mother still in her spot on the step.

Another damn disappointment.

"Yes, like the liquor down your throat," she said, turning to look out the peephole at Hammer loading his things into the back of his SUV.

"Bull*shit*," Darla said, clapping her hands together between her open knees. "What's this about your daughter?"

Jessa pressed her forehead to the door and closed her eyes, ignoring her mother. At the sound of Hammer's truck cranking, she again looked out at him. His image increased in size as he walked toward the door.

"I see you looking at me," he said, tapping the peephole on his side of the door with the folder before he bent and pushed it through the black wrought iron mail slot. "Call me when you ready to talk."

Darla sucked her teeth. "Shit. The nerve of *that* Negro. Give a black man a big dick and a job and he think he invincible. Negro, puh-*leeze*."

As soon as he drove away, Jessa opened the door and claimed the folder, keeping it rolled up in her hand. She turned to point it in her mother's direction. "I promised myself twenty-four hours to deal with my ain't shit husband. My marriage of less than a month is over. And the child I had by my own father, that was *taken* from me, has returned and she hates me. I mean, she fucking *hates* me," Jessa wailed, her shoulders slumping as the very thought of that overwhelmed her. Her hands trembled and her tears were unstoppable. "My twenty-four hours to be selfish and worry about nothing or nobody is not up. So you got lucky that your bipolar ass is sitting here in my house drunk when you know you can't mix alcohol with your meds. Now try me tomorrow. That's what you do. Try this shit again *tomorrow*. It's not gonna work out well."

She rushed across the foyer and up the stairs past her mother, ignoring the words she mumbled under her breath.

No. I can't. Not today.

She entered her bedroom suite and locked the door. She felt like crawling under the bed and sleeping away her troubles, but she needed to wash away her tryst with Mr. Halston. *A stranger to me no more.*

There was a soft knock at the door. "Come in," she called out.

Winifrid entered, carrying Delaney's video monitor and wearing a comforting smile.

"How is she?" Jessa asked, taking the monitor from her.

"She's playing. She's good," the nanny assured her.

"Winifrid, I'm sure you picked up that I'm dealing with some stuff—personal stuff—right now," she began, running her free hand through her disheveled hair. "I'm a mess and I don't want this energy around my daughter. I don't want her to see me like this. Just not today."

Winifrid reached out to lightly squeeze her wrist. "Yes, ma'am, I can understand that," she said. "I can stay over in the guest room and keep her if you like."

The kind gesture in the midst of her turmoil and betrayal touched her. "Yes, please, thank you," Jessa said emphatically.

"No worries," she said, turning to walk back into the bedroom and softly close the door behind her.

Jessa knew she had to get it together for the sake of her daughter. She smiled as she watched Winifrid swing her up into her arms and circle the room as she sang a lullaby in her native tongue of German.

Just the rest of this day. That's all I need.

She drew a bath and was anxious to remove her trench and teddy to slide into the steamy depths of the scented bubble bath. She tried her best not to think of any of it. Georgia. Hammer. Her mother. Mr. Halston. The Rev.

She tried, but she was an emotional wreck, and soon her head was tilted back over the side of the tub as she covered her face with her hands. She was so sick of being near the brink of tears nearly every moment of the day. Her despair pumped through her blood. It all had turned so bad so very quickly, and her head was still spinning from it all.

The memory of Hammer and Georgia mating like dogs in heat came back in a rush.

She winced.

Followed by the hate in her daughter's eyes that was burned in her memory.

Do you finally see me? I'm Georgia, Mother. *Don't you see me?*
Jessa shook her head.

I stopped being yours the moment you gave me away . . .

"I didn't give you away," she whispered, sinking lower in the water until her chin touched it.

Mama, save me.

That thread from the sweater was slowly unraveling again. *All chickens come home to roost.*

Jessa slept through the night. Pure depression, and she knew it. But that was yesterday. Today was another day.

The wounds to her soul were there on the inside. Buried. Hoped one day to be forgotten. But her façade? Cool and unshaken.

She studied her reflection in the full-length mirror inside her walk-in closet. The brilliantly red tailored suit, shoes, and lipstick she wore only hinted that she was out for blood. Her mission was simple: Destroy those who tried to destroy her.

She clung to her old ways. They once saved her from the pain. They would save her again.

It was time to go to war, and she would be the victor... by *any* means necessary.

Chapter 12

Jessa purposefully avoided a chance meeting in the elevator with Mr. Halston by arriving at work long after her usual start time. She took a chance on his punctuality and was right. Not that she didn't want to partake of him again. She would. Her focus was currently elsewhere. *More to life than a good nut right now.*

As she came up on the door to the Mistress, Inc., offices, Jessa paused, wondering if the business meant anything to her anymore. Her passion for helping save people from being duped by the affairs of their spouse had lost its shine.

Why am I even here? And who am I to help people discover what I missed in my very own marriage?

She walked into the office, glad to find the reception area free of her agents or clients.

Felisha immediately picked up the phone and whispered into it. Seconds later Keegan flew out of her office. "Jessa, where in the great hog heaven have you been?"

Jessa ignored her and eyed Felisha with a stare meant to make her toes quiver in her boots. "You're fired. Gather your shit and get out," she said as she made a circular motion with her finger in the air and then pointed toward the door.

"What!" Keegan exclaimed.

Felisha looked aghast. "But, Mrs. Young—"

Jessa walked past her to her office. She paused in the doorway. "Matter of fact, just to be clear, read the contract you signed that gives me the explicit right to fire you at will with no cause," she said, before entering her office and setting her bright red crocodile Louis Vuitton city steamer tote atop her desk as she took her seat.

"Wait here, Felisha, don't you move," she heard Keegan say.

Jessa cut her eyes up from removing the file Hammer gave her on Georgia from her bag.

Strike one.

She turned her attention to also retrieving her iPhone as Keegan stormed into her office. It vibrated in her hand and she flipped it over. Another of Hammer's series of text messages either pleading for her forgiveness or demanding to know the name of her lover. She ignored it just as she had all the rest.

"Jessa, what's going on?" Keegan asked, her hands on her hips as she looked down at Jessa from where she stood in front of the desk. "First you're no show, no call to work yesterday. Late today. And now you fire Felisha for absolutely nothing?"

Strike two, bitch.

Jessa set her phone face down on the desk and leaned back in her chair to eye Keegan. "When the fuck did you become the boss?" she asked, her voice cold.

Keegan was taken aback and her stance stiffened. "I never said I was," she countered.

"Actions speak louder than words," Jessa said, stroking the tender spots on her neck from when Hammer had gripped her there the day before.

Keegan eyed her suspiciously. "What's up with you, Jessa?" she asked.

Bzzzzzz...

"Lacey Adams is fired as well," she said, turning over her phone. "That's not her real name and she got a job here just to retaliate against me, which she did by sleeping with Hammer."

Another text from hubby.

She opened it.

ALL I CAN SEE IS ANOTHER MAN FUCKING MY WIFE. HOW COULD YOU? PLEASE SAY YOU'RE LYING. PLEASE JESSA. PLEASE.

She sighed and turned the phone back face down.

I really need to make that appointment with my lawyer.

"I didn't know. I'm so sorry about Hammer, sweetie," Keegan said.

Jessa remained quiet.

"Why didn't you call me?"

She arched a brow. "As a friend in need of compassion or to explain an absence?" she asked.

Keegan opened her hands. "Both," she said. "We had a couple of small fires to put out yesterday, and you wouldn't answer our calls."

This bitch.

"Like what?" Jessa asked.

"Mrs. Montgomery wanted to speak to you yesterday, and it sounded urgent."

That reminds me, I need to do something about her, too.

Jessa nodded. "And?"

"We usually have our monthly dinner with the staff, but I canceled it," Keegan said.

"I am so sorry. I just had my entire world as I knew it destroyed, but boo-hoo for *you* and a couple of small fires that obviously didn't burn the business down," she drawled sarcastically, giving her an unblinking stare as she crossed her legs. "I haven't heard a damn thing that absolutely needed my attention. You had to take a message and the staff missed a free fucking dinner. Are you serious?"

Keegan bit her bottom lip as she glanced down at the floor and released a heavy breath.

Jessa rolled her eyes. *All reflective and shit.*

"I hate that you are in such pain," Keegan began. "It's clear that you're lashing out—"

Jessa applauded. "Wow. Interior decorator. Top-grade deliverer of one-liners. Business manager. *And* a therapist. Whoa."

"You're being a bitch, Jessa."

"Good," she said, drumming her fiery red fingernails against the desk. "Trying so hard not to be one left me wide open. It's a mistake I won't repeat."

Keegan frowned. "How can you just fire Felisha like that? What is she supposed to do for money?"

Jessa eyed her. "I'm done with the matter," she said.

Keegan squinted as she eyed her. "So, to hell with everyone else's life and livelihood because your hubby did you dirty?" she asked. "You don't think that's just a little crass, Jessa. Good Lord, you're better than that."

Strike three.

She gave her a slow smile. "Anything else you want to get off your chest?" she asked pleasantly.

She can't be that gullible to walk into that *trap.*

"I think learning one of the employees was here under false pretenses so easily has exposed another flaw in the company," Keegan added.

So she is.

I really could do without the headache.

"I think it's time we part ways," Jessa said. "Over the years you have more than made back the money you invested—"

"You have to buy me out," Keegan spouted.

Jessa arched her brow. "No, I don't. I was just obligated to ensure you recouped your initial investment, and you've done that plus some."

"You can't be serious," Keegan snapped.

"I'll tell you the same thing I told Felisha, read your paperwork," she said, reaching for the phone.

"I was warned about you and your bullshit," Keegan said.

Jessa waved her hand at her dismissively. "Hello, Security? Yes. Could you send up a guard? I have two *employees* that need to be escorted from the premises," she said. "Thanks so much."

"There's no way you can be this heartless."

Jessa nodded. "Call it what you want, and please do not remove any electronics on your way out. They belong to the business—*my* business," she stressed.

Keegan slammed her hand on the desk. "I will sue you before I let you screw me like you have screwed so many others."

Jessa leaned forward to lock eyes with her friend. "Your balls ain't big enough," she said in a whisper that still carried the chill of her voice. "I will end this business, liquidate everything for little to nothing, and start fresh with a new a tax ID and LLC. Nothing from nothing leaves *nothing.*"

Keegan stepped back from her, her anger softening into pity as she shook her head. "I feel for you, sugar," she said. "You must really be hurting to have become this pathetic in so little time. Or was it there hidden beneath your bravado and false pretenses of being saved?"

"You can have Hammer *now*," Jessa said spitefully. "I'm done with him."

The front door to the office opened and then closed. Two security guards stood in the foyer.

"No, honey, thank you for getting fucked over by him before I could," Keegan said with a sarcastic chuckle before she turned and walked out of the office.

Jessa came over to lean in her doorway as she watched Keegan and Felicia gather their personal items into containers and take their leave, flanked by the security guards.

Fuck 'em.

Back in her office, she took her seat behind the desk and opened the file of Georgia Coletti. There wasn't a lot about her adoption. The files were sealed, but there was enough to know she led a good life in Connecticut. Private school. Good grades. College graduation. Good income. No arrests. Decent credit score. A trendy apartment on the Upper West Side.

For years, she wondered what had become of her child. She worried the legacy of her parentage would affect her. She wasn't naive to think these couldn't be more to her story beyond what appeared in the file, but her life was still far better than what she'd imagined it could've been.

Do you finally see me? I'm Georgia, Mother. *Don't you see me?*

I stopped being yours the moment you gave me away . . .

Mama, save me.

All chickens come home to roost.

Jessa picked up the office phone and dialed the number from Georgia's file. She paused before she dialed the last digit. *And what if she asks me who her father is?*

"I'll lie," she answered herself aloud before punching the button.

It went straight to voice mail.

"This is Georgia. No essays or soliloquies, please."

Jessa actually smiled, remembering the soft-spoken young woman she'd interviewed for a job as an agent and not the cold-blooded shrew who relished in her destruction. "Georgia, hello, this is Jessa. Your mother," she said, finding the words an oddity to say. "I wanted to speak to you, not about Hammer, to hell with him. He doesn't matter. That's over."

Jessa released a breath as she tucked the phone between her shoulder and ear and turned on her computer to pull up the Lacey Adams employee file. "Right now, making sure that I speak to you and try to understand that hatred for me is important," she said, zooming in on her photo to finally notice she had her eyes.

Do you finally see me? I'm Georgia, Mother. *Don't you see me?*

She looked upward. "I hope you will meet with me. Talk to me. I am your mother, and there is one thing I can promise you—that I have loved you and wanted nothing but the best for you *every* day of your life. Please call me."

Jessa softly placed the handset back on the cradle before she leaned back in her chair and swiveled in it to look out the window. Georgia was back in her life. Neither her anger nor the pain of knowing the child she bore hated her, clouded the fact there was no way Georgia could have found her alone. She had signed nothing giving away her rights to her baby. Georgia had to be presented to authorities as abandoned—she figured that out long after her grandmother died and the truth of the baby's existence was no longer a question that lingered unanswered between them.

Georgia had a benefactor who gave her information, and the facts had obviously been pissed upon.

Was it Hammer? He knew of her first child. He spoke of finding her. Perhaps he had done just that. But what was there for him to gain—certainly more than sex?

Her mother had neither the resources nor the free time to locate a missing grandchild.

Her grandmother was dead.

Jessa tapped her nails against the desk as she released a bitter little laugh. The Halls. Eric's parents, and unfortunately the grandparents of her beloved daughter Delaney. This was right up Eric Hall Sr.'s alley.

She bit her bottom lip and focused on a pigeon landing on the roof of a nearby building. "How apropos," she said. "A dirty bird."

What was any dirtier than trying to sleep with the

woman who 1) once slept with your son, 2) had a baby by that same son, and 3) you blamed for your son's suicide after he attempted to murder that same woman? Jessa recalled the hell of them suing her for custody of Delaney. He had threatened to expose the sordid details of her rape and the birth of her first child. She had to get low and fight as dirty as he had. She seduced the duplicitous man just enough to capture video footage on her nanny cam to blackmail him into not only dropping his suit but agreeing to step out of Delaney's life for good.

Is he back? Is this some backdoor shit?

Mrs. Hall's anger at her during their accidental meet-up at Serenity Spa had been palpable.

And now so is mine. But first things first . . .

For the next hour, she got the affairs of Mistress, Inc., in order, calling all of her agents, any current clients, and her webmaster to alert them that the offices were closed for two weeks. After a final call to the management company for the locks to be changed and a quick change to the outgoing voice mail message, she tucked her tablet, iPhone, and the Georgia file back into her bag.

She walked around the office, turning off the lights and unplugged their Keurig coffee machine. As she stood in the middle of the foyer and looked around, she knew a short reprieve was for the best. Her focus was elsewhere.

Jessa walked out of the offices of Mistress, Inc., shut the door, and locked it.

Darla tucked her hands inside the pockets of her lightweight jacket as she walked down the driveway of her daughter's home and her prison. The walls seemed to mock her because she had no power within them.

It's Jessa's house and Jessa's rules.

She nodded, thankful to the voice that had recently returned to her and understood her like no else. They were longtime friends, and she missed her.

I missed you, too, Darla.

She smiled. The voice was always present. Always there. Always understanding. Always listening. Boosting her like a battery in her back.

Who is she to tell you not to drink? Fuck her. She's not the only one dealing with the shame. Right?

Darla shook her head as she stopped at the corner and reached out to press her hand against the lamppost. She panted and squeezed her eyes shut as she envisioned the man she once loved raping the child she bore for him. "How could he?" she whispered harshly.

She knew he drank.

She knew he could strike out in anger.

She knew he hid a darkness within him with far too much ease.

That's why she left him and took Jessa with her.

But then she left Jessa, foolishly thinking he would never reappear in her life, and never warning her mother to not allow him to do so.

It wasn't your fault, Darla. You weren't there.

"Lies!" she spat. "I shouldn't have left her behind."

Darla opened her eyes to find one of their white neighbors staring at her oddly as they walked their dog. She gave the woman a wide-eyed, unblinking stare as she hurried past her.

Relax, Darla. Re-lax.

She looked over her shoulder, grimacing as the woman upped her walk to a jog.

The breath she released was shaky.

A drink will calm your nerves.

She knew where to find it. She smiled as she patted the pole and continued down the block, taking in the tree-lined streets with wrought iron lampposts and large pots with colorful perennial flowers. She turned the corner, widening her stride as the street inclined.

We're almost there. Can't you just taste it, Darla?

"I sure can," she said, licking her lips as she came to a stop at the brick house on the corner with the beautiful gardens—floral in the front and vegetable in the back—all behind a metal gate designed like lattice.

Darla opened the gate and walked up the brick-lined path to the double doors painted a bright red.

Your heart's pumping.

She rang the bell, not sure why she felt so nervous as the door opened. "Hello, Frankie," she said, smiling at the tall gray-haired man with a fair-skinned complexion like shortbread cookies. He looked at her over the rim of his glasses.

Months ago, she'd spotted him from her bedroom window sitting in his yard, listening to jazz and drinking snifter after snifter of some brown liquor. The little buzz she had from the eggnog before Christmas and her boredom had stoked her hunger for alcohol. Two walks past his house and Darla finally caught his attention...and an offer to sit a spell and have a drink. Not long after that she discovered he really poured one on after a hand job and took a nice nap that allowed her to pilfer from his stocked bar.

"Hey there, neighbor," he said, waving her in with the gardening gloves he held in one hand.

Cheers!

Jessa sat outside her house for at least an hour listening to old-school rhythm and blues on her XM satellite. She checked her phone. There was nothing but voice mails and text messages from Hammer. She ignored them all.

She was hoping Georgia would call.

She looked out at day turning to night as she mouthed

along with the O'Jays singing "Forever Mine." *Ain't no such thing as forever when it comes to love.*

Jessa scratched her scalp with her nails as she shook her head. Her attorney said she couldn't even file for divorce for six months and then there was still time before it was processed. The separation would have lasted longer the marriage. *In the words of Keyshia Cole: I just want it to be over.*

She could claim residency in Nevada and get a divorce in six weeks or get one in the Dominican Republic in a day *if* Hammer legally agreed to the divorce being filed in that country. *Easy to get into and hard to get the fuck out of.*

"Thank God for that prenup," Jessa muttered.

Bzzzzzz...

She picked up her phone from the console. "Winifrid?" she said, before she answered.

Her eyes widened at the commotion in the background.

"Mrs. Bell, please hurry home," Winifrid said.

Delaney let out a wail that seemed to reverberate.

She hopped out of the car. "What's wrong with her?" she asked, her heart pounding.

"Your mother fell with her—"

Jessa ended the call and rushed toward the house at a full run. She pushed the front door wide open, leaving it that way as she took the stairs two at a time in her heels.

"Give me my grandbaby, you bitch. You don't know who you fucking with!" Darla screeched.

Delaney let loose another shrill cry.

"Mrs. Darla, please leave her be. You're upsetting her!" Winifrid said, her voice calm in the midst of the storm.

Bzzzzzz...

Jessa ignored the vibration of the phone against her palm as she rushed down the hall and into Delaney's bedroom. Winifrid looked grateful as she handed Delaney over to her.

"What happened?" she asked.

Winifrid shook her head and released a heavy breath. "I

left her alone in her playroom while I went to the bathroom. Just a minute or so. When I stepped back in the room, your mother was dancing around the room with her, and she tripped on something and fell backward—"

"I didn't hurt her, Jessa," Darla said, her words slurring.

Jessa could hear her drunkenness in her voice and smell the liquor that seemed to press the fresh air out of the room. She closed her eyes and shook her head as Delaney finally being to settle down, her wails diminishing to whimpers.

"Grandma scared me," she whispered as she buried her chubby little face against Jessa's neck.

That broke her heart and infuriated her beyond belief.

"I got one granddaughter you won't let me see and another one I ain't never met," Darla said, pounding on something behind her. "What kind of shit is *that*?"

God help—

She shook her head. It was a habit that she would soon break. There was no turning to Him when she felt he had forsaken her. It felt like the worst betrayal of them all.

"Please take her down to my car and stay with her until I'm done here," Jessa said, forcing calm into her voice and momentarily shielding the anger boiling over inside her.

Winifrid nodded, attempting to take Delaney from her arms.

Delaney shook her head and tightened her grip on Jessa.

"Jessa, I'm sorry. It's all my fault. I'm sorry," Darla said from behind her.

"I'll walk y'all down," Jessa said to the nanny, leaving the room and avoiding even looking at her mother.

They descended the stairs and reached the front door.

A crash from upstairs echoed, breaking the quiet.

"Delaney, I need you to sit with Winifrid for a little while I talk to Grandma," she said softly into her ear, desperate to protect her by all means—the way she had not been sheltered. "Be a big girl for Mama, okay?"

She patted and rubbed Delaney's back as she gave Winifrid a nod to take her. She did and Delaney outstretched her arms for her, but Jessa turned her back and looked up the flight of stairs.

"Mama!" she roared as soon as the front door closed.

Her fists were clenched as tight as they could be with her long nails, and her chest heaved with every breath as she released the anger and bitter disappointment she felt about her mother.

Darla stumbled into the railing lining the second floor and leaned against it as she sought stability. Her eyes were clouded and bloodshot. There was a fine sheen of sweat on her brow and across her upper lip. Her soft black and silver hair was plastered to her head. The neck of the T-shirt she wore was damp with it. She swayed back and forth as she looked down at where Jessa stood.

"You off your meds?" Jessa asked, her tone ominous as she rubbed her thumb against her index finger in a futile attempt to calm herself.

Darla shook her head vehemently.

"Liar," Jessa said. "Tell me, Mama, why does it *always* have to be about you?"

Darla stumbled back as she reached into the pockets of her slacks to pull out a small bottle of liquor.

Jessa's face crumpled with her emotions, but she closed her eyes and released breaths through pursed crimson lips until she felt the welcome sensation of her soul going numb. "You made a choice to drink...just like you made a choice to leave me at that window that day and you made a choice to never come back for me."

Darla nodded and wiped her lips with her trembling hands. "I know it. I'm sorry. I'm so sorry, Jessa," she said, opening the bottle and taking a drink.

"You abandoned me. My father raped me. My grandmother tore my baby out of my arms and gave her away. Now that daughter hates me. My husband crushed me," Jessa said, walking over to tilt her head and look up at her mother as she wiped the liquor that spilled onto her mouth with the back of her hand. "Ain't that enough, Mama? Huh? Your crazy wants me crazy, too? Huh?"

Darla leaned onto the banister again, the bottle in one of her hands over the side. "I want you happy," she said. "I do. I want my little girl happy."

Jessa shook her head, denying her words. "You were a lousy mother then and you a lousy motherfucking grandmother *now*," she stressed, drawing out the word for emphasis.

Darla let out a little moan. The bottle slipped from her hand. She cried out and bent over the railing, outstretching her arms as if to reach for it. She failed. The bottle crashed against the floor of the foyer, the stench of the liquor quickly rising to fill the air as the brown liquid pooled amongst the shards of glass.

"No!" Darla cried out, pounding her fists upon the railing.

Jessa sent up a bitter laugh. "Did you cry that hard for me? *Ever?* Huh? When you were off screwing men and looking for love in a bottle or with drugs? Did you every cry for the daughter you abandoned? Did you ever cry when you learned I was raped? Did you cry when you heard I watched my rapist takes his own life right in front of me? Huh? Did you shed one *fucking* tear when your mother took my baby from me? *Huh?*"

The air was electrified with their emotions, swirling and clashing and creating an explosive backdrop that fed into the very worst of it all. The shame. The hatred. The anger.

Darla covered her ears with her hands and wobbled back and forth on her feet. "Stop it, Jessa, please."

Jessa refused to cry. She wouldn't allow it. With her lips snarling with the same ferocity as a pit bull she pointed at her mother. "Delaney and I are not staying here tonight. You go on and have what you love most in the world. Enjoy it. Live it up. Drink it up. Right?"

Darla stumbled to the top of the stairs, grabbing the railing as she flopped down onto the top step. "I did the best I knew how," she said, wiping away the tears that mingled with the clear snot running from her nostrils. "I did my *best*—"

"It wasn't fucking good enough," Jessa told her before she turned and left the house.

Ding-dong.

Darla's eyes opened and she was looking up at the ceiling. She grunted a little as she sat up, surprised to find she was still sitting atop the top step of the stairs. "Oh Lord," she whispered, leaning against the railing before she gripped it and fought to rise to her feet without toppling down the stairs.

You're all alone, Darla. Everyone's gone. You're the queen of the castle now. Top bitch in charge.

Darla laughed and puffed up her chest before falling into another fit of giggles.

Ding-dong.

Darla frowned at the door, squinting as she continued down the stairs, tumbling down a few a few as she did. "Who is it?" she called out.

Don't answer it. Now you don't have to share, Darla. The house is all yours.

"It's Georgia. Georgia Coletti," a voice said through the door.

No, Darla. You don't know her. Who is she? She could be a killer. Don't go to the door without a weapon. Protect your house. It's your house now, Darla.

Darla pushed her bob back from her face as she looked around for a weapon. She spotted the broken liquor bottle on the other side of the foyer and walked over in a haphazard zigzag fashion to pick up the broken neck. She cried out as its point dug deeply into her palm, puncturing the flesh and drawing a steady stream of her blood that dripped across the floor as she made her way to the door.

That's right, Darla, now you're ready.

"I'm ready," she mumbled, so grateful for the voice as she reached out to press one hand against the wall for stability and opened the door with the other while still gripping the neck of the broken bottle.

She eyed the young woman standing there from the topknot of her hair down to the red flats she wore with the strapless jean jumpsuit. "What?" Darla asked, barely registering the piercing pain in her palm.

"Is Jessa Bell home?" the young woman asked, obviously taken aback by Darla's appearance.

"No, no, no," Darla repeated softly as she shook her head. She patted her chest with her hand, leaving a bloody smear across the white shirt.

"You've hurt yourself," Georgia said, her eyes shifting from Darla's hand and back up to her eyes.

She's nosy. Make her go, Darla. Make her leave.

"You're nosy. You have to go. You have to leave," Darla said, licking the dryness from her lips.

"Don't you want to talk to your granddaughter?" Georgia asked.

Darla peered at her, "No, I've seen you before," she said. "I've never seen my granddaughter."

She's lying. She wants your house, Darla.

Darla stepped back and pointed the sharp edges of the bottle in Georgia's direction. "You're a liar," she spat.

"Look, is Jessa here?" Georgia asked as she took a step back. "She called me to talk."

Liar, liar.

"But what if it's her?" Darla asked herself, tilting her head to the side as she looked back over her shoulder. "I never met her. I want to say I'm sorry. I want to tell her not to hate Jessa. It's not Jessa's fault her own daddy raped her. That bastard raped my baby. I'm so sorry."

"What?"

Darla turned her head quickly and looked at Georgia, her mood and affect changing in the blink of an eye. She blinked her lashes rapidly. "Get from here!" she spat. "Don't come back here no more."

She stepped forward, jutting the jagged edge of the bottle toward her.

Georgia continued to back away, her eyes wide and confused.

She wants to hurt Jessa, Darla. Don't you let nobody else hurt your baby.

"Stay away from my Jessa. You hear me?" she screeched as she watched the young woman turn and sprint until she reached her car.

Darla watched the vehicle until it took off at a high speed down the driveway.

Good job, Darla.

She nodded, tossing the makeshift weapon from her hand. It crashed against the driveway.

"See, Jessa, I can protect you," Darla said, before closing the door and locking it.

Interlude

I feel like shit.

Today I looked in the eyes of a crazy woman, but I believed every word she said.

"I want to tell her not to hate Jessa. It's not her fault her daddy raped her. That bastard raped my baby."

My grandmother's words seemed to echo. I didn't know if it was inside my head or inside the toilet bowl I clutched as I vomited for the countless time at the thought of my grandfather also being my father. The thought of the hate I had for her, the revenge I plotted and executed against her, and the pain I caused her, was too much.

I pressed my eyes closed, squeezing them as if that would erase the memory of the tortured look on her face when she caught her husband fucking me.

I fed off her embarrassment like a savage.

When I left Hammer's bathroom and saw her on the floor like a discarded crumpled piece of paper, I felt nothing but pleasure that I brought her to knees. That cry she released seemed torn from her very gut, and I only wanted to mock her more. Push her. Hurt her.

Denigrate her. Never did I imagine that some of her anguish was the violent history of how I was created. The impact that left on her life.

"Are you my daughter?"

"I stopped being yours the moment you gave me away."

So clearly, I remember her eyes washing over with so much agony.

"I never gave away my daughter. That's a lie. That's a lie. That's a *lie!*"

And now I wondered if it was. It was possible Eric Hall Sr. used me to get back at her and I was his silly, foolish little pawn. I was so starved for information on her that I willingly swallowed lies from someone I later discovered had reason to hate her as well. Still, I was so focused on my course of destruction that common sense never prevailed.

"I want to tell her not to hate Jessa. It's not her fault her daddy raped her. That bastard raped my baby."

Her daddy raped her.

Her daddy raped her.

Her daddy raped her . . .

My stomach wretched again, but it was empty and there was nothing left to purge. I shook my head and pressed my hands into fists, pounding them against the commode.

I was a child of rape.

My life was shitted on from the very moment of my conception.

It was all too much to bear.

Ding-dong.

I rose from the floor of my bathroom and rushed across the length of my apartment, dressed in nothing but a sheer thong and strapless bra. I paused long enough to grab money from my wallet before I opened the door, quickly snatching the plastic bag of Chinese food from the tall, dark-haired man with pockmarks on his face. He openly stared at my nipples pressing against the material. "You've never seen titties before, Jay?" I snapped, pushing a folded hundred-dollar bill into his hand.

"*Haven't heard from you in a while,*" *he said, using a pen to check if the bill was counterfeit.*

"*Fuck off, Jay,*" *I drawled before I slammed the door shut in his face.*

I trembled from my hunger, dropping to the floor by the door to tear the plastic and remove the containers of food. There nestled atop the beef and broccoli I wouldn't dare to eat was my old friend. Nothing made me feel as good as OxyContin. And I was anxious to feel any kind of good. To forget.

It was all too much to bear.

I knelt on the floor, crushed the pills beneath the weight of a Buddha statue by the door, and used the side of my pinky finger to break the powder into two separate lines. As I snorted my savior from the floor, I realized I was in the same position as my mother in her husband's apartment that night I sought to destroy her world.

Tears raced down my cheeks and wet the residue I left behind. Pain and disgust haunted me as I lay on the floor on my back and waited to rise high above the pain.

Chapter 13

The next morning

"And I'm feeling good," Jessa sang along with Nina Simone playing on her satellite radio.

Her day was jam-packed with plans, and she couldn't wait to get started. All night long as Delaney slept in the bed of the two-star, midlevel hotel they were forced to check in to, Jessa nursed cheap champagne that locked her jaw with every sip and made devious plans. She plotted with the same selfishness and reckless abandon that she had when she decided to send that message all those years ago. Being deceitful felt good and familiar, like a well-worn coat that she easily slipped on.

"Today is going to be a good day," Jessa said as she glanced up in the rearview mirror to look at Delaney happily munching away on the McGriddles from her McDonald's breakfast meal.

Bzzzzzz . . .

She reached for her iPhone on the console but was disappointed when it was Hammer. She answered, hating that there was even one instance when she needed him . . . but she did. "I want you to sign a special power of attorney allowing us to get divorced in the Dominican Republic," she said without hesitation, her tone cold.

There was a long pause.

"Jessa, I'm not giving up on us that easily," he said. "No. I'm not giving up. I will fight for this marriage. Can't you tell she set me up to get back at—"

"Don't do that. Don't you dare put your actions on her," she said, feeling disgust.

"Look, I'm sorry. I know this is a lot to handle at one time. I want to be there for you."

She turned her sports car onto the drive leading to her home. "Go fuck yourself," she said, ending the call.

She was thankful to see her nanny's car already parked in front of the two-car garage. Before she could get out of the car, the front door opened and Jessa knew from the look on Winifrid's face that Darla had done anything but sleep off her drunkenness last night. *What now?*

Jessa climbed from the car still in the clothes she wore yesterday and paused at the sight of the shattered glass on the drive. Some of the pieces were stained with dried blood. "Is she okay?" she asked when Winifrid walked down the stairs to stand beside her.

"She's asleep on the stairs," she said. "There's blood—"

"Stay with Delaney," Jessa ordered before rushing up the stairs and into the house.

Her once beautiful foyer now looked like a crime scene. There was a trail of blood spots from beneath the railing over to the front door. She turned her head and grimaced at the garish bloody handprint on the wall. "The fuck?" she said aloud, walking over to where her mother was slumped across the bottom four steps as she snored loudly through her open mouth.

Jessa's eyes dipped down to her mother's hand, punctured and covered with dried blood that had also spilled onto the stairs. For a few foolish moments she tried to piece together what might have happened, but then she realized the futility of that. There was no way to find sanity in the actions of the insane.

"Ms. Bell, your phone," Winifred called through the open door from outside the house.

Jessa rose and turned on her red heels to make her way back to her car. "Shit," she swore, when she saw it was Georgia.

She held her phone and sat down sideways on the driver's seat, tapping her feet against the pavement as she allowed herself a moment. She was torn, but she knew it was best to let Georgia go on with her life without the same burden carried by Jessa and Darla.

In the light of day, with her emotions firmly in check, she rationalized it was better for her to be hated than for Georgia to know the truth of her conception. She didn't dare risk the horrid secret being outed. *No, it's for the best.*

Bzzzzzz...

She turned the phone over in her hand, biting her bottom lip to see a voice mail notification on the screen. Allowing herself a ten count before she retrieved the message, Jessa debated deleting it. She couldn't. She entered her passcode and pressed the phone to her ear. She shook her head at the sound of tears echoing.

"Forgive me. He u-u-u-used me. My mama...enemy is my enemy, right, M-m-m-mama?" Georgia said.

She recognized that familiar thickness in her tongue that revealed a lack of sobriety.

Jessa pressed her lips into a thin line, fighting not to let the sound of her daughter addressing her as Mama tear into her. Emotions were a weakness.

"I didn't know. I...I didn't know you were...raped, Mama."

How does she know? What all does she know?

"Your daddy is my daddy. I . . . I . . . can't . . ."

Jessa sat up a straighter in her chair, pressing the phone to her ear.

"I wish I didn't–didn't–didn't know. I wish your mother never told me," Georgia wailed, her voice now dragging.

Mama, save me. "I'm too late," Jessa whispered, rising to walk back up the stairs and into the house. She stood by her mother's feet, one bare of a shoe, and nudged it with her toe. "Wake up."

Darla stirred, smacking and licking her lips as her eyelids fluttered. The smell of alcohol seeped from her pores and tainted the air around her.

Jessa nearly snarled as she pressed the tip of her toe to the wound in her mother's hand.

Darla cried out as Jessa stepped back from her. She looked up at her daughter with bloodshot eyes. "Mornin'," she said, her voice hoarse.

"Good morning," Jessa said with false calm. "You hurt your hand."

Darla looked down at it.

Jessa watched her closely and knew her mother could not remember. "Put your shoe on and let's go to the emergency room to get it checked."

Darla's eyes shifted left and right several times before she looked up at her. "It's fine," she said, wincing as she attempted to close her hand into a fist.

Enough is enough of this shit.

"Let's go, Mama, so they can give you some pain pills," she said, luring the addict in her with the bait.

Her mother began mumbling under her breath, her expressions swiftly varying. "I thought you said I couldn't have pills," she asked, her tone accusing.

Jessa gave her a false smile. "I did, but you're hurt and I don't want you to be in pain," she said, stepping back again as her mother rose to her feet with effort and stepped into her missing shoe.

She turned and rushed to the open front door. "Take Delaney in through the side entrance and please call Valeria to come in and clean this foyer," she said to Winifred, who immediately did as she was told.

Darla's feet dragged against the floor as she crossed it. When Jessa felt her mother's hand on her arm to help steady her gait, she purposefully eased out of her reach and rushed ahead to climb into the driver's seat. She couldn't stand her touch. She couldn't stand her.

From behind the wheel she watched her mother, usually composed and neat in dress, looking disheveled and out of sorts. She shook her head as Darla used the hood of the car as her crutch until she opened the door and dropped down onto the passenger seat, letting out a gush of breath that made Jessa gag from the mix of overnight breath and liquor.

They rode in silence, and for that Jessa was thankful, but she was also aware of her mother mumbling under her breath and clutching the door handle with both hands as if prepared to jump out and roll. Not trusting that she wouldn't, Jessa hit the button to lock all the doors.

Darla shot her a look of aggravation before her chatter increased in volume and speed.

"I don't trust her," she said, giving Jessa another sidelong glance before pressing herself against the passenger door.

Jessa pressed the accelerator, anxious to be free of the burden.

Needing a diversion, she sang the words to Nina Simone's "Feeling Good" again, wishing that she was.

Mama, save me.

She couldn't imagine how Georgia felt knowing the family's dirty little secret. She had wanted to spare her—*to save her*—from the truth. And Darla, in her drunken and crazed stupor, had obviously laid that burden on her daughter's life. Her mother was a liability. *She* was the burden Jessa was no longer willing to bear.

Jessa pulled up to the county hospital and turned off the car, removing the key from the ignition and grabbing her iPhone as she climbed out. She called her mother's psychiatrist at his office nearby as she eyed Darla through the rear window of the car.

"Dr. Zevin, please," she said, crossing one arm over her chest as she inhaled the spring air.

"Would you like an appointment?" the receptionist asked.

"No, this Jessa Bell. I have my mother, his patient, Darla Jordan, here at the ER and I would like her evaluated for an emergency psych hold," she said. "She is off her meds and I'm afraid I can't contain her to keep her or others safe."

"Hold, please."

Darla twisted in her seat to look at Jessa through the rear glass. When she turned and reached for the door handle, Jessa rushed over to the passenger side to press her hip against the door to shut it. She pressed the lock with her keys as she turned to look down at her mother trying her best to unlock the door and open it.

"Jessa, let me out," she said, knocking lightly on the glass.

She shook her head.

Darla's eyes widened, quickly filling with alarm and then anger.

"Ms. Bell, the doctor is at already at the hospital and coming down to the ER with an orderly to have your mother admitted," the receptionist said.

Bam-Bam-Bam.

Jessa nodded as the force of her mother's ramming her shoulder against the door caused her body to jolt with each hit as she continued to lean against it. "Please let them know I am right outside with her in my car and I need help with her."

"I will," the receptionist said, before ending the call.

Bam-Bam-Bam-Bam-Bam-Bam!

"Stop it," Jessa said calmly.

Bam-Bam-Bam-Bam-Bam-Bam!

"Let me out, Jessa!"

Bam!

"Let me out!"

Bam!

"Let me out!"

Jessa turned her back on her. "And I'm feeling good," she sang softly, looking down to study the chipped nail of her index finger.

Bam-Bam-Bam-Bam-Bam-Bam!

She was thankful the interior of the car was too small for her mother to climb from one seat over to the next to try to escape via the driver side door. She heard the grind of the hospital's automatic doors and looked up from inspecting the rest of her nails to see Dr. Zevin, a tall and broad middle-aged man with a smooth bald head and a long gray beard. "Thank God," she said, moving from the door.

Moments later, Darla pushed it wide open and climbed out. She swung to slap Jessa, who effortlessly leaned back to avoid the hit.

"Darla," Dr. Zevin said, his voice calm. "It's good to see you."

She turned, shaking her head as she eyed him, before turning back to Jessa. "You tricked me," she said, pointing her finger.

I damn sure did.

Jessa felt nothing. No shame. No guilt. No remorse.

Mama, save me.

"Darla, I'm going to have one of the ER doctors check your hand and then you and I will talk, okay?" Dr. Zevin said, motioning someone forward with a hairy hand.

Jessa looked past him to see a tall and burly man in dark

blue scrubs pushing a wheelchair out to them. *Let's see how much of an ass she makes out of herself with this . . .*

And Darla did not disappoint, taking off at run. Unfortunately, one of her shoes slipped off and she tumbled down to her knees screaming obscenities at Jessa, who casually leaned against the trunk and waited for the melee to end.

"Ms. Bell, are *you* okay?"

The orderly helped her mother up into the wheelchair as she continued to release a string of profanities made all the more vile by her pain.

"Yes, I'm fine," she said, looking up at the psychiatrist. "Why?"

"You seem different. Your behavior is a little disconcerting," he said.

Oh no the hell you won't.

She feigned concern about her mother, forcing a tear to her eye. "It's been very hard, and I admit I've disconnected a bit to be able to function," she lied.

He nodded. "Sometimes being the caregiver can be just as overwhelming as the person dealing with a mental illness," he said. "If you ever need to talk, I'm available."

Fuck you and fuck off.

"Actually, I think long-term care for my mother is now necessary," she said, as her mother glared at her as she was lightly strapped to the wheelchair.

"Let me evaluate her and then we'll talk," Dr. Zevin said, offering her hand a consoling pat before he strode away, leading them all inside the hospital.

Jessa accepted the forms the unit clerk handed her when she came to the admitting desk.

"She's going straight in the back," the woman said with a polite smile. "I'll let you know when you can go back and be with your mother."

"There's no need," Jessa said unapologetically before turning to kneel beside her mother.

"I'll be good, Jessa," she whimpered, her anger and belligerence fading.

"Telling Georgia about my father and what he did to me was cruel, Darla," she whispered for her ears alone. "Somewhere inside this crazy, you know exactly what I'm talking about. So let me be clear. I will *never* forgive you for that, and you will rot in some facility wishing like hell that you didn't fuck with me or mine. The next time I lay eyes on you, it will be your corpse. I *promise* you that."

Darla gasped and reached out for her. "No, Jessa, no!" she begged as her wheelchair was backed through an open door that soon closed and divided them from each other's sight.

Jessa took a seat in the waiting room and began filling out the forms, quietly mouthing the words: "And I'm feeling good."

When Jessa walked inside her home she paused in the doorway. It was back to being spotless and beautiful. All signs of whatever her mother's crazy drove her to do was gone. Everything was still. Quiet. Winifred had taken Delaney to a nearby park, and Valeria was done for the day. Jessa kicked off her heels before jogging up the stairs and then walking down the hall to pause at the open door to her mother's bedroom.

"I'm free," she whispered with a small smile, glad for Darla's absence.

She entered and walked around, pulling everything from the dresser drawers before searching odd places she'd thought would expose all the secrets her mother held. She was disgusted by the bag of dirty underwear, remembering how her mother used to live in filth like a hoarder back in her apartment in Harlem. This was yet another sign that her mental illness had once again taken control.

The discovery of the pills she'd been hoarding inside the tip of one of her shoes truly baffled her. Keeping them there instead of easily flushing them was like mocking her. To have some convoluted sense of control in a life where she felt she had none.

Crazy ass.

At the rear window, Jessa paused and looked out at the afternoon sun high in the sky creating a beautiful landscape. She pushed the window open, wanting to invite in the fresh air, and the sounds of jazz music in the distance reached her. It was fast and up-tempo, reminding her of the Sundays she used to spend with Aria, Renee, and Jaime's brunch at one of their favorite restaurants that had a live band.

To hell with them, too.

Wanting distance from the memories, she reached to pull the window closed. She paused when she spotted the elderly man in his backyard across the street, tapping his foot in time to the music as he refilled his snifter from a tall bottle of some brown liquor.

"She went walking around the block."

Jessa shook her head, remembering Winifred's words about her mother's location while she and Hammer were on their sham of a honeymoon. So clearly, she could envision her mother standing at this very same window plotting on that old man, his liquor, and who knew what else. *Slick ass.*

She closed the window and left the room, closing the door on her involvement in her mother's life once and for all.

Ding-dong.

She made her way down the stairs, acutely aware that she still looked and smelled like the day before. "Who is it?" she asked, her hand on the doorknob.

"It's me. Hammer. Open up, Jessa. Let's talk."

Her hand went up to her neck to lightly stroke the dark bruises that remained from his tight grip. *He cheated on me, fucked my daughter—knowingly or unknowingly, and then assaulted me because he couldn't take my payback.*

"I asked you not to come here again, Hammer. We're through," she said, her eyes glittering as she reached for her iPhone in the pocket of her red pantsuit. "Please leave me and my business alone."

Another pause.

"Your business?"

She arched a brow. "Did I need to say the words 'you're fired' for you to understand that?"

She dialed 9-1-1.

"I love you, Jessa," he said, knocking on the door.

She moved away from it as the dispatcher answered. "Yes, I need the police to my home. My soon-to-be ex-husband is here. I'm afraid. I don't want to be hurt anymore. I'm tired of being beat upon. He refuses to leave."

"Is he inside the home?"

Knock-knock-knock-knock.

"No, I'm safe inside, but I would feel better if the police came and talked to him before he breaks in or something," she said, feeding false fear into her voice as she rolled her eyes.

"Jessa, open up and let me talk to you face-to-face, baby, please—"

She moved close to the door, leaning back against it. "Leave me alone, Hammer, please! I asked you not to come back here after you choked me," she said, her voice loud and expressing a fear she did not feel.

"I was so mad. I'm sorry for that," he said through the door.

"He choked you?" the operator asked.

Jessa arched a brow. "Yes, the other day. I'm so afraid," she whispered. "Lord, please tell the police to hurry."

She turned and kicked her door several times.

Thud-thud-thud.

"I think he's trying to knock the door down. Oh God, hurry, please, hurry," she said, suddenly longing for a cigarette to cap off the drama.

"Please stay on the line with me, Ms.—"

"Bell," Jessa supplied.

The wail of sirens soon filled the air.

"I think I hear the police," she said, turning to look out the peephole just as a cop car turned up her driveway. "Yes, it's them. Thank you so much."

Jessa ended the call and opened the door just as a male and female officer stepped from their vehicle.

Hammer had turned to eye them, but turned back to look at her in shock. "Really, Jessa, the police?" he asked.

Her eyes were brimming with insolence as she stroked her neck. "Yes, really," she said, giving him a look of pure malice before she changed her expression and fought to fill her eyes with crocodile tears.

"Sir, step away from the door," the male officer said, his hand already on his holstered weapon.

Hammer immediately held up both hands and turned to face them. "I am unarmed," he said.

"We'll be right with you, miss," the cop said.

She nodded, looking forlorn as the red and blue lights of the siren silently played against her face. Hammer was walked over to the back of a police car as she slumped down to sit on the door saddle.

A uniformed female police officer walked over to her. "Are you okay?" she asked.

Jessa looked up at her, purposefully extending her neck. "Yes, we split up and I've asked him to stay away from here—"

"What caused those bruises?" she asked.

"He did the other day," Jessa said, closing her eyes and letting tears fall as she continued to stroke her neck. "He choked me. I didn't call the police, though. I never did when he gets that way."

"What way?"

"He beats me when he's mad," Jessa exaggerated.

"I need to take photos of those," she said.

Jessa nodded as she rose, following the officer's directions to turn and hold still as she took pictures with her cell phone. In the distance she saw the moment Hammer looked over at them and did a double take before he shook his head and looked downward.

All she could see as she looked at this man she once loved, trusted, and built her dreams upon was the sight of his buttocks clenching and releasing as he thrust inside another woman. His lies, deceit, and disrespect nearly stifled her.

I hate him.

They stared at each other as the officers conferred, and when the male officer walked over and asked Hammer to turn and place his hands behind his back, Jessa wondered if he regretted every moment he lied and used her.

"Ms. Bell, your husband is being arrested for assault. We do suggest that you pursue a restraining order to ensure he does not continue to bother you."

I guess getting a quickie divorce in the Dominican Republic is out.

The rest of her words faded into the background as she watched him give her one last look over his broad shoulder before the cop palmed the back of his head and pushed it down as he was placed inside the police cruiser.

His destruction was the easiest. He'd handed it to her.

How could I resist?

She took the card the officer handed her with the incident number to identify the case report. As the car pulled away, she tapped the card against her cheek and turned to enter her home without another look back.

★　★　★

After a long bath and change of clothes, Jessa felt rejuvenated. She pulled her hair up into a tight topknot and slipped on her black Gucci frames that matched the lightweight fitted black tee she wore with wide-leg pants and patent leather Louboutin flats. She finished off the outfit with her platinum and diamond jewelry and watch.

As she applied her bright red matte lipstick in the mirror, she knew the woman in the reflection had changed. Gone were any illusions of happiness.

I see you happy, my Jessa, and that makes me so happy for you. I don't care what anyone says, I know that you deserve it after everything you have been through.

She smirked and shook her head, using the pad of her pinkie to clean any lipstick that overlapped her mouth. Happiness wasn't one of the cards she was dealt in life, but she was taking back control and swore she would never feel such pain again.

"Never again," Jessa swore, turning from the mirror and tossing her iPhone inside her black Chanel bag.

Mama, save me.

"Shit," she swore, reaching into the bag for the cell phone she'd just dropped in it to dial Georgia's number. It went straight to voice mail.

"This is Georgia. No essays or soliloquies, please."

What to say? Jessa was at a loss. She shook her head and ended the call, dropping the phone back in her pocketbook and grabbing the bag by the handles before she left her bedroom suite and made her way down the hall. She wanted to say the right thing. Make it better for her. In the past she would have turned to Bible verses and prayer for clarity. She refused to lean on that falsehood again.

There was a time when fear of hell dictated her life. Now she didn't believe in the heavens and the only hell she acknowledged was the one burning inside her.

Revenge was her fuel, and she was brimming over with

the need to feast upon it. Although Georgia had infiltrated her life and plotted to destroy her, Jessa held no ill will against her. She was a distraction—a door to emotions and regrets Jessa was unable to handle. She needed focus.

Georgia Coletti was not on her list, but plenty more were.

Jessa left her house and drove to Manhattan in silence. Her thoughts were full. Her schemes were wicked.

She pulled into her parking spot and leaned forward to peer through the windshield at a note tucked between the wall and a metal pipe. She grabbed her phone and briefcase before exiting, taking the steps to lead her to the wall to retrieve the note. "Come see me. H.," she read aloud, before shaking her head and tucking the note into the side pocket of her bag.

It was clear Mr. Halston was in need of more.

Do I even have the time?

She'd only come to the office to retrieve files she needed. Sex hadn't been on the agenda.

Jessa stepped on the elevator along with two men and a woman, all in business attire. She looked down at the panel of numbers as the door closed before finally pressing the button for the twelfth floor. *Why the hell not?*

And when the lift slid to a stop on that floor, she bit back a mischievous smile as she made her way to his offices. There was the same high-energy, almost frenetic pace of his employees. The receptionist eyed her as she came to a stop in front of her desk. "Mr. Halston, please," she said coolly.

"Do you have an appointment?"

"Not at all," Jessa replied, giving her a chilly smile. "Ms. Stranger, please. *If* he's available."

"One moment."

Jessa crossed the area to set her bag in one chair and bend her body to sit in another.

"You can go right in," the receptionist said, before Jessa could press her bottom to the seat.

She nodded and grabbed her things. "I guess I didn't need an appointment after all. Thanks, dear," she said mockingly as she passed her desk and opened the door to the conference room.

Mr. Halston was already standing in the open doorway of his office sans a jacket with his tie loosened around his neck and a stylus pen tucked behind his ear. "You got my note?" he asked, walking back inside the office and smiling in pleasure as she closed the door and strolled toward him.

"I did," she said, pausing to rise on her toes and press her cheek to his as she stroked the front of his zipper. She looked up at him and bit her bottom lip. He was already hard.

"Well, damn, Mr. Halston," she whispered, her words coating his lips.

He wrapped a strong arm around her waist and held her body close to his. "I can't get you off my mind," he said before pressing his face against her neck and kissing her there.

Jessa shivered, dropping her bags to the floor as she tilted her head back and ran her fingers through his blond hair. She tugged the silky ends, lifting his head and meeting his eyes with her own. "Did you wish it was me when you were fucking your wife last night?" she asked.

His eyes smoldered. "I haven't touched her since I had you," he said.

She pouted. "Why? Her pussy not as good?" she asked, stepping out of his embrace to step out of her shoes and remove both her pants and her lace thong.

"Hell no," he admitted emphatically.

"Pants off," Jessa ordered him as she walked over to his desk to roll the chair from behind his desk to the center of the office. She patted the seat for him. "Condom."

Mr. Halston rushed to pull out his wallet and retrieve

protection before dropping his pants and boxers down around his tanned ankles and atop his handmade Italian shoes.

"Sit."

He did. His erection pointing toward the ceiling.

Jessa straddled his lap, rising onto her toes and reaching between their bodies to guide his hardness inside her with a hot little gasp. He moaned in pleasure at the feel of her as he jerked her T-shirt and bra up above her breasts and sucked one brown nipple deeply. She squatted up and down on him, enjoying the feel of him and their salacious act there in his office as the afternoon sun shone through the window onto their bodies.

It was hot and frenetic and just what she needed.

She was so aroused that her clit ached and her nipples throbbed as she closed her eyes and rode him, alternating between up-and-down motions and slow grinds of her hips that brought the base of his dick against her spot.

"Am I the first black girl you ever fucked?" she asked him in a hot whisper, entwining her fingers behind his strong neck as she leaned her upper body back to look at him.

"Yes," he admitted, bringing his hands up to gently stroke her nipples as he thrust his hips upward to deepen the length of him inside her.

Jessa cried out as her body rolled.

"Shit, you're beautiful," Mr. Halston swore, his dick hardening inside her. "Please don't make me cum yet."

So. Damn. Good.

Jessa released him and turned her body on his dick so that her back was to him before moving her hips back and forth, sending her core gliding across the length of him to press her walls against him when she reached the smooth, round tip.

He cried out, pressing kisses to her spine as he snaked his hands around her body. One gripped a full breast and teased her nipples between his fingers, while the other stroked down across her stomach to bury his fingers against her moist and throbbing clit in sweet circular motions that made her entire body quiver in anticipation.

Damn, white boy. Damn.

She wanted to cum on him so very badly. Warm him. Wet him. Clutch her walls against him.

"I love your pussy," he moaned against her back with a grunt of pleasure that came from deep within him. "Shit!"

Beep.

She felt his face swipe against her back as he looked over his shoulder.

"Mr. Halston, your wife is here to see you," his receptionist said via the intercom.

Jessa was too close to her climax to even *think* about stopping. "Let her wait," she gasped, biting her bottom lip as she rode him. Harder. Faster.

He backed the chair toward his desk. "Tell her I'm wrapping up a meeting and will be right out," he said before releasing the intercom button.

Jessa flung her head back and giggled in pleasure. "Should I stop?" she asked, reaching for his hands to put them back on her body. Her breasts. Her clit. His touch would intensify her nut.

"Hell no."

"Fuck her?" she asked, looking back over her shoulder at him.

"*Fuck* her," he emphasized.

Moments later they both softly cried out as they came together, both working their hips to satisfy themselves until their climaxes receded and nothing was left to feel.

Jessa's legs were wobbly and she stumbled a bit when she climbed off him. "Damn," she swore, fighting to find the energy to put on her clothes, her extremities still trembling.

"It's nice to meet you, Ms. Bell," he countered as he stood as well and removed his filled condom to drop it into the wastepaper basket.

She couldn't hide her surprise.

"My receptionist recognized you and knows you have an office in the building and wondered if I was working on renovating it for you," he explained as he bent to pull up his pants and boxers.

Nosy bitch.

He knew who she was. The fun for Jessa was the anonymity, and now that was lost.

They finished dressing in silence and left the office together.

Jessa's steps faltered when she saw his wife sitting in the conference room. She was a tall and waiflike stylish blond with bright emerald eyes. The woman gave her a friendly smile as she came over to press a kiss to her husband lips. Jessa cleared her throat.

"Darling, this is a new client of mine, Jessa Bell," Mr. Halston said, his hand now on his wife's lower back. "Ms. Bell, my wife, Elizanne."

"Very nice to meet you, Elizanne," Jessa said, her eyes going from him to her as she extended her hand to the woman.

"I hope you're satisfied with Halston Architecture," Elizanne said.

"Oh, *very* satisfied," Jessa stressed, a little taken aback by his calmness. "Enjoy your lunch."

He is slick as hell.

Jessa walked to the door.

"How's the love of my life?" he asked.

Jessa paused with her hand on the handle.

"In need of a little *attention*," his wife said, so low that Jessa almost didn't hear her.

"Last night wasn't enough?"

The shared a soft laugh that spoke of intimacy.

She turned in the doorway. "Wow, you're really amazing, Mr. Halston," she said.

"What's that?" he asked, still calm, cool, and collected.

Elizanne's face was mildly inquisitive as she smoothed her hand against his tie.

"That you have the stamina to have fucked your wife last night, fucked the hell out of me few minutes ago, and you plan to fuck her again tonight," Jessa said, enjoying as she watched his face lose its composure and Elizanne's hand tightened around his tie until her knuckles were truly white. She applauded as she sighed and bowed to him mockingly. "You are amazing."

"What?" Elizanne gasped, looking up at him with a wide-eyed stare.

"If you don't believe me, check his garbage for the condom," Jessa said. "It's *very* full."

"Elizanne," he roared when she roughly pushed past him to enter his office.

Moments later her cry of anguish pierced the air.

"Lie to your wife, Mr. Halston, but *never* to me," Jessa said. "It's a pity because you really do have an amazing dick that I'm going to miss...unless you want to *reconnect* once things cool off."

"You bitch," he snapped, his eyes filled with fury.

"No, no, no. You *black* bitch," she reminded him gently before she left the conference room and closed the door behind her.

Chapter 14

Same day

Jessa gave Mr. Halston and his wife not one other thought as she left Halston Architecture and made her way down the hall to take the elevator to her own offices on the twentieth floor. She went to the restroom and cleansed herself with rough paper towels and the commercial soap from the dispenser. "Now *this* a ho bath," she said to her reflection in the mirror over the sink before quickly avoiding looking into her own eyes.

She moved quickly to her office and called her favorite car service for a chauffeured SUV before turning on her computer to print off hard copies of the files she needed. With a flourish, she used her personalized stationery to draft a personalized note. "Wu-Tang ain't the only one not to fuck with," she said, grabbing the still-warm papers from the printer in her office before she eased the stack and the note into her tote.

She cut the lights and left the offices of Mistress, Inc., locking the door securely before she hurried to the elevator, pressing the button for the lobby floor and not the parking garage. When the elevator zoomed past the twelfth floor, she chuckled at the trouble she'd caused. *Being bad again feels so damn good.*

The stylish and modern lobby was bustling with activity as she moved easily through the crowd to exit the building through the automated glass doors. A chauffeur standing in front of an all-black Tahoe awaited her with her name on a sign. She moved toward him, offering the short and stout driver in a black suit a polite smile.

"Ms. Bell?" he asked, turning to open the rear door for her when she nodded.

Jessa slid on the seat and immediately retrieved the first file, flipping through the pages until she found Hammer's report detailing the daily activities of Horatio Montgomery. "Cigarros, please," she said, speaking of the eighty-year-old private cigar club known for its Dominican and Cuban tobacco products and its exclusivity.

"Yes, ma'am."

As the driver easily maneuvered through the congested traffic, she settled back against the plush leather seat, focusing her attention on the hustle and bustle of the city to keep her thoughts from wandering, from thinking of those she had already chosen to leave behind. To forget the years she had fought so hard for redemption, begged for forgiveness, and accepted disrespect.

I played myself for the fool. Time and time again.

"Ms. Bell."

She turned her head, surprised to find the vehicle was double-parked and her driver stood there with the passenger door wide open. Shaking her head a bit, she gathered her tote and accepted his hand as she climbed from the SUV. "Thank you. I shouldn't be any more than ten or twenty minutes," she said.

Jessa paused to take in the sight of the three-story red-front building with its brass adornments. It was decidedly different from a lot of the more updated designs of the towering buildings on the street, but appeared more regal and respected than out of place. She approached the building and gave the uniformed doorman a stiff smile as he blocked her entrance to the red-frame glass door.

"I would like to meet with Mr. Horatio Montgomery, who is a member here," she said, reaching inside her tote to withdraw her handwritten note to hand to him. "Please give him this for me."

The doorman took the note with a stoic expression and entered the building, securing, shutting, and locking the glass door behind him. He was back within minutes, unlocking the door and pushing it wide for her to enter.

"Right this way," a tall woman in all black said to her with a slight wave of her hand.

Jessa barely took note of her dim surroundings, the wooden interior that seemed a throwback to another century. She glanced back over her shoulder and noticed the glass in the mirrored doors was one way, and the busy back-and-forth pace of New Yorkers was clearly shown to the men sitting in the club chairs that were staged in groups of four around the first level of the cigar shop. She inhaled the scent of the cigars, not finding the smoky interior a bother, as she was led past different brass-trimmed glass cases housing pipes, ornate lighters, and humidors.

This was a place ideal for serious business discussion in a casual atmosphere.

And what I have to discuss with Mr. Montgomery is very serious.

She was well aware of the wealthy, elderly men in their tailored suits staring at her through the haze of fifty-dollar cigars and over the rims of their snifters filled with expensive liquor. She ignored them all as she was led to a trio of soft camel leather club chairs nearly hidden beneath a wrought iron stairwell leading to the upper level.

Jessa eyed the two men sitting there with their eyes on her. She immediately recognized them from Hammer's surveillance. The tall one with smooth skin nearly as dark as a midnight sky and neatly groomed stark white hair and beard was Horatio Montgomery. The other, his attorney, was a fair-skinned balding man with freckles and a broad build that could only be described as barrel-chested.

She took the third seat, setting her tote on the seat beside her. "Thank you for agreeing to see me, Mr. Montgomery," she said, leveling her gaze directly on him.

"You made it difficult to ignore you after this," he said in a deep and rich voice as he tossed her note onto the center of the table.

She eyed it and then shifted her eyes up to refocus her gaze on him. She knew what it said.

I have proof your wife is planning to divorce you.

"That was the point," she said, reaching inside her tote for the copy of his wife's folder. She dropped it atop the note. "I didn't appreciate your wife using my business to plot against you, Mr. Montgomery."

"Horatio," he offered as he picked up the file and began to read through it. Montgomery's face soon filled with disbelief and then a hint of sadness.

Jessa knew that in that moment, the man's heart was broken and his belief in his wife shattered. She connected to exactly how he felt. The disappointment. The hope lost. The shattered dreams.

Fool. Don't worry, you're not the only one.

"Is your business...legal?" Horatio asked, shifting in his chair as he crossed his legs and then shifted the crease of his pants.

Jessa gave him a slick smile, aware of what he was asking in the politest way possible, before she looked over her shoulder and motioned for the nearby server to come to her. "I'll have whatever the gentlemen are drinking," she said.

"One thing about words is that they're varied. They can

mean many things. Like yellow can be lemon or butter or saffron, but in the end it's still yellow," she said, pausing to accept the drink from the server and take a sip. It was an aged brandy, and smooth. "So, being asked if my business is *legal* is a trussed-up way to ask me if I'm a whore. Let's not play with semantics, gentlemen."

Jessa finished her drink and pulled her credit card from her wallet to hand the server. "Let me be clear," she stressed, standing with her phone in hand to quickly turn her back to them and take a selfie with them both clearly in the background, "my business is very legal. My soon-to-be ex-husband served as my private investigator. Neither my agents nor I are whores. I married for love and not for money, unlike your scurrilous wife, who I suspect is trying to backdoor a private prenuptial agreement between you."

The look the men shared told her she was correct.

She gave them a frosty smile as she signed her bill on the tray the server held. "One thing about whores. Some sell their pussy on the street. Some take calls and deliver the pussy. And some *really* put on a show and pretend to be the good wife when they marry strictly for money. A whore is a whore is a whore."

She turned to leave.

"Ms. Bell, could you wait one minute?" the attorney asked.

Horatio had risen and was on his phone with his back to them.

She paused before facing them again. "Why? To receive more insults?" she asked.

"No," Horatio said, turning to reclaim his seat. "To give me the opportunity to close my wife's credit and bank accounts before you gloat to her about your payback, Ms. Bell."

Jessa chuckled and did a mock applaud.

"I presume that's why you took the photo."

"Absolutely," she assured him.

He gave the attorney a look, and he immediately rose to take his leave.

Horatio extended his hand toward the seat the man had vacated. She eyed it before she crossed the small space to sit down. "My apologies for insulting you," he said.

Jessa inclined her head but remained quiet as she watched him relight his cigar.

"I mistakenly hoped I could reclaim some of my wounded pride by buying some time between your thighs," he said, resting his eyes on her.

"Listen, old man, there would be nothing between these thighs of mine but a heart attack for you," she said, her tone soft and slightly mocking.

He chuckled, exposing bright white teeth that gleamed against his dark lips.

"I have done many things in my lifetime, but sell pussy was never one of them," she said, reaching over to take his cigar from his mouth to clamp between her lips.

"I think you'd make a fortune," Horatio said.

She tilted her head back and blew a stream of thick smoke through pursed lips. "I agree."

"Every man in this place is eyeing you, Ms. Bell."

Jessa lowered her head and looked around, confirming what he said. "There's something about women's lips and phallic objects in public," she explained, handing him back his cigar now stained with her crimson lipstick.

"I haven't been with another woman during my entire marriage," he said, his voice regretful. "It seems fidelity is outdated."

"You think she's cheating?" Jessa asked.

He nodded. "Don't you?"

Jessa nodded as well. "Yes, I just didn't get a chance to prove it."

"Probably some young cat with a strong back and no damn money."

She leaned in and tilted her chin toward him. He blew a thin stream of smoke toward her nostrils and mouth. She inhaled it all. "They were working on the money part," she reminded him, as she exhaled.

His grip on the cigar tightened.

"Can I offer you some advice?" she asked, leaning back in her chair. "Don't cheat and risk losing a good chunk of your money behind some kitty-cat. Get rid of her ass first. Once you're all good and divorced—or at least legally separated— than you find you some young, supple pussy to pump away *all* your frustrations."

"Thank you, Ms. Bell," he said, settling back in his chair with a melancholy expression.

"Jessa," she offered as she rose to her feet. "I have to go. I have a meeting I don't want to miss."

He looked up at her.

"Good-bye, Horatio," she said.

"Not good-bye, see you later," he said, with a smile that did not overshadow the sadness in his eyes.

"Perhaps, Horatio, perhaps," she said as she walked away from him.

Bzzzzz...

She looked down at her phone. An AirDrop notification. "Horatio's iPhone would like to share contact information. Accept or decline?" she read, shaking her head at the wonders of modern technology as she accepted his info and also sent hers to him.

Her car service was waiting for her when she exited Cigarros. By the time she reached the vehicle, the driver had already exited the driver's seat and come around the car to hold the door open for her.

"Where to next?" he asked, once back behind the wheel.

"One second," she said, lowering the rear mirror so that the door to Cigarros was in her background before she FaceTimed Bella Montgomery.

Her image soon filled the screen. Jessa was instantly able to make out she was in Saks Fifth Avenue. "What has taken so long for you to return my calls?" she asked.

Jessa pouted, ready to relish the moment. "Are you shopping, Bella?" she asked.

"As a matter of fact, I am," she said.

"Well, unless you have cash, I wouldn't skip my ass to the counter," Jessa said, enjoying the look of confusion filling the woman's eyes.

"Excuse me?"

"I just left a meeting with your husband, Horatio, here at Cigarros." She moved her head out of the frame and showed the building. "I told him how you're trying to backdoor your prenup by setting him up, and he canceled your card and froze your bank accounts. Trust me, ain't nothing there, darling."

Bella gasped before she ended the connection.

"She'll call back," Jessa said, sure the woman was checking her online accounts.

"Driver, head toward Bedford, New York. I'll give you directions once we're closer," Jessa said as she closed the window and leaned back in her seat as he merged the vehicle with a break in the busy traffic.

She pulled out her tablet and stylus, drawing a red line through Bella Montgomery's name. "Driver, could you turn on a little air?" Jessa asked as she added Mr. Halston's name to the list and then proceeded to draw a line though that as well. *Collateral damage. Fuck it.*

Bzzzzzz . . .

She turned her phone over in her lap, chuckling as she picked it up and accepted the connection as she set her iPad to record. "Was I right, Bella? I hope you have cash on you. Then again, it's not the best time to go on a shopping spree," Jessa teased.

The woman was livid and that was clear. "You treacherous,

low-life, red-lipped, deplorable-ass trick!" she screeched, her tone high-pitched.

Jessa held the iPad with one hand and the phone with the other. "Just so we're clear, you fucked with the wrong one, Bella," she said, her tone hardening with coldness. "And I hope I get called in to testify because my—what was it again—treacherous, low-life, red-lipped, deplorable ass will be *right* there."

Bella licked the gloss from her lips. "Do you understand what you have done skulking after my husband with your files and worrying about our private prenup?" she asked, shaking her head. "What proof did you have? That I tried to make sure my husband wasn't cheating on me, so I tested him? Whoopee-fucking-doo, Jessa. You played your hand too soon, bitch, you have to know when to hold them and when to fold them."

Jessa squinted at the change in her demeanor and the tone of her voice—nothing like what she presented herself to be when she first came to Mistress, Inc., months ago. "Once we caught on to your bullshit, Bella, I sent my dog after you, and your husband is very aware that you're fucking his attorney," she said, calling her bluff and making sure the iPad recorded her reaction.

Bella's breathing became labored and she looked shocked. *Got 'em.*

"Your husband knows it all. And I took great pleasure in being the one to deliver him the nail to hammer into your coffin," Jessa gloated.

"You have destroyed my life," Bella said between clenched teeth. "And if you think I'm going to let you get away with this, then you are one dumb-ass little bitch."

Jessa tapped her nail against the screen. "Listen, I have to go, and you can't afford any more of my time anyway," she said with a slight shrug of her shoulders before she ended the call.

She made sure to block Bella's number before pulling up Horatio's info and calling him.

"That was quick," he said, when he answered.

"New developments," she said, momentarily taken aback at how his voice was richer and deeper in her ear. "Have you spoken to Bella?"

"No, not yet, my attorney advised against it until we get some more things in order."

"It didn't stop him from calling her and telling her about the file I gave you," she said, sending him the video she'd recorded of Bella. "I lied and told her I gave you proof of her affair with your attorney, and she didn't deny it on the video. I'm sure if you put the right pressure on his ass, he'll tell it all to save his license."

"I can't believe this shit."

"Life is a no-good, bald-headed, toothless son of a bitch, Horatio," she drawled, noticing the driver's eyes on her in the rearview mirror.

He quickly looked away.

"Good luck with everything, Horatio," she said before ending the call.

"Boy, you are hell, Ms. Bell," the driver said, shaking his head in wonder.

Jessa arched an eyebrow. "Humph, yes the *fuck* I am."

Forgive me. He u-u-u-used me. My mama enemy is my enemy, right, M-m-m-mama?

Jessa wanted so badly to reclaim the distance between herself and Georgia, but it seemed during any moment of extended quiet her thoughts turned to her.

Mama, save me.

Jessa reached for her phone, looking for a diversion. It was on Do Not Disturb with only calls from Winifrid allowed through, and there were a few notifications of calls she'd avoided that were sent straight to voice mail. She called her attorney back first. It rang just once before he answered.

"You're really working me for that monthly retainer fee, huh?"

"Just trying to balance out the times I pay you to do nothing at all," she countered.

He chuckled. She did not. "I don't have time for chitchat, Mr. Nitzan," she said, her tone curt.

He sighed, ever good-natured, which camouflaged his shrewdness and made many people underestimate him. "Just yesterday I was Nadav," he said wistfully. "Okay, let's see. Your husband was granted bail and your temporary restraining order was issued. He should be processed and released within the hour. As soon as he steps outside of the jail, he will be served with the divorce papers. Now, I did want to make it clear that this charge and the TRO may be enough for him to lose his private investigation license in the state of New York."

"And? Fuck him. Next," she said, pulling out her tablet and making notes to her hit list.

"Keegan's attorney has reached out to me, and she plans to go forward with a lawsuit against you, but I sent him a copy of the business's operating agreement clearly outlining that once her initial investment was repaid to her, she in fact is considered an employee although she receives the same percentage of payout. Hopefully, that will cool her heels."

"Seems like she should have hired him before she signed the agreement. Next."

"Based on the video footage from the spa of Mrs. Hall, I suggest you file a police report, and with that I would be able to also secure a TRO against her," he said.

"Don't worry about her right now. I got her," she said, reaching over to pat her bag. "But send me a copy of that footage."

"Jessa, I wouldn't advise you reach out to the Halls, even with the upper hand. A misstep could severely hurt you and put them back in the position to sue for visitation rights with your daughter."

"Yeah, you're right," she said, even as the SUV pulled to a stop in front of the Halls' beautiful two-story brick home on the Lake Valley Golf Course.

"Last thing. Jaime Hall—"

"I'll call you back, Nadav," she said, ending the call.

Forgive me. He u-u-u-used me. My mama enemy is my enemy, right, M-m-m-mama?

"Right," Jessa said, eyeing their home through the window.

"You said something, Ms. Bell?" the driver asked, looking back at her over his shoulder.

She shook her head and opened the rear door, climbing out with her tote in hand. Jessa had no doubt Eric Hall Sr. was behind not only the reemergence of Georgia, but also the pumping up of her hatred of Jessa with bold-faced lies. He had refused to be bested and used her own child against her like a pawn in a game. For that he would pay.

Forgive me. He u-u-u-used me. My mama enemy is my enemy, right, M-m-m-mama?

"Park up the street," she said to the driver before shutting the door and striding up the street.

She cared not one bit about the picturesque surroundings. Inside their stately home with its flower boxes at each window and manicured lawns dwelled evil, but she was prepared to show them just how dirty life could get.

They too had to learn, like all the rest, that she was not the one with whom to start a battle. She was built for war.

As her car service pulled away she knocked on the door, ignoring the doorbell—that was too polite. Moments later the door opened, and she took pleasure in the look of shock on Kittie's face. "I need to speak with you and your husband," Jessa said. "Once and for all we need to handle this issue with *my* daughter."

"Bitch, go somewhere and die!" Kittie exclaimed, moving to close the door.

Jessa reached out and pressed her hand to the solid wood, stopping her. "Don't you want to know why your husband truly ceased pursuing custody of Delaney?" she asked.

Kittie's eyes blazed with her fury, but in the brown depths also lingered the doubts she obviously had.

Jessa gave her a mocking smile as she reached into her bag and withdrew the small teddy bear. "It's the nanny cam I used to record him the last time he came to my home to discuss Delaney," she began. "I was surprised he was alone. Were you surprised he left you behind?"

Kittie's eyes dropped to the teddy bear as she stroked the pearl necklace she wore with a pretty peach cardigan set. "What are you trying to imply? What lies have you come up with now?" she asked, her voice low and bitter as she shifted her gaze up to Jessa.

"I'm not trying to imply anything. That's why I have *proof*," Jessa said, pulling out her iPad and playing the video she already had cued. She held it up in front of Kittie for her to see.

It was grainy and in grayscale, but it gave a clear shot of the room as Jessa sat there and beckoned for him to join her in the living room.

"In here, Mr. Hall."

Jessa remembered so clearly her plan to shoot and kill them in the same room where their son had taken his own life. She had loved the irony of it. And now she closely watched every single emotion on Kittie's face as she closely watched the video.

"I wasn't looking to hear from you for a few more hours," he said.

"And your wife? Where is she this morning?" Jessa asked.

Kittie frowned a bit, and Jessa knew she saw the look her husband gave when she crossed her legs.

"She's at home getting Delaney's bedroom ready for her," he said.

Jessa remembered his cockiness. His confidence. He had been so sure she would sign the papers giving him custody of her daughter. *I had one snatched from my arms and there was no way I was handing another over so easily. I was ready to kill them with the same gun I have in my bag right now.*

Kittie coolly took in their argument over the unsigned papers, but her eyes widened and she gasped as Jessa pulled a gun from behind the pillows on the video.

"I would love nothing more than to kill you in the same room where your son killed himself. Have a fucking *seat," Jessa ordered.*

Kittie looked up at her with contempt. "You could have hurt him," she scolded.

"I meant to do *just* that," Jessa promised her.

"Do you understand that I would rather see you dead than have you raise MY CHILD?" Jessa asked.

"So you threatened him with death?" Kittie asked.

Jessa saw the reflection of her pressing the gun to Eric Sr.'s head in her eyes.

More played out. More angry words and bitter declarations. Jessa didn't need the video, she remembered like it happened yesterday.

And so her eyes became steely as she knew the next words from his mouth would destroy whatever illusion this woman had of her husband.

"I'll tell what you what. Sign the papers, put down the gun, and I'll forget you pulled this little stunt," Eric began. "Or you sign these papers, put that gun down, give me some of the good pussy I know you got and I'll let you visit your daugh—"

Kittie's face crumpled and her shoulders slumped under the weight of the truth. "Oh, Senior," she sighed in disappointment, turning away from the video as she pressed the side of her little fist to her mouth.

"There's more," Jessa egged her on.

"No more. I refuse to let you enjoy this," Kittie said, even as pain made her eyes appear glossy.

Jessa fast-forwarded the video to the part where she slapped him hard before she pressed the barrel against his dick.

"You talk a lot of shit when I'm the one with the motherfucking gun," she said, her anger clear.

Kittie turned and looked on, her eyes widening as her husband opened his legs and thrust his hips upward, causing the gun to stroke his privates.

"You are in between a rock and a hard place, Jessa. You don't want to go to jail and have those big dykes in there fucking you with broom handles and making you eat their pussy."

"Oh my God," Kittie wailed softly, the string holding her pearls together nearly snapping as she tugged upon them in obvious distress.

"I guess he wanted to know just what drove your son batshit crazy," Jessa said spitefully.

"Maybe there is another deal you and I can make," he said. "Give me a month—no, two months—of pussy on call and allow us to keep the baby once a month, and I'll convince Kittie to drop the lawsuit."

"Enough!" Kittie screamed, covering her ears with her trembling hands.

Yes, it was more than enough. Jessa turned off the video, sparing Kittie the sight of her allowing her husband to kiss her and fondle her pussy as he pressed her body down on the sofa.

Jessa remembered how in that moment she chose to forgo killing him because she wanted to see her daughter grow and teach her about men and the games they played. To one day give her child the wisdom and guidance she was never given. To help steer her from those same mistakes made by a little girl wishing for and missing her mother.

I want that for Georgia as well. I have to fight just as hard for her as I did for Delaney.

"What the hell is going on here?"

Perfection.

Jessa turned to find Eric Hall Sr. standing on the sidewalk in his golfing gear of plaid pants and polo shirt, glaring at her with such open hostility that she almost felt like stumbling back from it. Instead she gave him just as good as he gave it as she stepped out of the frame of the door to let him see his grief-stricken wife.

"Kittie, what's wrong?" he asked, dropping his leather golf bag onto the sidewalk and rushing up the stairs. He roughly pushed Jessa out of the way to reach his wife.

Jessa corrected her stance, looking on as Kittie reached her arm back until it was almost behind her and then swung, slapping him soundly.

Whap!

"Kittie!" he exclaimed, his cheek quickly reddening.

Jessa laughed.

"Get the hell away from us!" Kittie roared, looking past him and giving Jessa a glare like she wished it had been her that she hit.

This is not what she wants.

"No," Jessa said simply. "So you'll have to have your domestic squabble after I'm gone, because I am far from done with the two of you whack jobs."

Eric turned and got in her face. "I am not the one to fuck with, little girl," he said, his voice cold enough to evoke a chill of fear and intimidation.

If she didn't have the upper hand.

Jessa gave him a mocking smile. "I showed her the video," she whispered contemptuously as she matched his glare with her own.

In the quiet storm that brewed between them, Kittie's sobs filled the air.

His hands came up with a quickness to grip her neck.

Jessa brought her hands up to clutch at them, trying to dig

her talon-like nails in the soft flesh of his inner wrists and free herself. "You're just like your son. First you want to fuck me and now you want to kill me."

His eyes bulged as he tightened his grip.

Jessa felt the pressure against her windpipe. She was unable to swallow. Dropping her hands, she felt around inside her bag until her hand closed around her gun. She grunted as she pressed the muzzle against his gut with it still inside her bag.

Kittie cried out. "Stop it, Senior!" she wailed, coming over to wrap her hands around his arm.

He felt the barrel of the gun, and his mouth twisted in hate and anger just before he roughly pushed her away from him. "Bitch!" he snapped in disgust.

Jessa harshly gasped for breath.

"Call the police," Eric Senior snapped.

Jessa nodded as she swallowed and gulped in air. "Call them so I can show them this proof that you've been doing some insider trading during your retirement. You and Roderick Rivera would look really good in prison jumpsuits."

His body stiffened.

She chuckled and nodded. "That's right, you're not as slick as you think. I've been holding on to this little nugget just in case you stepped out of line, and you did just that when you turned my daughter against me, motherfucker," she said with contempt. "You are looking at a woman with nothing else to lose. No secrets to be held against me. No trump cards to be played. So, try me, *please*."

Jessa brushed her hair from her face as she walked down the stairs. Her heart pounded and her pulse raced as she took large breaths to steady her nerves and calm her anger. She turned to face them on the sidewalk and patted her purse. "This is the second time I spared your life. There won't be a third," she promised him before turning to walk up the street to her waiting car.

Her driver turned when she climbed into the car and

closed the passenger door. "Where to next?" he asked, his friendly demeanor in contrast to the explosive turmoil she had just faced and conquered.

He was oblivious.

She turned and looked through the rearview mirror just as Eric tried to wrap his arm around his wife's shoulders. Kittie roughly pushed away his show of comfort before entering the house and swiftly slamming the door in his face.

"You done for the day, Ms. Bell?" the driver asked.

"Not at all," she told him, turning to face forward as he drove them away.

As the SUV pulled to a stop in front of the red brick community center, she closed the file she had been studying and quickly checked her hair and makeup in her compact. She applied a fresh layer of crimson gloss before she pulled a stack of one-dollar bills from her wallet, folding and sliding them into the pocket of her pants. "I got it," she said to the driver, opening the door and exiting the car before he could leave his seat.

She settled her shades on her face as she made her way across the short sidewalk and opened the glass door leading into the building. The wood floor that spoke of the building's age was polished to a high gleam. The walls were painted a mint green that reminded her of schools. She ignored the glass cases filled with awards and plaques of local successes in sports and other activities as she made her way to the row of double doors with "Bedford Community Center" in faded bronze letters on the wall above it.

The space was wide open with no divisions and a modest stage on the far wall flanked by doors. The windows were frosted but still allowed the late afternoon sun to shine in on the floors with brightness. Metal chairs formed a circle in its center and a table with refreshments was just beyond, with a dozen or so people gathered around it. Some looked at her with open curiosity and others spoke with a nod or brief word before losing interest in her.

Jessa took a seat and crossed her legs, looking for her target. *He's not here.*

She decided to wait.

"Is this your first meeting?"

She pushed her shades atop her head and looked up at a full-figured dark-haired woman with skin almost the color of milk.

"Yes, I'm just observing. I'm not sure if it's for me," Jessa lied.

"I'm Olive," the woman said, extending her hand as she sat down.

"Jessa," she said, avoiding the woman's hand and giving her a stiff smile instead.

Olive shrugged and gave her attention to devouring an onion bagel. "You are going to be a *huge* trigger for some of these guys... and girls," she said, in between bites.

Jessa truly didn't care as she checked her watch.

"Good luck with your recovery."

"Olive, you talk too much. Would you mind moving?" Jessa asked, pointing at the other empty chairs in the circle.

The woman gasped in shock. "Wow, you're a megabitch," she said.

"Yes, I know. Bye-bye."

The door to the left of the stage opened and her eyes went to it as Olive gathered her snack and her purse and moved several seats down.

He's still fine as fuck, I see.

Jessa allowed herself to enjoy the sight of Pleasure strolling toward them. His body was still sculptured and strong, the navy button-up shirt he wore with faded denims unable to hide the physique that once made him a popular exotic dancer and skillful man-whore. His dreads were neat and pulled back from his handsome bronzed face. She could tell from the quality of his shoes, clothing, and watch that he was not suffering from his change of occupation.

She couldn't help the little moan she released as she remembered paying him well to go down on her. In the aftermath of her message to her friends all those years ago, she had wasted his tongue talent on just pissing Jaime off. She'd known Jaime was one of his most loyal clients.

Why didn't I fuck him? Silly, silly me.

"I apologize for running a little late," he said, clasping his hands together as he looked around at the small crowd with a grin.

His steps faltered a bit and his smile faded when his eyes landed on her. She arched a brow and offered him a nod of her head.

"If everyone will take their seats and let's get started," he said.

Jessa continued to stare at him, enjoying that he was unsettled by her sudden reappearance in his life. She bit her bottom lip as she gave him a sultry look.

"My name is Graham and I am a sex addict in recovery for a little over a year," he began, taking a deep swallow before he deliberately shifted his gaze away from her.

That's right. He goes by his real name now. Graham Walker.

Pleasure suits him better, Jessa thought, crossing her legs and leaning back against the uncomfortable metal chair as she continued to take in the beautiful male specimen.

"Hello, Graham," the group said in unison.

She looked around at the faces of the people in the circle. *I bet I'm not the only one who is here to get some Pleasure.*

"Um...uh...listen," Graham began, his face bewildered. "Will you all excuse me for a moment?"

Jessa looked to him as he rose to his feet and focused his attention on her.

"Can I speak to you in private, please?" he asked.

Now the fun begins.

"Sure," she said, rising to follow him.

Olive reached out to grab her wrist as she neared her. "I bet you two would have the most amazing sex ever," she whispered up to her, assailing her nostrils with the scent of onions on her breath.

"I think so, too," Jessa agreed before looking around at the group. She felt reckless, and it was a rush. "Does everyone else agree? Because I plan on doing just that right now."

A middle-aged woman with curly salt-and-pepper hair smiled and shook her head. "Oh, you remind of me myself. It wasn't healthy at all, but Jesus, it was *fun*," she stressed.

Several group members agreed and began retelling stories of clandestine sexual hookups in odd public places.

"Jessa!" Graham barked.

She walked away, leaving the excited chatter behind as she proceeded through the door he held open for her. The smell of his cologne was warm and spicy, and she inhaled deeply of it. "Tom Ford," she said, as she looked around at the oil paintings and charcoal sketches lining the wall of the spacious room.

"What?" he asked, adding confusion to the other myriad of emotions flittering across his handsome face.

She glanced back over her shoulder at him. "Your cologne is Tom Ford. Not sure which one, but definitely Tom Ford," she said, coming to a stop near a large easel right by the windows of the room.

The painting seemed to be of a rose but was actually a woman's vagina. "Is this mine?" she asked, aroused by the memory of his tongue stroking her to an explosive climax. "You've seen it up close."

"What do you want?" Graham asked.

"You," Jessa said, raising her hand to lightly stroke her neck. "I am here for you."

His brows furrowed.

"I want to finish what we started that day at my house in Richmond Hills."

He crossed his arms over his chest. "I'm out of the business."

"No business, just ... pleasure," she said softly, giving him a little wink at her clever wordplay.

"Please leave."

"No, not yet. I'm not done with you, Pleasure."

His face tightened, and she could tell he clenched his jaw.

She turned again and smiled, releasing a breath as she looked at a large charcoal sketch of Jaime's face. "If you're so obsessed with her, then why haven't you two spoken in a year?" she asked. "Does she know you're living right here in your hometown just a few miles from your mother? Did you invite her to your art show next month?"

"Are you stalking me?" Graham asked, his face incredulous.

"Don't be silly," she said.

Graham eyed her critically, remaining silent.

Jessa gave him an alluring smile and began to remove her shirt as she walked up to him. "Just the thought of how good you ate my pussy makes me want to cum. *So* good," she whispered over to him. "I could really use a good fuck session. You sure you can't backslide just once for me?"

He continued to study her face, his eyes never lowering to the sight of her breasts pressed against her lacy bra.

She reached out to stroke his crotch and press a kiss to the corner of his mouth. "My intel tells me it's been a long time since you got that big dick wet," she said, impressed by his length even at rest.

He knocked her hand away.

Her eyes lit with anger and she gave him a hard stare. "Now you have boundaries?" she asked, her tone slightly mocking before she turned and bent over at the waist to press her buttocks against his groin.

"Man, get the hell up off me and get outta here," he said in disgust, instantly stepping back from her.

Jessa turned to him as she reached in her pocket and

pulled out the stack of bills. "I was going to make it rain on you *after* we fucked, but you're so damn dedicated to your celibacy. So here it goes. There's more where that came from."

He remained stoic as the money floated in the air around him. Jessa giggled as she replaced her shirt, but a wave of anger and hurt about her marriage rose quickly, and the giggle turned to a small wail before she pressed her lips closed and covered her face with her hands.

She winced at an all-too-vivid memory of Hammer having sex with her daughter.

Get your shit together, Jessa.

"There is something wrong with you," Graham told her, frowning as he rubbed his hand over his mouth. "There always has been. Trust me, I've seen crazy, and you're not far from it."

Jessa dropped her hands from her face as she eyed him, her emotions swirling around her like a tornado. She chuckled. "The only thing crazy about me is my crazy good pussy," she told him.

He shook his head as he turned his lips downward into a frown. "Go away and don't come back with your selfish and devious bullshit trying to wreck my life and, in the meantime, jeopardizing the recovery of these people who don't know you and don't give a fuck more about you than I do. Get your crazy ass out of here and don't come back."

Jessa turned from him, looking around at his artwork again, and her eyes landed on Jaime's face. It was created with love, and she saw that emotion in the strokes of his charcoal. And it wasn't for show or to impress, but simply an expression of how he felt for her even during their separation.

She hated it. Her envy was palpable.

This was the love she foolishly thought she'd found in Hammer.

She strode over and picked up a paintbrush sitting in a

can of red paint, bringing her arm up across her face as if to deliver a wicked backhand blow.

He reached her in time and tightly gripped her wrist with one hand and jerked the paint brush away from her with the other.

"No better way to work off anger than a good sweaty fuck, Pleasure," she said, licking her lips as she eyed his mouth.

She so desperately wanted him to stop rejecting her, and it had nothing to do with sexual gratification or making her feel desired. It would take more than rejection from a man-whore to make her feel less than. He was nothing but a pawn. Something to be used toward strategizing a win against a foe.

The loss of her marriage had created a hunger for triumph. He released her and moved away. "I have to get back to the meeting," he said, dropping the brush back into the can and then wiping the small splatter on his hand away with a cloth.

"Your loss," she said, turning to walk to the door.

"Stay the fuck out of my life, Jessa Bell, I *mean* it," he said, his voice hard.

"Don't worry, the only use I had for you was your dick," she assured him, meaning to be low and insulting as she opened the door. "I mean, what more is there to you? You're just a big, dumb fuck. Not much better than a dildo. Good luck with trying to forget you were—and will always be—nothing more than a dick for hire."

She slammed the door to his little studio and quickly strode across the floor, dropping her shades back over her eyes. She had failed to seduce him. *What a waste of my fucking time.*

"How'd it go?" Olive called over to her.

"Fuck off, Olive!" she spat, not sparing her or the rest of the group another glance as she sped past them and out of the building.

Chapter 15

Same day

The skies were just beginning to darken in color. Late afternoon was transitioning into early evening. The streets were relatively busy with those trying to make it home from their jobs.

Jessa was still working.

It was time to go back to where it all began.

Bzzzzzz...

She picked her phone up from beside her on the rear seat. "What?" she said.

"Do you really believe it's worth destroying my life over an affair?"

"How long?" she asked, her voice soft.

"What?" Hammer asked.

"How long were you fucking her?" she asked.

"Jessa—"

She shook her head. "How long? How many times did you betray me?"

Hammer fell quiet.

"And don't lie because I already know. I just want to see if you if you have the truth in you," she lied.

"Jessa—"

"I'm hanging up," she threatened.

"The night at the restaurant right after she first got hired," he admitted. "You had on that short gold halter dress."

Jessa arched her brow as she remembered Lacey—Georgia—still in the bathroom when she left it and ran into Hammer. They had just shared a cigarette, an indulgence Jessa rarely shared with anyone, but the younger woman had known, proving her observation skills.

"Did you fuck her in that bathroom?" Jessa asked, closing her eyes as a vision of it flashed in her mind with heartbreaking clarity.

"Jessa—"

That's a yes.

Foolishly, she and Keegan had assumed it was the glamour and poise of Charli that had interested him as they watched the two talk during dinner, and all the while it was her daughter posing as sweet and innocent Lacey Adams.

"You came back to that table fresh off fucking another woman, probably still wet and smelling of her juices, not giving a damn that you were in my company," she said, the softness fading from her voice as it hardened with anger. "How was I so blind to your shit? How did the player get played?"

"I never deliberately meant to hurt you, Jessa."

"Shut up. Shut. Up. Shut. The. Hell. Up." She pressed the bridge of her nose with her fingers.

"I'm so sorry."

"Yes, you are sorry as *fuck*," she said with a low laugh that was mocking. "Don't worry, I don't have any more questions. I have no more fucks to give about you or your dick. I couldn't care less whether there were more women. It doesn't matter. One was enough, and especially the one you chose being my daughter."

"I will prove to you that I am the man you want me to be."

She shook her head. "You have already proven that you are the man I don't want," she said, reaching into her tote for her cigarette case and lighter.

"No smoking in the car, Ms. Bell," the driver said, his face apologetic.

"Pull over," she ordered.

He parked on the street outside a Laundromat, and she immediately climbed out to light her cigarette and take a deep inhale of it. "Let me be clear, Robert," she said, reverting to his given name. "This marriage is over, and you will not get one red cent out of me. In fact, you better hope my attorney can't figure out a way for me to take everything you have. I look forward to the day your ass is on a Greyhound bus headed back to Bumfuck, California, with your bitch of a mother—"

"Don't you ever disrespect my mother."

"Fuck her."

"Fuck *you*."

Jessa exhaled a long stream of smoke and tucked her iPhone between her ear and shoulder to applaud. "Nice to meet the real you, Robert Young," she said. "But your mother made me feel like I wasn't good enough for you. Ain't *that* some shit. No, fuck her and them tough-ass, no-seasoning-having chicken feet with the clumpy gravy. She can't cook and she can't raise a man right. The little old bitch. *Fuck* her. Fuck *her*."

"You *wish* your trifling ass could be my mother."

"I will tell you who I won't be is Mary, and you're not Kendu. This ain't California and that prenup is airtight."

"Don't push me, Jessa," he warned, his voice low and menacing.

"Don't push you to what? Choke me? You did that. Cheat on me? You did that, too. What's left?"

"If you think I'm gonna let you destroy my life and just skulk away like some punk instead of the grown man that I am, then, bitch, you just as crazy as everybody say."

Jessa tossed her head back and laughed from her belly. "Hey, Robert. Come on, be you, motherfucker. Don't front. You might as well get it off your chest because the sight of you fucking another woman took us to a place where there ain't no coming back from. I couldn't care less if you lose your license. I couldn't care less if you drop dead. Be gone. Deuces. Kick rocks on the way."

She ended the call.

Jessa took another draw of her cigarette, releasing a controlled stream into the night air as she quickly dialed his mother.

"Hello."

"Listen, LuBell," Jessa said, leaning against the passenger door of the car. "I just wanted to clue your ass in on the fact that your son got chickens of his own that came home to roost."

"Who is this?" she asked.

"You soon-to-be ex-daughter-in-law—"

"Ex? Well praise God," she sang out. "Hallelujah!"

Jessa arched her brow when she soon heard the clang of a tambourine and foot stomping. "While you celebrating to your God, ask him to send a vision of me walking in on your perfect son screwing another woman. He ain't shit, and he raised him to be that way."

The impromptu revival ceased.

"What you say, gal?" she asked.

"You heard me, LuBell," Jessa said, tossing the butt of the cigarette onto the street and crushing it beneath the pointed toe of her Cardi B red-bottom bloody shoes. "And ask him about that assault charge for choking me. Ain't you *ever* so proud, LuBell?"

"Your evil spirit has led my son down the wrong path—"

"My evil spirit told me to do this, LuBell," she said sarcastically, ending the call.

She looked up and down the length of the street. Her gaze landed on the sign for Premiere Wine and Liquor. Her mouth watered, hungering for not just the taste of alcohol but craving the effects. The anger she clung to; it was the soul-searing pain she wanted to escape. In that moment she understood a little bit better about just why her mother turned to alcohol and drugs to cope. She turned to open the door and retrieve her wallet. "Be right back," she said before heading down the street and into the store.

She returned with a large bottle of José Cuervo, climbing in the back before she opened the bottle and took a healthy swig that burned her throat as it went down. She gasped with wide eyes. The driver eyed her in the rearview mirror.

"You good?" he asked.

"I haven't been good for a *long* time," she said, feeling her world spin as she took another sip and pointed her finger forward, signaling for him to drive.

The liquor warmed her belly as she looked out at the streets of the community she once called home. When the driver turned the SUV down the road leading to the security gate of Richmond Hills, she was a ball of emotions she had been fighting so hard to squelch during the days since Hammer betrayed her and Georgia revealed herself.

"Hold up," she said, pulling out her phone to call Renee.

"Why are you calling me?" she asked.

"I have more information on your husband I wanted to give to you," Jessa lied with ease before taking another sip of tequila with a wince before she capped the bottle and set it on the seat.

Silence.

Jessa removed her compact mirror with lighting and tube of lipstick to touch up the matte red on her lips. She smoothed her hair up into her topknot and checked her brows.

"Where are you?" Renee asked.

"At the security gate," Jessa said, snapping the compact closed.

"Okay," she said.

"Driver, pull up to the gate, please," she sang to the beat of Beyoncé's "Partition."

He chuckled and nodded, acquiescing.

Jessa lowered the rear window as the vehicle slowed to a stop. "Jessa Bell . . . or Jordan, either way," she said.

"Yes, she just called," he said. "Go right ahead."

The gate opened.

"Little pig, little pig, let me come in," she said with a calculating smile, quoting the big bad wolf from "The Three Little Pigs" fable.

With the skies darkening, the lights lining the path leading around the curve to the first house in the subdivision made the view picturesque. She gave the driver directions to Renee's house, and soon he pulled up in front of the beautiful Mediterranean-style home.

Jessa looked up the street at the house she'd once owned with her first husband. For a moment she allowed herself to wish he had never passed away and left her behind. She had relied on him—perhaps too much—and once he was gone from her life, she had been twisting in the wind ever since.

Did you let me down like everyone else and I just didn't know it?

She pushed aside that train of thought. The very idea of that would push her completely over the edge, and she was clear she was already straddling the line as she welcomed the darkness in her soul that she had ignored over the last few years.

It was Renee who had permitted her entrance to the subdivision, but she focused her attention on Aria and Kingston's house. "Needs a paint job," she said, as she picked up her phone from the seat.

She waited. When her driver didn't leave his seat, she

cleared her throat and gave him a pointed look when he glanced back at her over his shoulder.

"Oh. Okay. My bad," he said, jumping out and coming around the vehicle to open the door. "I didn't know you changed your mind about the door opening thing."

"That's a woman's prerogative, driver," Jessa said as she exited, crossing the pristine sidewalk to take the steps leading up to the house.

The yard needs cutting, too.

"The struggle is real," she said aloud with a giggle as she rang the bell.

The door opened, and Aria's eyes instantly filled with hostility at the sight of Jessa. "What the hell do you want?" she asked.

Jessa gave her a slow and thorough once-over. "I really tried to do right by you boring basic bitches," she began. "Swallowed your insults and disrespect to make amends for my wrongs against you, but fuck that."

"So what you wanna do?" Aria asked, stepping down off the porch. "You act like you want that work. You can get it."

Jessa sighed but did not back down, so there were just inches between them. "Your house may be in the worst condition on the block, but you're not in the hood anymore, Aria. Elevate, boo. El-e-vate."

"Words of advice from your ho ass. Girl, bye."

Jessa was a lightweight with alcohol, and the effects of the tequila were already beginning to kick in. "Here's some more advice. Your husband and that dumb second practice of his is the reason your money looking funny, honey. Well, that and that bargain basement book you wrote," she said, laughing at her own wordplay.

"I know you fucking lyin'," Aria screamed, drawing the eyes of her neighbors who were lounging on their porches or enjoying a leisurely stroll through the subdivision.

"Aria, what's going on?" Heather Goines, Aria's mother,

came to the door to stand beside her daughter wiping her hands on a dish towel. She looked disappointed at the sight of Jessa.

Jessa eyed her hairdo with a slight frown. One side was shaven nearly bald and the other was as long as her chin with purple, fuchsia, and gold highlights. "I was just telling your daughter about her broke-ass husband and that second practice he need to strike a match to for insurance money."

Aria jumped at her, and Heather pulled her back. "The baby, Aria," she reminded her.

Jessa's eyes went down as Aria pressed a protective hand to her belly. "Wow, another baby with that womb you tore up with all those abortions, STDS, and trains you had run on you. Kudos, Aria, seriously," she said, with mock sincerity.

"I'll be glad when you're gone for good," Aria spat, before turning away from her. "Come on, Mama."

Heather looked at her with concern and pity in her eyes. "This ain't the way, Jessa, and you know it. You been down this destructive road before. Hurt people try to hurt people. The shit ain't cute. Not worth a damn."

Jessa released a breath and rolled her eyes.

"Now I'm asking you for the same respect I hope you give your mother, and leave my child alone," Heather said, her voice firm.

Mama, save me.

Aria had a mother to protect her.

Again, something in Jessa broke, and she dropped her head as tears rose. She shook it off, pressing her eyes with her fingers and wiping her tears viciously as she turned and jogged down the stairs and Heather closed the front door. She quickly composed herself as she buried her feelings once more. She was on a mission—retaliation was her fuel.

Her driver climbed from the car and rushed to hold the passenger door open.

She shook her head. "I'm not done yet," she said, holding

out her hand to him as she strode past the car and crossed the street headed for Renee's home. Midway there, she turned and headed back to the SUV to retrieve the bottle of tequila. She chuckled at her pettiness.

Bzzzzzz . . .

She checked her phone.

Hammer.

She answered. "You should be working on your résumé because when I get done with you, that PI license will be just as worthless as you are," she said. "Walmart *always* hiring."

She hung up on him before he could say anything.

Bzzzzzz . . .

She sent him to voice mail.

As she climbed Renee's porch, the front door opened. "I thought you changed your mind," Renee said, as she leaned in the doorway with her arms crossed over her chest.

"And miss the opportunity to share a drink with you while I tell you what I have to tell you?" Jessa said, holding up the bottle of liquor.

Renee eyed her with open hostility.

Jessa feigned shock. "Oh, that's right, you're an alcoholic in recovery—that's the right term, right, because I actually attended one of those addiction groups today and learned that word, so it's pretty cool to be able to use it with an actual addict," she said, taking a step forward toward the door.

Renee blocked her from entering the house. "My kids are home from college," she said, closing the door.

Jessa shrugged as she sat down on one of the rocking chairs lining the porch. She looked around and opened the bottle of liquor to take a small sip as she rocked. "I understand that," she said, crossing her legs. "The last thing you want is for your children to be around a bad influence and pick up habits."

"That's right," Renee said.

"It's just a shame it's a little too late for that since your daughter, Kieran, is experimenting with pills—I guess she has *your* addictive gene. And did Aaron tell you he's been to consultations to do a Caitlyn?" she asked, her voice cool and her eyes hard as she took dark pleasure in delivering her verbal blows.

Renee was shaken.

Jessa could see it and relished it, her smile slow and wicked.

She was surprised when Renee reached her with quick strides and backhanded her across the face, knocking her from the rocking chair. The smell of her tequila rose in the air as it poured from the open bottle onto the porch. She laughed as she unsteadily rose to her feet. "Still pretty," she said in a high-pitched voice, imitating Kimbella from the reality TV show *Love & Hip Hop.*

Nothing could hurt her. She was on a wave of reckless and hurtful behavior that felt deliciously fun.

"Get the hell away from my house and don't ever come near me or my family again, Jessa," Renee threatened her, pointing toward the stairs as if speaking to a disobedient child or a naughty dog.

The front door opened. Both Aaron and Kieran stepped out onto the porch. Their faces showed their surprise at seeing Jessa.

"Is everything okay, Ma?" Kieran asked.

Jessa picked up the bottle of tequila that lay on its side next to the tipped-over rocking chair. "Your mom and I was just talking about she's having an affair with your dad, who is now married to the same woman he left your mom for," Jessa said as she descended the stairs.

Renee gasped in shock.

"You will make a pretty woman," Jessa said, nodding as she eyed Aaron. "Good luck with the surgery."

"Come inside, Ma," Kieran said, trying to pull her mother in by her arm.

"I think the next husband you get shouldn't be okay with

living in a house another man paid for. That was clue number one he wasn't shit, Mrs. *CEO*," Jessa said mockingly as she backed her way across the street. "Oh, and in case you're still clueless, your hubby moved right out of your house—or Jackson's house—and in with his mistress."

"Somebody needs to do the world a favor and put you out of your misery," Renee said, her tone ominous.

Jessa held the bottle up in a toast as Renee shot her one last angry glare before finally following her children inside. "One more," she said, eyeing Jaime's home. "Just one more and this day can end."

She waved for the driver to follow behind her with the car as she walked down the street and climbed the stairs onto the porch. She tapped on the door with the bottle of tequila before sitting on a small wicker table between two chaise lounges. She felt slightly dizzy and closed her eyes, massaging her temples with her fingertips.

You're doing good, Jessa. Pay these bitches back for all the years you put up with their anger and let shit slide for the sake of your redemption. Fuck that and fuck them.

Fuck Hammer.

Fuck your crazy mama.

Fuck them all.

"I heard you were slinking around the neighborhood."

Jessa looked up at Jaime standing in the doorway, ever pretty and perfectly poised. She gave her a tight smile. "I won't be slumming much longer," she said.

"Care to explain these?" Jaime asked, holding up court papers.

Jessa looked around at the front of the house. "Yes, I'm suing you on behalf of my and Eric's daughter for half the value of this house," she explained, before taking a sip of tequila and wincing at the slight burn of it to her throat. "Your daddy's a judge, if you need help deciphering the big words."

"I told them you hadn't changed," Jaime said with con-temptuous eyes and a twist of her lips. "Same old Jessa Bell, maybe even worse from the stunts you pulled today. Just wrecking lives for no damn reason. I thought it was impossible to top the fuckery of the past, but you have done it."

Finish her.

"And when I saw Pleasure—I mean Graham—today, I told him to stop hiding from you and reach out," Jessa countered, with a lick of her lips. "Didn't he call? He might be busy, being back in business and all."

Her lies caused Jaime's complexion to pale a bit before she quickly recovered her equanimity. "You're a liar."

"No, I saw him today," she assured her. "It was good to see him . . . and feel him . . . and fuck him."

Sometimes a lie went even further than the truth.

"So, you always want my leftovers?" Jaime asked.

Jessa arched a brow and frowned. "Leftovers implied you ended it, and we both know that's not true. Right?" she mocked, chuckling. "He's ducking and diving you like Ali trying to avoid getting hit."

"Excuse me, ma'am."

Jessa turned to find the subdivision's security guard standing beside his small white pickup truck with the yellow lights flashing. "Yes, can I help you?" she asked.

"Yes, ma'am, we received a complaint that you were no longer authorized to be in the subdivision," the guard said, his hand on the top of the flashlight hanging from his duty belt.

"Unlike the other ladies, I don't have time to play with you," Jaime said from behind her.

Jessa noticed a movement from the corner of her eye and turned to find Renee, her children, Aria, and her mother standing in the street looking on. "All of this for little ole me?" she asked, touching her fingertip to her chest.

"Ma'am, I'll escort you and your vehicle out," he said, taking steps to climb onto the sidewalk.

Jessa laughed. "And what are you supposed to do with that flashlight rent-a-cop?"

"Go away, you're not wanted here," Aria yelled.

Aaron and Kieran applauded.

"Deuces," Kieran said, holding up two fingers.

Jessa turned and eyed Jaime. "And what will you all do when I force you to sell this house? And I look forward to it. If you think this little stunt is going to get rid of me, then you are dead wrong," she warned her. "I will keep you tied up in court until every cent you owe my daughter is hers. I gave him the child you did not. Remember that. This house is hers. Not yours. I am far from done with you."

"Eric should have dragged you to hell with him. Careful someone else doesn't get the job done," Jaime said in a low voice.

"There hasn't been a motherfucker born bad enough to do it. So, dream on, bitch." With that, Jessa turned and descended the stairs with her head held high. She flung the bottle of tequila down onto the street, and the crash echoed into the early night air.

As she reached the SUV, her driver climbed from it and came around to open the rear door for her. It took everything she had to maintain her cool façade. She was embarrassed as they all began to applaud. She gave him a soft smile of thanks as she slid her hands into his and accepted his help into the back of the vehicle. She was thankful when the door closed, shutting outside some of their joviality at her dismissal.

"Where to now?" the driver asked with politeness as he did a K-turn and followed the security truck down the road leading out of the subdivision.

"I'm done," she said, her voice barely above a whisper. "Take me back to my office building."

"Yes, ma'am," he said.

She picked her shades up from the passenger seat to slide

on, shielding her tears from his eyes as they rode away in silence.

Jessa awakened with a start. Her neck felt stiff and her temples pounded as she held her head up to look around at her surroundings. At first, she was surprised to find she was at her office on the sofa in the receptionist area.

She struggled to sit up, wincing at the discomfort of her joints from the awkward splaying of her body across the couch. "Damn," she swore with a soft grunt.

By the time they made it back to Manhattan, the tequila had truly taken its toll on her and she was afraid to drive and reluctant to leave her car in the parking garage overnight. She rode up to her office, spent from the alcohol and a full day of malicious deeds, and barely made it to the sofa before she fell asleep.

"I thought you were never going to wake up."

Jessa yelped in alarm, her heart pounding as she looked over at Georgia sitting on the floor across from her with her knees to her chest and her chin settled in the groove between them. "Georgia," she said, in surprise, raking her fingers through her hair and longing for a breath mint.

"I was waiting for you outside your house, but I never saw your car and I was too scared to knock," she admitted, her speech slow and sluggish. Her eyes were much the same.

Jessa knew she was high. A wave of deep sadness and regret washed over her.

"I figured you were here, so I Ubered. You didn't even lock the office door, so I just came in and sat and waited for you to wake up," Georgia said, a tear racing down her cheek. "And watched you. And...and..."

Jessa walked over to her and dropped onto her knees beside her, pulling her daughter into her arms. "I have never held you before," she admitted, her throat tight with her emotions. "I never got a chance to be your mother, Georgia. It wasn't my choice. Please believe me and please give me a chance. I know it's tough and I know our story is crazy and sick, but we can get through it, me, you and your little sister, Delaney."

Georgia nodded against Jessa's neck, her tears staining her shirt. "All my life I wanted to know you, and I fucked it all up," she moaned. "I fucked it all up, Mama."

"There's a lot of that going around," Jessa said. "I promise there is nothing you can do to make me turn my back on you. *Nothing.*"

"Mama, help me," Georgia whispered in her ear. "I don't want to be on this shit no more."

"I got you," Jessa swore, rubbing her back.

The door to the office opened. They both turned their heads just as the barrel of a gun with a silencer was eased through the crack.

The sound of the shot was followed by a fiery explosion as its expulsion lit up the air.

Georgia leaned across Jessa, sheltering her and taking the bullet into her body with a force that caused her to jolt as she cried out in pain.

"Noooo," Jessa screamed, bringing her arms around her daughter as the blood began to spread across her chest.

"Forgive me, Mama," Georgia whispered as she looked up at Jessa, the light of life already fading from her eyes.

"Hold on, Georgia," Jessa begged her fiercely, easing her body onto the floor. "Don't you dare leave me. I just got you back."

Jessa eyed the door, desperately wanting to chase down the gunman to discover which of her enemies had been pushed to the point of taking her life. Instead, she rushed over to the reception desk to call 9-1-1, choosing the love of her daughter over her desire to identify the gentleman and make them pay. As she finished the call and returned to Georgia's side to pull her head into her lap, Jessa regretted the anger she'd purposefully stoked in someone capable of murder.

The list was long.

Hammer. Keegan. The Halls. The Halstons. Della Montgomery. Horatio Montgomery's attorney. Warrington Sachs. Renee, Aria, and Jaime, plus any one of the people who cared about them or were collateral damage in the bombs she dropped.

Even her mother.

Jessa's head dropped to her chin.

One of them had attempted to take her life and put her daughter at risk instead.

She looked down at Georgia and her heart ached. With trembling fingers, she stroked her daughter's chin, scared beyond measure that these were the last moments they would spend together.

"Father God, please," she whispered, glad to be on her knees as she closed her eyes, released a shaky breath, and began to pray ceaselessly to the same God she shunned.

Epilogue

One week later

Shit. Did I almost die *again?*

Her body felt heavy. The pain was there, but it was a dull ache, and she knew drugs lessened its power. She couldn't open her eyes, and her tongue felt dry and out of place in her mouth. It felt like being trapped inside her own body.

But I'm alive. Thank God. I am alive.

Emotions flooded her. She could almost swear she felt a lone tear fall, but she couldn't be sure. She felt disconnected from her physical form.

The events of that night were a blur. Pain and blood loss had been the victor over her consciousness. She had been shot. And in the moments before she slipped into total blackness, her mother's prayers to the Lord had comforted her. Hearing Jessa beg for her life and to forgive the sins she believed caused it had given Georgia strength to hold on. To fight for her life.

"Georgia. Georgia. We're here. We're right here."

She felt a mixture of happiness and disappointment at the voice of her adoptive mother.

Did Jessa leave me to be mothered by someone else again?

Georgia felt her warm hand pressed against her cheek and was comforted by it, but the question she yearned to open her mouth and ask was: Where's my real mother? Where's Jessa?

She listened as they settled in by her bedside, and soon their conversation turned to normal daily living. What to have for dinner. The due date of bills. Days off from work.

Where is Jessa Bell?

Georgia was thankful when the rush of narcotics in her veins soon lulled her back into a deep sleep.

"Yes, Nadav. I'm sure. Drop all the lawsuits. Thank you for your help with everything."

Mama!

She wasn't sure if it was the sound of Jessa's voice that stirred her, but she couldn't deny the happiness she felt at hearing her. To have her near. Georgia longed to open her eyes and see her mother again.

"Keegan, thank you for being here after everything," Jessa said.

"There is no other place I'd be than right here by your side, darlin'," Keegan replied.

Georgia could hear the reconciliation and warmth in their tone. She liked that her mother had a friend again. She'd discovered from her days working at Mistress, Inc., that Keegan was loyal to Jessa.

"I think we made the right decision to end Mistress, Inc., don't you?" Jessa asked.

"Abso-fucking-lutely," Keegan stressed.

"I have my daughter back, and it's time for me to leave all the other shit behind and focus on getting to know Georgia and raising Delaney."

"So, you and Hammer are done?"

"Completely," Jessa stressed. "So much so that I dropped the charges against him and he can have his career and whatever else he wants out of life . . . except me."

"It's for the best," Keegan agreed.

Kick rocks, Hammer!

"My disappointment and betrayal by men has gotten me into so

much trouble. I feel like I lose who I am in them, and then I'm lost when I discover they're not worth it."

"And your mother?"

Yes, what about my grandma?

Silence reigned for a bit.

"She forgave me, too, but I think it's best she remains at a facility . . . for now."

More silence.

"The day Georgia got shot, I was in a bad place and I did some fucked-up shit, Keegan," Jessa confessed, her voice barely above a whisper and filled with her remorse. "I almost can't blame any one of them—or even you—for wanting to kill me. I just hate that my actions put Georgia in the crossfire."

"Any news on just who did shoot her?" Keegan asked. "Because it damn sure wasn't me."

"No. None."

"So, they may get away with it?"

Georgia grunted as she felt the fog being lifted and she began to flutter her eyelids. "Mama," she mouthed. It was painful to even try to speak.

"I have to focus on Georgia getting better and on Delaney. My girls," Jessa said. "Fuck everything else. Seriously."

Georgia felt a soft hand wrap around one of hers.

"I was hell-bent on revenge, and look where it got my daughter," she finished.

Georgia grunted softly again as she wiggled her fingertips. She wanted so badly to speak and reassure her mother that everything would be better.

"Georgia!" Jessa exclaimed, rising to her feet as she held her daughter's hand in both of hers.

I finally opened my eyes and looked up at my beautiful mother, feeling assured that we were united and would help each other through it all: my addiction to drugs and hers to revenge. I never believed in happy endings. They were meant for the fairy tales and the romance novels I used to read when I was younger. But now I do believe in a happy medium between hell and heaven. Reality. Not all good and never all bad. Just the best it can be.

As they called for the medical staff to alert them I was finally awake from my coma, I used all the strength I could muster to hold on to my mother's hand and took comfort that her embrace was just as tight.

This woman I once schemed to betray and destroy was now the center of my world. I was okay with that. She, Delaney, and my grandmother were my family. It was time to put our horrible past behind us. I wanted to get to know them and to love them. We were blood.

And so, on behalf of my mother, farewell, because any further stories about Jessa Bell will hopefully not be told.

Meet Jessa for the first time in Niobia Bryant's sexy, unforgettable novel about love, infidelity, and the importance of keeping your friends close and your enemies closer...

Message from a Mistress
Available wherever books are sold

Jessa's intro

Where do I begin? How do I tell the story? Our story. His and mine.

He was my lover and her husband. You would think that wasn't possible—like saying dry rain or cold heat—but it was true. She had the ring and the license . . . but I had him. From that first heated moment in their kitchen when his strong hands reached beneath my skirt to grab my soft, bare ass, I knew I had him.

I don't recall the specific moment when our lust turned to love. When our time spent together became about more than just fucking, more than just rushing through electrifying sex that left us both panting, sweaty, and in various stages of undress. We shifted so easily from sharing clandestine and wonderfully sneaky moments—even in their house while she was there—to him sneaking out of their home to be in my arms and in my bed.

I hated to lie alone at night surrounded by nothing but cool cotton sheets and plush down pillows while she had his hard and warm body to hold close.

I knew the time would come when I would want more from him than just his dick. I wanted his love, his time, his all . . . for me and only me.

She was my friend—true, but he was my lover, my love, and in this game there could only be one winner, as far as I was concerned.

Me.

Chapter 1

Jaime Hall enjoyed the feel of the steam pressed against her shoulders and her legs where she sat in the glass shower of their bedroom suite. The thick swirling vapors felt like a lover's gentle touch against her skin and those intimate parts of a woman's body. Her breasts. Her nipples. Her thighs. Her lips—both sets.

She relished it. She needed it.

Sadness weighed her shoulders down and soon she felt tears fill her oval-shaped eyes and race down her cheeks. Jaime brought her shaking hands up to hug herself close. "God, I can't take much more of my life," she whispered into the steam as her head dropped so low that her chin nearly touched her chest.

She heard a sudden noise in her bathroom. Her head jerked up as she immediately swallowed back any more of her tears and frantically wiped any traces of them from her face. The last thing she wanted was for him to see or hear her crying.

"Eric," Jaime called out to her husband of the last seven years.

No answer. Nothing to acknowledge her. Seconds later the bathroom door opened and then closed. Disappointment nudged the door to her heart shut as well. The body's automatic defense mechanisms were amazing.

Jaime rose from the bench, turned off the shower, and walked out of the stall. The vapors swirled around her nude curvaceous frame like fog as she stepped down onto the plush white carpeting that felt like mink against her pedicured feet. As she wiped a clear spot in the grand oval mirror over the pedestal sink, she came face-to-face with her unhappiness. She forced a smile and put on her usual mask, but even she could see it didn't reach her eyes.

She grabbed a towel and wrapped it around her frame. She raced out of her bathroom suite through their spacious cathedral ceiling master bedroom and out to the hall. As she raced down the curved staircase, her towel slipped and fell behind her on the stairs, but she didn't break stride.

Thank God she was home alone, because she wouldn't want anyone to see her stark naked and racing through the house like she was crazy.

"Eric!" she called out, striding through the circular foyer to the kitchen.

The house was quiet. She covered her exposed breasts with her arms as she looked out the kitchen windows over the driveway. The sun was just starting to rise. She just made out his tall and slender figure headed down the street toward their friends' home with his tackle box and fishing rods in hand.

He left to go deep-sea fishing and didn't even bother to tell her good-bye. *How much more can I take?* She turned and let her body slide down to the polished hardwood floor as tears racked her body and she could do nothing but wrap her arms around her knees and rock to make herself feel a little better.

★ ★ ★

"Shit!" Renee Clinton swore as the gray acrid smoke rose from the frying pan with fury. She hurried to turn off the lit eye of the Viking stove before shifting the pan to one of the remaining five burners.

"Damn, damn, damn it all to hell."

Renee could only shake her head in shame at the blackness of the bacon she'd been frying. It was *beyond* crispy.

"Is something on fire, Ma?"

Renee looked over her shoulder as her fifteen-year-old daughter, Kieran, walked into the kitchen on dragging feet in her oversized fuzzy pajamas. "Just breakfast."

"*You* were cooking?" she asked in disbelief as she leaned her hip against the island in the center of the kitchen.

"I wanted to fix your father breakfast before he left to go fishing." Renee slid the halfway-decent-looking slices of bacon onto a clear glass plate.

"You never cook." Kieran moved across the kitchen to the pantry.

"I know how to cook," Renee protested as she ran a hand through her deeply wavy natural. "It's remembering that I have food on the stove that I have a problem with."

Kieran stepped out of the pantry digging into a box of cereal before throwing a handful of some sugary-sweet cereal she loved into her mouth. She moved over to stand beside her mother and looked down at the bacon with a frown. "Good thing Daddy loves you," she joked before turning to walk out of the kitchen.

"Yeah, good thing," Renee said hesitantly as she cracked eggs into a large red Le Creuset ceramic bowl and whisked them with a little extra ferocity.

She poured the eggs into a stainless steel pan and left them so that they would set before she scrambled them. She moved back to the end of the island where her briefcase was opened and instantly became absorbed into the facts and figures of the report she'd brought home to review.

At forty-three, Renee was the vice president of marketing for the CancerCure Foundation, one of the largest nonprofits serving cancer research and awareness in the country. It was her job and her passion to develop partnerships with major corporations for invaluable donations and increasing the national visibility of the foundation. She took her work very seriously—not just for the six-figure income she received, but because it intrigued and challenged her every day. It was very easy for her to get deeply absorbed in her work.

Renee picked up an oversized cup of gourmet coffee with one hand and the open report with the other. Her lips moved as she read. Her face showed her shifting feelings: interest, surprise, discontent. She leaned her hip against the island as she took a deep and satisfying sip of her drink.

"What the hell is burning?"

The words on the report disappeared as Renee closed her eyes and frowned as she thought, "Damn," at the sound of her husband, Jackson's, voice from behind her.

She dropped the report and snatched the burning pan from the stove in one continuous motion. "This just isn't my morning, Jackson," she told him, looking over her shoulder at her tall, solid husband of the last eighteen years.

His handsome square face shaped into a frown as he took in the papers and files on the island. There was no mistaking the immediate look of disapproval.

Renee hated the guilt she felt at that one look that spoke volumes about their marriage. "I thought I would cook—"

"*And* work?" he asked, moving past her to fill the thermos he held with coffee.

Renee swallowed her irritation. She looked down at the burnt bacon on the plate and the brown eggs in the pan and scraped them both into the garbage disposal. "I'm trying, Jackson," she stressed, her eyes angry and hurt.

He just snorted in derision.

Renee felt tension across her shoulders. She jumped a little as he moved close to her to press a cool kiss to her cheek. She closed her eyes, absorbing his scent as she raised a hand to stroke his bearded cheek. He felt familiar and strange all at once. It had been so long since they showed each other simple affection.

She tilted her head back to look up into those eyes that had intrigued her from the first time she saw him on the campus of Rutgers University. "I love you, Jackson," Renee whispered, hating the urgency in her voice as her eyes searched his.

For what seemed forever, his eyes searched hers as well. "We need to talk. We *have* to talk," he said, his voice husky and barely above a whisper.

A soft press of his lips down upon hers silenced any of her words or questions.

Moments later, he was gone and Renee felt chilled to the bone.

"You didn't have to get up so early with me, baby."

Aria Livewell shrugged as she followed her broad-shouldered husband, Kingston, down the stairs of their three-thousand-square-foot home in the family-oriented subdivision of Richmond Hills. A home meant to be filled with children. "It's no problem. You know me and the girls are hanging out today and I wanted to get some housework done before they picked me up."

Kingston sat his fishing equipment by the wooden double doors. "Think you four will be back on time? You know we're supposed to meet at the Clintons' tonight to fry up all the fish we'll catch today."

"Just three, actually. Jessa said she had *something else* to do today." Aria made a playful face and waved her hand dismissively.

Kingston put his broad hands beneath her short cotton

robe and pulled his beautiful mocha-skinned wife close to him. "If we whup our friends in bid whist tonight, I have one helluva surprise for you."

Kingston was *so* competitive.

She tilted her head up to lightly lick his dimpled chin as she pushed her hand into the back pocket of his vintage jeans to warmly grasp his firm, fleshy buttocks. "Can I get a hint?" she asked huskily with a teasing smile, the beat of her heart already quickening with anticipation.

"Damn, I love you," he said roughly, his eyes smoldering as he slid one hand up to her nape.

Aria moaned softly in pleasure at the first heated feel of her husband's lips. As she gasped slightly, he slid his tongue inside her mouth with well-practiced ease. She shivered. Her clit swelled to life. Her nipples hardened in a rush.

"Do we have time?" she asked in a heated whisper, barely hearing herself over her own furious heartbeat as Kingston undid her robe and planted moist and tantalizing kisses along her collarbone.

"We'll make time" breezed across her flesh.

As her robe slipped open and his familiar hands caressed her silky skin, Aria enjoyed their passion and wondered if the time would come when she didn't cherish and yearn for her husband's touch. His dick. His kisses. His love.

With his mouth, Kingston made a path to the deep valley of her breasts, bending his knees to take one swollen and taut dark nipple into his mouth. He sucked it deeply and then circled it with the tip of his clever tongue.

"Yes," Aria whimpered, flinging her head back.

Kingston turned them and pressed Aria's back to the towering front doors as he quickly undid his belt and zipper. His hands shook as he placed them on her plush hips and lifted her with ease until her pulsing and moist pussy lips lightly kissed the thick tip of his dick. "Why is your pussy so good?" he whispered against the pounding pulse of her throat.

Aria didn't answer, she just smiled wickedly—and a bit cockily—as she caused the swollen lips of her vagina to lightly kiss the smooth round head of his dick...twice.

Kingston dropped Aria down onto his erection, her pussy tightly surrounding and gripping him like a vise. "Damn," he swore, his buttocks tensing as he froze. He didn't want to cum. Not yet.

Aria pressed the small of her back to the door and began to work her hips in small circles, anxious to not just have his dick pressed against her walls but to feel his delicious strokes.

Kingston's jaw clenched. "Don't make me nut, baby." His voice was strained.

Aria raised her hands to tease her nipples with her slender fingers as she enjoyed the tight in-and-out motion of his penis when Kingston began to work his hips. She felt wild and free, uninhibited and sexy. "Umph. I'm gone cum, baby. Please make me cum," she whispered with fevered urgency as each of his deep thrusts caused her pussy juices to smack and echo in the foyer like applause.

Kingston's chest and loins exploded with heat as his primal need to feel as much of Aria's pussy as he could. He pushed deeper up inside her, drawing quick and uneven breaths as his heart thundered. His buttocks clenched and then relaxed as he touched every bit of her ridged walls with his solid inches. "Damn, Aria," he swore, planting adoring kisses along her collarbone as his dick filled her several times with warm shots of cum.

Connect with

Visit us online at
KensingtonBooks.com
to read more from your favorite authors, see books
by series, view reading group guides, and more.

Join us on social media

for sneak peeks, chances to win books and prize packs,
and to share your thoughts with other readers.

facebook.com/kensingtonpublishing
twitter.com/kensingtonbooks

Tell us what you think!

To share your thoughts, submit a review,
or sign up for our eNewsletters, please visit:
KensingtonBooks.com/TellUs.